OUT COLD

A ROOK RADCLIFFE MYSTERY
BOOK 1

E.J. RIDLEY

WN

ISBN: 978-1-969863-01-1

Published by Wayward North Press

First print edition.

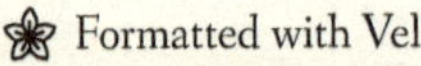
Formatted with Vellum

For all the girls with barbells
And the ones who bring them chicken.

ONE

The weight room at Lakeview High stank. Industrial-strength cleaner couldn't mask the reek of sweat, but Rook Radcliffe breathed it in deep. It smelled honest.

"Line up," said Coach Gonzalez, a faded Seahawks cap shading his eyes in spite of the fact that it was 6:45 a.m. and the sun hadn't risen outside. Octobers in Washington were dark.

Gonzalez pressed one end of his clipboard against his stocky torso.

"Everybody should be able to squat more today than six weeks ago," he said. "You're warmed up. Let's go. Nolan, beat 160."

Rook barely resisted scoffing as Nolan Becker stepped up with his tawny buzz cut, nervously popping his thumb knuckle. He was sixteen like her, and also a sophomore, but he was taller and built heavier. He should've been squatting way more than 160.

Nobody here pushed like she was used to.

Nolan loaded 170 on the bar, ducked under, and gripped it. His squat didn't hit depth—no rep in a real meet.

But this wasn't Nationals, and no one cared but her. She watched, unimpressed, as he stood and racked it.

Coach Gonzalez gave Nolan a beady look. "You could've done more."

Good, Rook thought. *Somebody said it.*

Nolan shrugged. "You want 180?" his voice was quiet. "I'll try."

"Next time." Gonzalez waved him aside. "Destiny, beat 55."

"I'm texting my sister to bring me some Midol," Destiny said, blonde beach waves falling forward, fingers moving fast on her glitter explosion of a phone. The thing looked like a rainbow had thrown up on it. Rook almost winced at the rhinestone glare. A tiny, cracked heart charm hung from a tassel, and near the camera, a pink cursive sticker read *Stronger Than the Storm*.

"Put your phone away," said Gonzalez.

"Hold on." Destiny's tone was more flat than rude. She yawned, fingers still moving on her phone, pink nails tapping occasionally against the plastic, her face lit by the screen.

"You want credit for zero period weight training, you're gonna have to lift something. Or drop the class."

"Come on, Des," said Nolan, passing a hand over his buzz cut in a brief, self-conscious gesture. "Squat 65. I'll spot you."

"It's too heavy," said Destiny. "I'm tired."

Nolan raised his eyebrows. "You live next door. I've seen you carry eight grocery bags in heels. While texting," he added.

Destiny didn't smile. She thumbed off her phone. "That's life, right?" she said. "Pick up and shut up."

Rook barely nodded. That was life.

AJ Ellsworth stepped up to the other side of the rack. He was as tall as Nolan, but broader. Built better, like he pushed harder. Sandy-haired and self-assured, with a crooked nose that worked for him. Rook watched him, unable not to.

"Do it," said AJ, shooting Destiny a grin. "Get over here. Let me see you hit this."

Destiny's blue eyes moved from Nolan to AJ. Unreadable.

She tossed her glitter bomb phone into her bag and stepped up to the rack. She gripped the bar, squatted, and stood so effortlessly that Rook had no doubt that she could have handled twice as much and was simply choosing not to try.

AJ gave her arm a light punch when she was done. "Looked good."

She bit her lip, leaned toward AJ, and nudged him with her shoulder. It looked like flirtation, Rook thought—and Nolan didn't seem like he approved. His worried glance flicked from Destiny to AJ and back again.

"Ellsworth," said Gonzalez. "Beat 200."

AJ loaded 230, ducked under the bar, and squatted shallow. Rook shook her head.

Coach Gonzalez, however, looked a little more awake. "Fifteen percent increase," he said with energy, giving AJ a look of approval. "Doubt anybody'll beat that."

Rook snorted louder than she meant to. Everyone looked.

AJ swept his eyes over her.

"Something funny, new girl?" he asked. "Think you can get fifteen percent? What would that be for you?"

Coach Gonzalez ran his pencil down the clipboard until he reached her name. "180."

Somebody laughed.

Rook clenched. 180 was nothing. She wanted to step up and lift her *real* max. Freak them all out. But if people at Lakeview knew she squatted 350, someone would get curious. They'd start paying attention to her. If anyone figured out who she really was—who her mother was—she'd be swamped by paparazzi, just like back in New York.

She only had to think it, and the memories flooded in, filling her head. Cameras flashing. Strangers in her face, demanding answers. Trying to climb the courthouse steps, to keep her head down as she moved through the gauntlet of reporters who crushed in on both sides, her own breath white in the frozen air, Greta's hand gripping the back of her coat, steering her toward the huge doors as she winced at their shouts.

Did she really pull the trigger, Ms. Chase?

Ms. Chase! Look over here! Did you see your mother with the gun?

She couldn't go through it again. She would keep the weights light, and no one would ask any questions.

She loaded 180. Her ego begged her to keep adding. She eyed the 45s, wishing she could slide them on and melt all their faces off.

"Don't do it if you're not ready," Gonzalez warned. "This isn't a dare—I don't want to see you getting hurt."

Rook almost laughed at him, because that was hilarious.

"Ellsworth, help me spot," said Gonzalez, when she didn't back down.

"Oh definitely," said AJ.

"Jesus Christ," said Rook, incensed. "Like I need a fucking spot."

"Language," said Gonzalez. "This is school, keep it clean."

Rook ducked under the bar and packed herself tight against it. Metal on skin. Tight grip. She squatted all the way to depth, in case the rest of them wanted to see what it was supposed to look like—and then she paused there for a few extra seconds. Might as well make it fun.

"Help her," said Gonzalez. He and AJ grabbed the bar and stood her up.

Rook turned on Gonzalez. "Did I ask?"

"You were stuck in the hole. Common problem, we'll work on it."

Rook couldn't take it. Hiding her strength was one thing. Being seen as weak was another. She was stronger than everybody in this place—they had no idea who she was, and she didn't want them to know, but she wasn't letting them stand her up like she was some beginner.

Cool it. Don't freak out. Stay small.

"I'm going again."

"Next time."

Rook ignored him, unracked the bar, and squatted. She wanted to do another one. Another five—another twenty.

She forced herself to rerack. It burned.

"Damn," said AJ, and now when he ran his eyes over her, it was a promise. "What else can you do?"

"Radcliffe, sit down. Ellsworth, that's enough." Coach Gonzalez exhaled. "Juárez? Your turn."

Rook headed for the benches, past Destiny, who was already on her phone again. There were tears in her eyes, and when she caught Rook looking, she turned away, wiping them with a furious hand. She snatched up her bag and headed for the door.

"Des," said Nolan, who was also watching her. "Can I—"

"My sister's coming," Destiny replied, and was out the door before Gonzalez could stop her.

As soon as Gonzalez was busy with the next student on his roster, Rook loaded plates onto the floor barbell. She could finally lift how she wanted.

Wide grip. Deep breath.

She bent, jumped, pulled—slammed her feet to the floor, dropped into a deep squat, and caught the barbell overhead. Arms locked. Back straight.

The snatch was who she was. What she loved. As long as she could still do this, even if the weight was low, maybe she'd make it.

The door opened. Chad Perkins swaggered in late, baseball duffel in hand, brown hair pomaded up too high for anybody to take him seriously. His buddy Keanu entered right behind him.

Chad's eyes fell on Rook, and he pointed at her, already gleeful.

"Co-oaach, she's doing it again."

"Nope." Gonzalez turned on Rook, who dropped the barbell in front of her. "No unsupervised snatches in here, we talked about this."

Rook glared at Chad, who was too busy cackling at the word *snatches* to care.

The intercom went off to call Gonzalez to the office.

"Safety while I'm out," he warned. He pointed to Rook's barbell. "Unload that."

"But—"

"You heard me."

He didn't leave until Rook had unloaded all the plates and stowed the barbell. Frustrated, she grabbed dumbbells and propped her foot up behind her on a box so she could do split squats.

"Dudes, you're screwed," Chad said, already on the bench, incline benching dumbbells. The other guys clustered around him. "I'm so glad I don't play football like you losers. First Mateo dips, then you lose your QB? Cooked."

"Dips?" said Nolan, wincing. "Mateo *died*."

Chad truly sucked, Rook thought, as she bent her knee and sank low. She had shared space with a lot of insensitive jocks in her life, but Chad Perkins was the complete douche package. Ratting her out to Gonzalez for snatching? Screw him. She glanced at his dumbbells and smirked to herself. He was only benching 40s.

"We're good," said Keanu, in his deep, calm voice, tying his long dark curls into a topknot on his head. "Ellsworth's crushing QB."

AJ fist bumped him. "Thanks, bro." His gaze traveled to Rook's dumbbells, and when he saw that she had 60s, his eyebrows went up. He went to the dumbbell rack and picked up the 70s. Rook watched, amused, as he carried them back to his bench. What did he think he was going to do with those?

She set down her weights, swigged her water, and switched legs for the other half of her set.

Keanu bent for the curl bar, showing the tattoos on his knees and lower thighs more clearly. Tight, black, geometric patterns in thick, deliberate bands around his legs. They looked like they would have been painful.

Chad put his dumbbells down and got up. "What's the Indian kid doing?" he demanded, jerking his head toward a skinny kid who was struggling to press 20s.

"Cambodian," Nolan corrected, giving Chad a look like he was an idiot. "His name's Sareth."

Sareth looked over at the sound of his name and found them all watching. He tossed his black hair out of his eyes.

"Yes?" he said, his tone arrogant, despite how out of his depth he appeared to be. "Can I help you?"

Sareth was an interesting guy, Rook thought, descending on one leg as she watched him. He didn't look like he wanted to be here, and he definitely didn't mix with the sports bros, but came off like he thought he owned the place anyway.

She could get behind it.

Nolan held his fists up, palms in. "Neutral grip, like this."

Sareth corrected his grip, and the dumbbells went up easier. He gave Nolan an appreciative nod.

"Thank you."

Rook refocused on her legs. They were good and on fire now. She bit down and braced hard as she ascended, core tight, heart pounding. It felt good. She heard AJ's voice.

"Look at *that*."

"What, her?" Chad sounded unimpressed. "Whatever, that's not even hard."

Rook knew they were talking about her. She descended again. Held it again. Let it burn, and let them watch.

"You and Jill," AJ said, after a moment. "Homecoming?"

"She wants a corsage," Chad complained. "Sixty bucks for a dead flower is dumb."

Rook had always thought so too. But she couldn't agree with Chad for any reason, so she changed her opinion about corsages on the spot. They were awesome.

"Get her one," said Keanu flatly.

"I heard Jill won't even wear your letterman's jacket," said AJ, grinning. "Doesn't want to be your woman, huh?"

Keanu gave a low laugh.

"She should wear it," said Chad, indignant. "It's a lucky charm."

"Softball made regionals without it," said Keanu, curling the bar with a last shaking effort before he set it down. "Jill carried them on the mound."

Chad made a *pshh* noise. "I won *State*," he said, and then he looked at his friends with seriousness. "You're my catcher," he said to Keanu, placing a hand on his shoulder like he was knighting somebody. He put his other hand on AJ's. "You're my shortstop. Ride or die."

He walked away. AJ and Keanu gave each other looks like they weren't sure whether to laugh or throw something at the back of Chad's head.

"Tool," muttered Nolan, yanking on his thumb knuckle.

Neither AJ nor Keanu replied.

Rook eyed Nolan as he picked up the curl bar. He wasn't really in the center with the other guys. He was on the teams, he was in the crew, but he wasn't *in*. Too quiet. Too nice to people. Only assholes made it to the top.

AJ took over the bench and picked up the 70s. His neck and arms tensed as he lay back and tried to position the heavy dumbbells in his grip.

So he was going to bench those? Okay...

Rook followed his progress out of the corner of her eye.

"Those are heavy, bro," said Keanu. "Is that what you usually use?"

"I got it," AJ muttered, and he pushed the dumbbells up. His arms shook, barely. Rook watched him lower them—he had control, but not by much.

Keanu pulled a jar of coconut oil out of his bag. Rook could smell it when he popped the top off and started rubbing it into his black tattoos.

Nolan watched him, curious. "Did you get those in Samoa?"

Keanu looked up at him and nodded.

"Intense," said Nolan, with a shake of his head. "I'm doing one when I'm eighteen, but nowhere near that big. Was it tough?"

Keanu nodded again, looking a little friendlier. "I get the next part when we go back. I hope next summer." He glanced at AJ. "Who are you taking to Homecoming? Destiny, right?"

"Nah." AJ pushed the dumbbells up again. This time, when he lowered them, it looked a little rockier. "We're not serious. Although, last night?" He laughed.

Nolan stopped curling midway up and held the weight frozen.

"Last night what?" he asked, voice quiet. "If you're about to brag about her, don't."

"What are you, her dad?" said AJ, shoving the dumbbells up with a hard breath. One elbow wobbled. "She can do what she wants."

Nolan set down the bar and walked away.

AJ went for a sixth press—and failed halfway. He clenched his fists and shut his eyes, pushing like he meant it.

Rook watched him fight for it, willing him to break through the sticking point. That was a money rep. Real gains only came when it hurt.

"Up," she urged.

The word came from pure instinct. Years of gym time with real lifters. When someone fought, everyone got loud.

AJ finished the rep with a huff of exertion, dropped the weights, and looked at her—intense. Attentive. Heat rushed to her face. Why had she talked to him?

A horrible sound—part wheeze, part scream—made Rook spin toward the bench press.

Sareth was on the bench, pinned under the barbell, eyes wide. Panicked.

Rook's gut lurched—she dropped her dumbbells and lunged. Nolan got there at the same time. Together, they hauled the weight off Sareth and racked it.

"Hey." Nolan crouched down. "You okay? Why are you benching without a spot?"

Sareth trembled as he sat up. His black hair fell into his eyes. "Someone changed my weights. I went to refill my water, and when I came back, it was different."

From the corner, Chad snickered.

Rook turned on him, furious. "Are you trying to kill somebody?"

Nolan moved first. He was on Chad in three long strides and slammed him into the wall.

"Don't touch me!" Chad barked, but Nolan grabbed him by the front of his jersey. Chad wrenched away.

AJ stepped in. He glanced toward Rook—then looked at Chad.

"Apologize to Sareth."

Rook blinked. That was unexpected.

Nolan too gave AJ a look of disbelief. "Seriously?" he said. "You?"

"Yeah, seriously, Ellsworth?" said Chad. "I barely added any weight. It was ten pounds. If he can't lift that, why is he lifting?"

AJ's eyes checked Rook again, and she realized what was happening. She was no dummy—he was playing it up. Acting like a good guy. Seeing if she'd notice.

The bell rang for the end of zero period and Chad

walked out, giving AJ an angry look. Most of the others followed.

Nolan went back to Sareth. "Come on. Let's hit the locker room."

"I don't want to."

"I'll stick with you." Nolan gestured for Sareth to follow him. "You're good, I promise."

Sareth followed Nolan out, and AJ met Rook's eyes.

They were alone.

In silence, Rook put away her weights. AJ wiped down his bench.

"We're even," he said.

Rook glanced at him. "How?"

"Fifteen percent increases. We matched."

"Uh, you didn't get fifteen percent."

"Uh, you watched me squat 230."

"I watched you fail depth. That wasn't a squat."

AJ's eyes glittered at the challenge. "So give me a do-over."

"I need to get to first period."

AJ's gaze dropped to her mouth. "Do you?" he said. "I kind of feel like skipping."

Rook flushed. She knew that look, and she hated how much she liked it. She had never done drugs in her life—clean, disciplined, focused. Boys like him were her one vice.

Look away, she told herself. *He is* not *a nice guy*.

Like that had ever stopped her.

"Can't skip," she lied. "History test."

"Who do you have?"

"Mr. Nordmark."

"There's no test today. I have him too."

Rook tossed her ponytail like she was swatting a fly and picked up her gym bag. When she stood and turned, she found AJ almost close enough to kiss her. Warning lights flashed in her mind.

Do we need to discuss this? You heard how he talked about Destiny. You're about to be a belt notch.

"You're not boring," he said, almost like it surprised him. "Meet me later."

Sure, meet him later. What could go wrong?

No. She was stronger than this. She was supposed to keep her head down and stay off everybody's radar—that was the whole damn point of uprooting her life and coming here.

"What's wrong?"

Everything was wrong. Him, this school, this town, herself. Her mother. Gabe. Light weights. Pretending it was fine. Nothing was right anymore, and nothing mattered.

"The graffiti wall," he said. "You know where it is?"

She nodded.

"Meet me behind it after school."

Classy. Bet he just wants to chat.

"Yes or no?" AJ urged.

"I—shouldn't."

"But?"

The door swung open, and Coach Gonzalez walked back in. He scowled when he saw how close the two of them were standing.

"For God's sake," he said, "get out. You're gonna be late."

They left the weight room.

"See you at the wall," said AJ, as they went down the stairs. "Say yes."

No. You don't fool me. I know who you are. I know what this is.

"Maybe," she said. Because if nothing mattered, then neither did this. She could do what she wanted.

Even if what she wanted was a mistake.

TWO

Theo Locke sat in the guidance counselor's office at the end of sixth period, squishing a stress ball in his fist and willing himself not to cry. He was tired of crying. It had helped, at first—it felt cathartic, the only release for the grief that sometimes felt like it would detonate inside him. After two months, crying had become mundane. Inadequate.

"I'm checking in with students who had important relationships with Mateo Salinas. Is there anything you want to talk about?"

Ms. Winter had come to Lakeview a few weeks ago. Her calm, grounded demeanor felt real—and under normal circumstances, Theo would've found her easy to talk to. But talking would change nothing. If he'd started walking sooner, he would've arrived in time to use the EpiPen. He'd calculated it again and again.

The walk to Fenton Park: fourteen minutes. Mateo's anaphylaxis lasted about fifteen.

If Theo had started walking six minutes sooner, he would have made it.

Six minutes. Less time than it took to microwave dinner.

Such a small error. He should have been able to fix it. But he hadn't known those minutes mattered, so he'd sat in his room playing a video game while Mateo died alone, suffocating.

The most important test of his life, and he hadn't realized it was happening until it was over.

Those thoughts aren't true, but the feelings are normal. Part of grieving is wondering if we could've done something to prevent the loss. But you couldn't have prevented it, Theo. You didn't fail to act—you just didn't know. You're punishing yourself like this is your fault, when you did everything in your power to help once you arrived on the scene. You called 911. You performed CPR. Short of being psychic, there is nothing more you could have done.

"I have a therapist." He kept his voice steady, debate-club controlled. "My parents are psychologists. I have help."

"That's a lot of mental health support," Ms. Winter said.

She sounded kind. He didn't meet her eyes.

"But if you ever want to talk, or need a space to decompress, you can. Okay?"

He nodded.

"You're carrying a heavy AP load for a sophomore. But you handled it well last year. Perfect grades."

Theo nodded again.

"Sometimes, students at your level are afraid to miss class, no matter what's happening in their lives. I hope you'll give yourself space if you need it."

He crushed the stress ball. "Okay."

"Other students told me how close you were with Mateo. I'm sorry for your loss."

Sorry for your loss. Like he'd misplaced a set of keys. Like Mateo was a suitcase left behind at baggage claim, instead of the best human being Theo had ever known. The loss was cavernous. It swallowed him whole.

He turned to the counseling office window, where rain streaked down the glass in rivulets. He followed one drop, watching it slide, so his voice wouldn't break.

"Thank you," he said. "Yes. We were close—"

It was all he could manage. He bit the inside of his cheek to make it stop, but it didn't help. His eyes blurred until he couldn't see the rain, and tears streaked down his cheeks, quiet and useless.

Ms. Winter pushed a Kleenex box toward him. Theo dabbed his eyes, gritting his teeth to hold back the flood.

"Based on what other students have shared, I get the sense that Mateo was extraordinary," said Ms. Winter. "If I can help, I'm here."

The bell rang. Relieved, Theo picked up his backpack and walked out of school, ducking his head against the rain. His shoes grew wet as he walked onto the baseball field.

The walk to his house was short, but every step reminded him that he was alone. Last year, he and Mateo had often crossed this field together, jumped the chain-link fence that separated the Lockes' backyard from Lakeview's campus, and spent afternoons in Theo's room, gaming, studying, and laughing at everything and nothing until their voices grew hoarse.

He couldn't go home.

He cut left, toward the graffiti wall. It stood at the eastern edge of campus, separating a dead patch of grass from a dense thicket of woods, its concrete surface covered with the names, artwork, and gang signs of this year's senior class. Though Lakeview kids called it a wall, it didn't have a uniform height. It was more like a bar graph, with sections that started low and could be climbed like steps.

Theo climbed up until he reached the top of the wall, a dozen feet off the ground. Up here, no one would see him unless they were really looking—thick falls of cedar branches hid him from view. He lay down on the concrete, using his backpack as a headrest, and shut his eyes against the raindrops that slipped occasionally through the greenery. Unlike his tears, the rain felt good on his face. Cool. Impersonal. He breathed in and out slowly, letting the smell of the woods in. Letting quiet and rain work on him.

The snap of a branch below him jolted him out of his trance. He rolled onto his side and peered down through the cedar sprays to see a girl standing behind the wall, hidden from campus. Theo readjusted himself, rolling onto his stomach to see who it was. She wore her brown hair in a ponytail, and he couldn't see her face well, but he didn't think he knew her. She dropped her backpack and gym bag onto the dirt.

Ten seconds ticked by. Thirty seconds. After a minute, she gave a *tch* of irritation, got down on the ground, and started to do push-ups—strict, military push-ups, one after another, without slowing or breaking form. Then she got up, planted her hands on the ground, and kicked her feet up over her head to rest her heels against the wall. She bent her elbows until the crown of her head touched the ground, then straightened her arms, lifting herself into a handstand. She did it again, and then again, and she made it look easy. Theo didn't think he could have performed a single one of those things without falling on his head.

"Good. You're here."

The girl kicked her feet back down to the ground and wiped her hands on her leggings as AJ Ellsworth walked up to her. Theo had been friends with him back in elementary and middle school. Now they rarely hung out unless they ended up at the same party, and AJ was usually too busy trying to have sex with someone to be much of a conversationalist.

The girl smoothed down her ponytail. "I'm about to head home."

"Hold up." AJ grabbed the front of the girl's hoodie and brought her close to him. She let him do it.

Then he tried to lift it up.

It took Theo a second to register what was happening, and when it did, he panicked.

Oh shit. Was this about to be a hookup? He had to get out of here. But it was a dozen feet down.

He stayed locked where he was. Trapped. Rain bled through the cedars and onto the back of his neck, rolling down his skin, making him shiver.

"Jesus, we're at school," said the girl, blocking AJ's hands.

"Nobody can see us. I'll do it too." AJ removed his own hoodie and t-shirt, knocking the baseball cap off his sandy hair as he did. His state championship baseball ring dangled from a gold chain and glinted against his bare chest.

The girl pulled off her hoodie and threw it onto her gym bag. AJ grabbed her waist. Kissed her. She made a sound—sharp, almost hurt.

Theo's pulse spiked. Did she need help?

She pushed AJ up against the graffiti wall and kissed him fast. Hungry. Something about it was still off—her hands ran all over him, searching, like there was something she couldn't find.

Theo rolled onto his back as quietly as possible, wincing. He didn't know how to get out of here, but he didn't want to watch them do whatever they were about to do. He didn't want to hear them either. He pushed a hand into his pocket, silent, looking for his earbuds. He dug them out, and they slipped out of his hand.

Crap.

They clacked to the dirt in front of the wall, on the other side from where AJ and the girl were making out. Theo waited for one of them to notice the sound and look up, and say something. Yell at him, maybe. He glanced down to see if they saw him.

They didn't.

They were on the ground now, the girl straddling AJ, kissing him like she was trying to erase him. AJ's attention was focused on getting under the girl's shirt. Theo couldn't see perfectly, but he was pretty sure AJ was trying to take her bra off.

He cringed and closed his eyes. He should have just gone home. Maybe he should say something. But now it had been too long—now they'd think he was a creep who had been trying to watch them.

Analysis paralysis, huh?

The voice in his mind sounded like Mateo. Laughing. Nudging him.

Make a choice, brother. Come on, do something. It's not that hard. Worst-case scenario, they both yell at you. Who cares?

"What's your name again?" AJ said. "Brooke?"

"Rook."

"Where'd you move to Cedar Point from, Rook?"

"What is this, a job interview?"

AJ laughed. "You don't want to get to know each other?"

"No."

"Love that. You should come to Homecoming with me."

"No."

"You don't want to go with the new quarterback?"

Rook scoffed, and Theo understood. AJ wasn't as smooth as he thought.

"Party at Marna's before the dance," said AJ. "We go, we have a couple drinks. And privacy."

"Wow. Subtle."

She sounded tired. Bored, even. Then she sucked a breath that made Theo's eyes snap open.

AJ had rolled her onto her back.

"Damn, your body is crazy," he said. "I've never seen anything like you."

Rook's eyes glazed. She lay under AJ, staring at nothing.

Theo's chest tightened. Something was wrong. She looked *gone*. He didn't know what was happening, but he didn't like it at all.

He forced his mouth to work. "Hey," he said, but his voice came out dry, the word scraped in his throat, almost inaudible. Neither of them heard it.

Before he could try again, Rook came back to herself. Her expression shifted, fast and hard. She shoved AJ off her, and he pitched over onto the dirt. She got to her feet.

"The fuck?" AJ sat up. "What did I do?"

Rook yanked her hoodie back on.

AJ got up. "You're not leaving."

But she had already picked up her bags.

"You were having fun," AJ said. "Don't act like it was just me—you were into it."

"And now I'm not."

"Don't be like that."

She laughed, and it was hollow. The hairs stood up on Theo's neck.

"Hey." AJ's voice got quieter, like he was trying to calm

a skittish animal. He stepped into her path, closer to her. "It's okay. Tell me what you need."

Rook didn't bite. "Try that line on Destiny," she said.

"So you're *jealous*." He laughed. "Is that what this is?"

Rook tried to go around him. AJ sidestepped and got in her way again.

"Move," she said. "Now."

AJ's eyes narrowed, but he moved. Rook strode past him.

"You're cold," he said. "I thought you were different."

She didn't turn back.

AJ snatched his shirt and hoodie off the ground and dressed quickly. Violently. He stalked away toward the football field.

Theo climbed down from the wall and jumped from the last step to the ground. He snatched up his earbuds from the dirt and shoved them into his pocket. The rain fell harder now, but he stripped off his jacket, sweating in response to everything he had just witnessed. He swung his backpack onto one shoulder and headed for home, too unsettled to notice how soaked he was getting.

Who was that girl? What kind of name was Rook? What were those upside-down push-ups? And why had she thrown herself at AJ like that? She didn't even seem to like him. She'd seemed, in the end, to know exactly what kind of guy he was.

The whole thing left Theo with a bad feeling in the pit of his stomach.

He jumped the fence that stood between Lakeview and his backyard. He walked into his house, grabbed his meds and a Coke, and went to his room, where he fired up his computer and logged into *Dragon Hunger*. He usually played a mage healer, but today he was feeling something different.

He started a new character. Battle Maiden class. Human. Brown hair. He searched through the hairstyles until he found something close to a ponytail, and then he pulled up the armor menu and scrolled through the hundreds of options he had collected.

"Very impractical armor," he muttered, as he chose what appeared to be a wet, lizard-skin bikini. "Plus 20 cold resistance... sure, that tracks."

He rested the keyboard on his lap and the mouse on the arm of his gaming chair, stuck his feet up on the ottoman that was duct-taped together and covered in crumbs, and launched the prologue.

He'd been playing for an hour before it occurred to him that he no longer felt like crying.

THREE

At lunch the next day, Theo got the corn dog and chips. He headed through the commons, past his friends, avoiding eye contact. He didn't want to sit with them and feel Mateo's absence there.

He found an empty table in the back corner, and sat alone.

At the table nearest his, which was also nearly empty, sat the girl he had seen with AJ yesterday. Rook.

She had a corn dog, a scoop of something potato-like, and a giant pile of salad. She picked up the corn dog, holding it away from herself like it might crawl off her tray, and began to peel the batter off it. Once it was naked, she took a bite, grimaced, and swallowed without chewing, like taking a pill.

"Sick," she muttered.

"Um, *hi*."

Theo flinched. He hadn't noticed Colleen O'Hare approach until she slid into the seat next to Rook's, phone in one hand, oversized water tumbler in the other. "Colleen." She gestured to herself, sweeping a hand from her fuzzy sweater to her polka-dot skirt. “From second period. You’re Rook, right?”

Rook dropped the corn dog and opened a milk box.

Colleen shook back her red wavy hair and leaned in. “So what’s up with you and AJ?”

Rook shrugged, and Theo listened to see how the interrogation would play out. Their tables weren’t far apart—and Colleen wasn’t exactly quiet. She’d been a first-rate gossip ever since Pre-K and was always trying to find out everybody’s business. The lunchroom was loud, but not enough to drown her out.

“Are you two going to Homecoming?” Colleen asked.

Rook swigged her milk.

“Because if you *are*...” Colleen lowered her voice, and Theo couldn’t hear exactly what she said next. He caught *party*, and *Marna’s*.

“And you could be more comfortable,” said Colleen, louder now, like she wanted people to hear her. “Because I get it, AJ’s hot, but the graffiti wall?” She wrinkled her nose. “Nope.”

Rook gave Colleen a dead-eyed stare. “What?”

“I heard it from AJ’s friend,” said Colleen, watching Rook’s face.

“Heard *what*?”

“That you two hooked up.”

“AJ said that?”

“Well,” Colleen sipped from her tumbler, “I don’t know *exactly* what he said, but some people are saying you had sex.”

Theo almost choked on the chip he was eating. Sex? Was that how AJ was going to play this? Rook had walked away, so he’d smeared her in response? What kind of person did that?

What kind of person lets it happen?

Mateo's voice again. Theo's stomach hurt.

You do, I guess.

Rook stabbed her fork into her salad like she hoped it would bleed.

"So it's true?" Colleen nodded. "You're new around here, so, friendly word of advice? AJ's a player. Don't get attached."

Theo expected Rook to protest—to tell Colleen that she hadn't had sex with AJ, not even close—but Rook said nothing.

He could help her, he realized with some discomfort. He could say something right now. Tell Colleen he'd seen everything, and the rumor wasn't true. It would mean admitting that he'd stayed on the wall the whole time. He didn't know if he could make himself do that. Could he explain that he hadn't *meant* to be there? Would anyone believe that?

He was so deep in his mind, he didn't notice the ambush until it was too late.

"You're not eating?"

Marna Hauterman sat down beside him. Theo had avoided her ever since the funeral; he didn't want to talk to her, or Tuyet, or any of his real friends. He couldn't stand to look into their faces and remember how dead Mateo was.

"I know you need space," Marna said. "I don't blame you—I haven't texted, or tried to talk to you in class, and I'm not trying to push you now... I just wanted to tell you, I'm thinking about you every day." She touched his hand. "I'm not ignoring you. I'm giving you space until you're ready, okay?"

Marna was genuinely warm and empathetic. It was why he hadn't gone anywhere near her.

He looked at her, and that was the mistake. When he caught the expression of compassion on her brown, round-cheeked face, he gritted his teeth in self-defense. He didn't want to cry in the cafeteria.

"I don't mean to make it worse." Marna squeezed his hand. "I just wanted to tell you that if you need me..." She trailed off. "I'm having a party Saturday." She sounded less than excited about it. "I just need to try to have fun again. To be normal, even though *nothing* is." Her eyes drifted back to the cafeteria table where their other friends were still eating. "Maybe you could come."

Theo couldn't imagine going back to his friend group, the group where Mateo had always been the nucleus, and acting like he wasn't breaking apart. He glanced at the table where their friends sat, and Tuyet caught his eye. In her dark, unfiltered stare, he saw exactly what he was afraid of. His own grief, mirrored back.

He looked down.

"I know you're sad," said Marna.

Theo laughed in a way that made her draw back.

"You know I don't mean it in a small way," she said, her voice quiet. "I don't know how else to say it."

His heel started tapping. He picked up a chip off his tray and cracked it into pieces. He didn't want to have this conversation. Not here.

"I know nobody misses him more than you and Tuyet." Marna was near tears—he could hear it. "And I know there's nothing I can do, I just wish there was, because I love you both so much, and I *hate* this."

Her words punctured Theo's attempt at detachment; emotion snaked up inside him and wouldn't be denied. Tears pricked his eyes and he blinked them away, furious.

At the table across from his, Colleen still hadn't given up. "So, are you hanging with us for Homecoming?"

Rook grabbed her tray and left without answering. Theo's eyes followed her across the room. Her expression was stone. She left the cafeteria, dumping her uneaten corn dog in the trash as she went.

Marna touched his shoulder. "Tuyet's struggling," she said. "She needs you. I don't know how to help her, but you could—"

Theo pulled away. "No." His voice came out rough. "Just stop. I don't want to do this here, all right?"

He saw her face fall, and knew he'd stung her. He hated that—Marna was the kindest friend he had.

But he didn't apologize. And when she got up and left him alone, he was glad.

FOUR

Not this. Not again.

Rook ditched the cafeteria tray and walked. Fast. Gaining speed with every step. She didn't know where she was going. Not class. Not home.

AJ had told his friends. Of course he had. Of *course* he had. That was how guys like him operated. If they couldn't get it out of your body, they took it out of your name.

I thought you were different.

The comment had been calculated to make her feel guilty about ditching him. She didn't. Instead, those words had cut her in ways he couldn't possibly have imagined. Different? She was *only* different. But nothing had changed. She could move across the country, across the fucking solar system. She could change her name, her face, her fingerprints, trade her soul—it wouldn't matter, because she'd always be the same.

"I thought *you* were with AJ."

Rook slowed. A girl she didn't know stood with Destiny Bray near a classroom door. Destiny's beach waves looked dull. Messy. She stared down at her glittery phone like it had just punched her in the heart.

"Did he even break up with you first?" the girl asked her. "He didn't, did he? God, he's such a dick. I told you."

Destiny's eyes were puffy, but when she caught sight of Rook, her expression turned cold. "Guess he found someone who'll do anything," she said, and she pulled her friend with her into the classroom.

Rook headed for the nearest exit. She slammed the door with both hands and charged through. It flew open and hit the outer wall so hard she almost expected the glass panel to break. Her palms burned.

Was it worth it? her brain asked her, taunting.

He hadn't even been a good kisser. They almost never were. Why did she keep doing this to herself?

The list they'd made, back at Saint Catherine's, grated over the cracks in her mind.

Face—6. Body—10. Mommy-Daddy issues—priceless. Give Brooklyn a little attention, she'll do anything you want.

They'd laughed when they'd sent the list around for rankings. Laughed when they'd put it online. She had been at rock bottom already, and they had found a way to shove her lower.

If she was the same shitty person, she would win the same shitty prize. If she wanted it to be over? Then it had to be over.

She had to burn the evidence.

She went to the upper parking lot, flung open the door of her grandfather's beat-up Civic, and dug through the glove compartment. Her grandfather left stuff everywhere, tangled up and disorganized, but he liked his cigars when he went to the car shows, and she expected to find what she needed.

She closed her hand around a lighter, and shoved it into her pocket. She unzipped her gym bag and the inner pouch, and withdrew the last pieces of herself. Her New York license—the one with her legal name. The letter she had carried with her for ten months.

License. Letter. Lighter.

She left her bags and walked out to the farthest edge of campus. She heard the bell ring for the end of lunch, distant, telling her it was time to head to fourth period—she didn't care. She hid behind the graffiti wall and knelt in the dirt.

Time to end it.

She held up the license and pressed closer to the concrete wall to get under the ledge where she was protected. *Snick.* She rolled the lighter wheel under her thumb.

Burning plastic. Acrid smoke. She was far enough from the school buildings that nobody would smell it.

She watched her picture melt. Curl. Distort. Until it got too hot and her fingernails started to smart. She dropped the ruined thing in the dirt.

You're dead.

She took out the letter—creased, worn, fragile from rereading.

Gabe hadn't just coached her. He'd seen her. All of her.

Don't open it.

She opened it. Read the words. Felt the wound.

> *I've never seen anything like you,*
> *Brooklyn. Nobody has. Every fire you*
> *walk through makes you stronger. Put*
> *that pain in the tank, and you can fly.*

Rage cracked her open. She screamed into the trees until her voice broke, lighter in one hand, crumpled letter in the other. Her heart hammered. Rain touched her face but couldn't cool her.

Her mother had let this happen. Her mother had done this to her. God, she hated her. *Hated* her.

Hated herself for feeling anything at all.

If she couldn't burn it, she'd bury it.

She clawed at the earth, rain soaking the paper as she shoved it into the dirt with the melted license. Buried it like a body. Slammed the ground flat with her fists. She slumped on the ground against the wall, in the rain, in the graveyard she'd made, and looked at her muddy hands. She sat there long enough for the world to get dim.

"Enough," she said, when she was ready.

She got to her feet and left herself behind in the dirt.

FIVE

Rook woke in the Ford Ranger, feet on the dash. Black water—freezing cold—up to her waist.

The river kept rising. The truck was sinking. Oh God, she was going to die—

Her fingers fumbled for the seat belt buckle. She groped for the driver's seat, but couldn't find her dad, and now they were calling her name. It was her turn. She would miss the first event.

She crawled out of the truck through the window and landed on the floor in her mother's house, but it didn't look like Caroline's house—it looked like a weightlifting meet. She broke into a run, sprinting toward the only thing that she could still see: a loaded barbell on a platform. She had to reach it. Her feet got stuck.

"Dad! *Dad*!"

"I'm here."

Not her father's voice. Gabe stepped up close behind her and put his hands on her shoulders.

"Put that pain in the tank."

Her feet finally moved; she hurtled up the courthouse

steps toward Caroline's blood-spattered face. Her mother turned to her, slow, and her eyes rolled back.

"You won't live at home anymore." Her mother sagged toward the wall. The gun dangled from her listless hand. "You're not going to see your mother anymore."

A phone buzzed and kept buzzing, growing louder and more insistent, but the airplane didn't have a phone, and she didn't want to go on the airplane; she was three years old, and she didn't understand.

"You're too loud." Her mother reached over to buckle her seatbelt, because they were taking off now. "Everyone's looking."

"I want to go home." Rook pulled at the seat belt, but it was tight and she didn't understand how to work it. "I want my mommy—"

Her mother clicked a lighter. Held up the flame.

"Get used to it, you little bitch."

The alarm clock finally broke through. The dream cracked.

Rook woke up.

She lay in the dark, sweating and cold, disoriented. It had been two months, but she still got confused sometimes, and it took a couple of seconds to piece reality together.

She lived in Cedar Point, Washington, in Oscar Radcliffe's apartment. She was with her grandfather now. Everything else was behind her.

She flailed for her alarm and slapped it. "Shut up," she croaked. "Fuck."

That had been a bad one.

Rook waited for the nightmare to fully ebb away and adjusted to the quiet. No white noise. No cars. No sirens. Nothing like New York. Only the slow drip of a leaking faucet, and the intermittent sound of wind in the trees.

And a sense of gnawing dread.

Somebody was going to find her old stuff behind the graffiti wall. She hadn't buried it deep enough. Rain would erode the dig site, and students would go out there, and someone would kick up the dirt, and what the hell had she been thinking?

She hadn't been thinking. She'd been raw and reckless —not for the first time. But one good night's sleep, and her rational brain was back online.

It wasn't even six a.m., but she moved fast, driven by fear. She yanked on her sneakers, grabbed her backpack and gym bag, took a couple bananas from the kitchen, and got her giant water bottle out of the fridge. She opened the coat closet by the front door and felt around on the top shelf for the flashlight that Oscar kept there. She hated borrowing his stuff, but what choice did she have? She had to get to campus.

She drove to Lakeview without her license. She was going to be driving without a license for a while thanks to her little freakout yesterday. Not that she cared, but Oscar might get mad if he knew she was driving his car illegally. So she just wouldn't tell him.

Hers was the first car in the upper parking lot. Good. Nobody would be on campus yet except maybe custodians, but they wouldn't be out by the woods. She went silently down the parking lot stairs and onto the dark campus, flashlight in hand.

At the bottom of the steps, a brisk wind hissed down the outdoor hallway, rattling the chains that held the garbage cans' lids in place. Rook swung around, almost expecting to find someone behind her.

Disquieted, she stood still and listened. No footsteps.

No voices. Nothing but the rustling of the wind through the cedars and firs that ringed the school.

Her gut told her to turn around. To go.

She couldn't. The longer she left her real name out there, the more likely somebody would find it. She walked onto the unlit baseball field, toward the graffiti wall. She couldn't see, but she couldn't risk the flashlight yet. She had to reach the wall. Then she could dig.

Ten feet from the wall, her foot caught on something big and solid. She stumbled—pitched forward—dropped the flashlight and fell hard onto the thing that had tripped her.

The second she landed, she knew.

Legs under her chest. Sneakers in front of her face. Motionless. A person.

A body.

"Fuck," she gasped, and tried to get up. She grabbed a shin, a thigh—her hands were wet—blood? Rain? Her primal brain clawed at her, survival instincts firing. She had to run, to get out *now*—

She scrambled to her knees and saw who she'd been lying on. Adrenaline surged through her, disconnecting her brain from her limbs.

AJ?

She fumbled for the flashlight. It took her three tries to press the button. She shone the light on his face.

AJ.

He lay face down, one cheek to the grass, hair matted with blood, mouth open, eye shut. Ghostly white.

Rook stared, lightheaded with nausea, catapulted back in time to Christmas Eve, to the house on Lake George in upstate New York. Dead men and guns. Brains and bone and spattered blood.

"Oh God," said a voice.

Rook shot to her feet and swung the beam of the flashlight at the voice in the darkness. A boy stood in front of her—pale and blond, shielding his eyes against the flashlight beam.

"What did you do?" he said.

Rook's heart beat so fast she thought she might pass out. Her brain pounded, and she swayed. She wanted to run, but she couldn't breathe. She sat heavily in the grass, sucking for air, flashlight lolling in her hand.

The boy had his phone out, its flashlight fixed on her. A woman's crisp voice issued from the speaker.

"911, what is your emergency?"

"My name is Theo Locke," said the boy. "I'm on the baseball field at Lakeview High School in Cedar Point. One of my classmates, AJ Ellsworth—he looks dead."

"Is the person breathing?"

Theo dropped to his knees beside AJ and placed two fingers on his throat. He bent low to listen. "Yes, he's alive."

Rook cried out softly. *Alive.*

"Is the person male or female?"

"Male. He's sixteen," said Theo, "and his head is bloody, and it looks bad."

"Is he conscious?"

"AJ," Theo said loudly, "AJ, can you hear me?" He dropped his phone and shook AJ's shoulders hard. "Not responsive." He looked at Rook, his voice rising. "And there's a girl here. She was with him when I found him—maybe she—I don't know. We're alone."

"Get to a safe location if you feel in danger. Stay on the line."

Panic rose in Rook's chest like water.

He thought *she* had done this.

Everyone was going to think she had done this.

Just like her mother.

She staggered to her feet. She couldn't stay here. She heard the 911 operator's voice, but she couldn't hear the words anymore—she had to run, had to hide. She bolted, not thinking about direction. Away from AJ. Away from the scene. That was all that mattered.

Theo jumped up and reached for her—she didn't know if it was to stop her, and she didn't mean to strike him, but she lashed out on instinct, and he fell. She fled toward the chain-link fence that separated the field from a row of houses beyond—and that was the wrong way. She needed her car. She was about to turn around when she caught sight of a young girl, no older than ten, standing on the other side of the fence in her pajamas, her hair tousled, her eyes wide. She stared past Rook, toward the dark field.

"No." Rook flung out her arms, trying to block the girl's view. "Don't look. Go inside."

"Theo?" the girl said uncertainly. "I can't see you. Are you okay?"

"No, don't look, go back in your house."

"Leave my sister alone," Theo shouted behind her. "The police are coming—Savannah, go inside, wake up Mom and Dad, hurry."

Savannah fled.

Rook's knees caved. She sank down into the grass against the fence, hugging her legs and hiding her face as sirens drew nearer. She had no idea what to do, or where to go.

She only knew that wherever she went, she was never really going to get away.

SIX

Theo sat on the couch beside his mother, holding her hand tightly as he answered a police officer's questions for the second time in his life. The first was after he had found Mateo's body, and he had been in shock. He only remembered fragments—it felt like another person had been speaking.

This was different. The shock was real, but wearing off faster. AJ didn't matter to him the way Mateo had. Theo was rattled, but he didn't feel like someone had cut off his oxygen.

Officer Petros's mustache nearly eclipsed his top lip. His detective badge shone like it was brand new. He showed Theo a school picture of an unsmiling female student as red and blue lights sliced through the Lockes' front blinds, circling in their living room as the sun rose outside.

"This the girl? Sophomore at Lakeview? Goes by Rook Radcliffe?"

Goes by? thought Theo, nodding.

"You ever spoken to her?"

"No. Not until a few minutes ago."

"Tell me what you saw when you found her."

Theo described, in exact, careful detail, every step he had taken and every moment of the encounter.

"Sharp memory," said Officer Petros. "Thanks for being so clear. What do you know about Rook and AJ?"

Theo didn't want to answer with his mother listening. Nobody knew that he had been up on top of the graffiti wall the other day—maybe it was good that he hadn't told Colleen. Now he could keep it to himself.

Can you? Really?

Mateo's voice was clear in his mind. Quiet and grieved.

Hermano.

No. Mateo would have told the truth. He would tell the truth.

He pulled his hand out of his mother's and crossed his arms. "I saw them hooking up," he said. Eyes on the floor.

"When and where?"

"After school. The day before yesterday. Behind the graffiti wall on campus."

"How'd you see them if they were back there?"

"I was on the wall. Up at the top. I climbed up there before they showed up."

"Why?"

"I just... like it up there."

"What did you see and hear?"

"Word for word?"

"If you can."

Theo could, but he wished his mom would leave. Horrible heat flooded him as he repeated exactly what he had witnessed. Officer Petros took careful notes.

"Was he using force to make her participate?" he asked.

Theo glanced up. He wasn't sure how to answer that one.

"I guess... no?" he said. "He was force*ful*, he was—aggressive. But so was she, at first, and she didn't stop him. Until she did," he added.

"He tried to stop her from leaving, you said."

"He got in her way, but he didn't touch her. When she told him to move, he moved, but..." Theo rubbed the back of his neck. "It felt wrong."

"You have any other info about her and him?"

"Yeah," said Theo. "At lunch, I heard Colleen O'Hare tell her that AJ told his friends about what they did."

"Colleen told Rook?" Petros repeated, writing. "What did she say?"

"That AJ told his friends that he and Rook hooked up." He cleared his throat. "Behind the wall. Which they did—but Colleen said people are saying they had sex. Rook and AJ. Which they didn't." He clamped his mouth shut. He had never explained anything so badly.

"How'd Rook take that?"

"She looked angry—but that's just my perception," he hurried to say, his debate background kicking in. "I have no evidence, I'm going by her facial expression."

"How angry?" Petros asked. "Enough to hurt somebody?"

Theo looked at the officer in surprise. The question wasn't fair. "She might not have hurt anyone. I didn't see what happened."

The officer gave Theo a wry look that made him prickle. He wasn't wrong. He could have made a good argument that someone else had done the crime, and that Rook had simply shown up at the wrong moment, as he had. It was possible. Improbable, perhaps, but possible.

"Not saying she did anything," said Petros. "Just trying to get a read, is all. What were you doing on the baseball field so early?"

"I was going to the library early to meet someone from debate club," said Theo. "Sareth Sok. We said we'd meet at six-thirty—and I always go across the field, it's the fastest way from my house."

"You live right on the edge of campus," said Petros. "You could've left fifteen minutes later and still made it on time."

"I wanted to beat him there, for once," said Theo. "He's always earlier than me when we do research sessions. It probably sounds flimsy, but it's true. We're competitive."

"Got it." Petros closed his notebook. "You've been really helpful, Theo. And you did good calling 911 when you found your friend—you showed real presence of mind, all right? Lakeview's gonna be closed all day while we do some follow-up, so you stay home and get some rest. Get in touch if you think of anything else I should know." He gave them his contact information and departed.

In the heavy quiet that he left behind, Franny Locke put a hand through her fading strawberry-blonde curls and regarded Theo with green-yellow eyes that were just like his own.

"I can't imagine hurting another person that way," she said. "That girl must carry a lot of trauma. I hope she finds the help she needs."

"You mean Rook?"

His mother nodded.

Again, Theo's conscience prodded him. "She might not have done it."

His mother didn't reply to this. "I need time to process," she said eventually. "The last time I saw AJ, you kids were in middle school. In my mind, he's still twelve. It sounds like he's... changed."

"Yeah." Theo's voice was dry.

"Do you need space right now?"

Yes.

But he shook his head. "I'm all right."

"Can I ask a question?"

No.

"Sure."

His mother searched his face. "You and Ana," she ventured, and then, in spite of having gained permission, she left the question unasked. "Sometimes I think of *you* as twelve too. But you're a sophomore now, and she's a senior, so... I won't ask you today. You've been through enough. But maybe another time, we should talk about—"

"No."

Theo and his girlfriend were not having sex. Ana didn't want to, and he wasn't in a rush, and he didn't want to talk about her like that—not with his mother. Not with anyone. What they had was theirs, and what they did together—that was theirs too. His mother didn't get to know how far he'd been. Even if he hadn't been that far.

He wished he could call Ana now. Talk to her. She was at school, but maybe afterward she could come over and pull him out of here. Get his head out of all this.

He pulled out his phone and saw notifications flooding the screen. He scrolled, startled. A lot of people had tagged and texted him, even though it was barely 8:30 in the morning.

Somebody must've seen the emergency vehicles at his house. They must've seen AJ being wheeled into the ambulance and Rook being taken by the cops.

Ana had texted too. He tilted his screen so his mom couldn't see it, and he thumbed her text to read it.

[ANA] Estoy aquí. Si quieres hablar, llámame.

He had texted in Spanish with Mateo, too. He had found Mateo in the grass, like he'd found AJ. He had called 911. He had tried everything.

You did good. You showed real presence of mind.

They had said that after Mateo. He'd done a good job. He'd done everything he should. He hadn't done anything wrong.

Theo's hands started to shake.

"You're just so young," his mother said. "There's no rush. Even if the other boys don't think so."

He turned off his screen. "I'm not doing anything, Mom." His teeth chattered. It was hard to get the words out. "I promise."

Franny put her arm around him. "My baby. This is all so much. I'm glad you weren't hurt, but I wish it were different."

Theo tried to hold still as the flood hit him. He stared at the wall across from the couch, unmoving, willing the trembling to stop.

"Theo." His mother's voice was sharp. "Honey?"

"I'm... I'm here, Mom." He didn't want her to think it was a seizure. It wasn't. He didn't know what it was. "I need to lie down."

His mother went with him to his room. He turned off the lights and got under the covers, and she sat there beside him, one hand on his back.

"I'm fine," he said, "I promise. I'm not seizing, I just want to sleep."

She looked reluctant. But she kissed his head and left.

Theo took out his phone again. More notifications, more texts. But the only person he wanted to talk to was Ana.

His fingers trembled too badly to text her, so he called.

"Cariño, ¿qué pasó?" she said at once. "¿Qué puedo hacer?"

"Just talk to me," he whispered. "Tell me something normal."

"Okay." Ana was quiet for a moment. "You want me to bore you with cheerleading stunt stuff?"

"Yes. Please. Also, it's not boring."

She laughed softly. "Nice save," she said. "Even in an emergency, you're a really good boyfriend."

He tried to laugh. It didn't work.

"Shh," she said. "Okay, pyramids—no, extensions, this is good, you'll like this, I can make it about physics."

He lay there in the darkness, her voice in his ear, coming down from panic as Ana told him everything he had never wanted to know about how Newtonian laws applied to full-ups and extensions.

SEVEN

"This interview is audio-video recorded. Ms. Chase is present with counsel. Oscar Radcliffe signed minor-interview consent."

Officer Petros picked up his pen. Rook sat across from him in the Cedar Point Police Station, arms crossed, chin up.

Bring it, she thought. *Not my first rodeo.*

"State your full name."

"The one I use?"

"Your legal name."

"Brooklyn Chase."

"Age?"

"Sixteen."

Petros was young, beefy, and thickly mustached, with a nick on his chin that told Rook that he still hadn't mastered shaving his face, and a mustard stain on one cuff. Not the kind of fine motor skills, she thought, that inspired confidence in his ability to handle the gun that hung at his belt.

"And you're a sophomore at Lakeview."

Rook nodded. She was a sophomore. She was also tired,

right down to her bones, of being in places like this, with men like him. Over the past ten months, she had sat in so many interrogation rooms, with so many different officers of the law, that she should have been used to it by now. But being questioned by authorities always made her feel small and guilty and afraid, and the best way to deal with that feeling was to act like she felt nothing at all.

"Blunt force trauma to the head." Officer Petros looked her in the eyes, and Rook could tell that he thought guilt was a genetic condition.

He thought she was just like her mother.

Rook checked her lawyer, Greta Talty, to see if she had to reply.

Greta recrossed her legs and pushed back a glossy swath of expensively foiled and blown-out blonde hair. She was trim, tall, and well dressed, but her face couldn't hide that she'd been smoking for decades. She was in her late 40s, but she looked older.

"My client is here to give a statement about what happened on campus when Mr. Ellsworth was found," Greta said, flipping a page of her legal pad. She was only in Cedar Point to protect Rook's mother's interests. Still, it was good to have a kickass lawyer on her side. It steadied her nerves. It always had.

Officer Petros consulted his notes. "What time did you arrive at school on Wednesday?"

"Six a.m."

"What brought you to campus so early, Ms. Chase?"

Were you ever involved in your mother's business, Ms. Chase? Did she have other associates? We know how difficult this must be for you, Ms. Chase.

"I go by Radcliffe," she said.

"Answer the question, Ms. Chase."

"I have zero period weightlifting, Officer."

"Detective," he said stiffly.

"Cool."

He glared. "We know you're an Olympic weightlifter. What's your PR?"

"For what?"

The officer looked stymied. He swiped at his phone. "A clean and jerk," he said.

"Hundred and ten."

"Pounds?"

"Sure," said Rook, letting him hear how stupid she thought he was. "Pounds."

He swiped at his phone again. "Kilos," he muttered. "So that's 242 pounds." He looked begrudgingly impressed as he put the phone down. "You could easily overpower AJ, couldn't you?"

"Irrelevant speculation," said Greta.

"Noted. Moving on." Petros shifted gears. "How long have you known AJ?"

"Not long," said Rook. "I only moved here this summer."

"From New York. You moved here to live with your paternal grandfather, Oscar Radcliffe, is that right?"

"Yes."

"Because your mother's in prison." Petros checked his notes. "And your father is deceased. Correct?"

Rook gazed up at the gray ceiling, wishing for the millionth time that her dad was still alive and that the last six years had never happened.

"Yeah."

"Last night, at midnight, where were you?"

"Why?" asked Rook at once. "Is that when you guys think the attack happened?"

"Just answer the question."

"I was asleep."

"Any witnesses to that?"

"How would I have a witness to that? You think my grandfather watches me sleep? What is this, your first case?"

Officer Petros gave her a quick, startled look, and Rook leaned in.

"It *is*," she said. "Did you just make detective? Am I number one? You must be sweating."

"Brooklyn," said Greta, sounding tired, "don't make this worse."

Petros didn't continue the interrogation right away. He tapped his notes on the table a couple times to make the stack even, and he wouldn't look at her. Rook watched this, satisfied. If he was going to make her feel crappy, then at least she could return the favor.

"How did you and AJ first meet?" Petros asked, when he started up again.

"In the weight room."

"You ever spoken with him?"

"Yeah."

"What was the nature of those conversations?"

Rook checked Greta, who shrugged as though to say, *You might as well answer that one.*

"We have one class together," said Rook. "We don't talk."

"Is your relationship platonic?"

Rook wasn't sure whether AJ had regained consciousness. But if he did wake up, and they asked him about her, he would tell them. Better not to lie.

"We kissed," she said.

"How did that come about?"

"Uh, the usual way. He put his mouth on my mouth."

Petros rolled his eyes. "Describe the encounter."

"No!"

"Brooklyn," Greta said warningly.

"I'm not fucking *describing* what we did!"

"Keep the questions specific," Greta said to Petros.

"How long were you and AJ romantically involved?"

"We weren't."

"Sexually involved, then."

Rook flushed, frustrated with her own lack of composure. "We hooked up after school on Wednesday, all right? That's it."

"And then?"

"And then he got head-bashed, dickhole!"

"If you have no further questions for my client," said Greta, "and no reasonable evidence with which to hold her, we'll be on our way."

"Hold on." Petros pointed his pen at Rook. "You were on campus way earlier than zero period—and you weren't at the gym, you were on the baseball field. Way over by the graffiti wall. Explain why."

Rook folded her arms. "I was taking a walk."

"Get serious."

"I am. I was warming up. First I took a walk, then I was going to run a little bit. Then I'd hit the gym."

"You had a flashlight."

"It was dark. I didn't want to trip."

She wasn't telling Petros about her mental breakdown yesterday and the burial pit she'd made out behind the graffiti wall. She would sooner go to prison with her mom. The lie made sense, and she was sticking to it. The only way they'd find out the truth was if they dug around the wall themselves.

Which they might. She was sure they were out there looking for evidence. If they *didn't* find it, she would have to go back out there and get it, but she didn't know how she was going to pull that off, now that it was literally a crime scene.

Jesus, her luck was shit.

"You want to try that again?" Petros asked. "Maybe tell the truth this time?"

"I don't know what you're talking about," Rook replied, too fast. She knew just how guilty she sounded.

Fuck. Keep your cool.

"I'm talking about how AJ was out there to meet *you*," said Petros. "You think we didn't know that?"

"Meet me?" Rook echoed, looking blankly at him. "He said that?"

"He didn't have to. It's in his texts."

Greta sat forward. "You're saying you already ran digital forensics." She sounded disbelieving.

"Our techs imaged the phone," said Petros. "Full analysis takes time, but we can see the recent texts."

Rook frowned. "Who texted?"

"We have AJ's phone. We talked to his friends. Chad Perkins knew exactly where AJ was headed. We know what happened." Petros paused, watching her face. "Starting to remember now?"

Rook looked at Greta. "I don't have a phone," she said.

Petros gave a rich snort. "A teenager with your resources doesn't have a phone."

"It's true," Rook said hotly.

"It's true," Greta confirmed. "Check the records. Her New York phone was disconnected in August."

"Doesn't matter," said Petros, "you could've borrowed one."

"Who would I borrow one from?" said Rook. "My grandfather? He only has a landline."

"A friend, then."

Greta made a quiet, amused sound.

Petros opened a folder and withdrew a printout. "'It's Rook,'" he read. "'Meet me at the wall.'"

"*What?*"

"And then AJ says, 'Why, so you can bail again?' And you say, 'I'm sorry. Please come. Just don't tell anybody this time.'"

"The actual fuck," Rook said. "That was not me."

"Your prints are on him."

Rook opened her mouth, but Greta cut her off.

"And you ran that analysis *how* fast?" she said. "Save the bluffs for someone without counsel."

"You were on the ground right next to AJ," said Petros, pointing to Rook with his pen again. "Witness confirmed."

"Because I tripped on him in the dark!"

Petros put his pen down with a slap. "I thought you brought the flashlight so you wouldn't trip," he said. He let that one land, watching her. "Why wasn't it turned on?"

Rook hesitated.

Think. Say something. Now.

"I thought I heard a noise," she said. "I pointed it to the side."

Petros made a note. "Then you ran for it, shoved Theo Locke, and threatened his kid sister—"

"I didn't threaten anybody!"

"You told Savannah Locke to turn around and go in her house."

"Yeah, because she looked young, and I didn't—" She stopped, twisting her hands, wondering if they had interrogated Savannah. Of course they had—they didn't care who they messed up, as long as they got their answers. That poor kid had probably been terrified.

"Didn't what?" Petros prodded.

"I don't know. AJ was bloody. Kids shouldn't see shit like that."

"Did you take anything off AJ's person?"

"They searched me at the scene. You know the answer's no."

"Did you notice if anything had been taken off him?"

Rook sat back slowly, remembering something. AJ usually wore a necklace—a thick chain with a gold ring on it. When she had shone her flashlight on him, she hadn't seen it.

"That's a yes." Petros leaned in. "What is it?"

"I'm not sure." Rook checked Greta. "Should I say what I think I remember? Because I could be wrong."

Greta shook her head. "Just facts."

Rook said nothing more. She hadn't noticed the chain, but that didn't mean it hadn't been there. It could have been down in his shirt.

"All right, Ms. Chase." Petros shot an irritated look at Greta. "We've got your statement. We'll contact you if we have additional questions. You're free to go."

Once outside the station, Greta took out a pack of cigarettes and tapped it against the heel of her palm. Her smooth blonde hair and perfect manicure gleamed youthfully, in sharp contrast with the lines on her face.

"So, you're having fun out here in the beautiful Pacific Northwest."

Rook didn't answer. She was still in knots from that dumb prick and his dumb prick questions. She stuck her hands in the pockets of her leggings and lifted her chin. Fuck everybody.

Who had texted AJ?

"The texts AJ got," said Rook, trying not to sound as freaked out as she felt. "Should I be worried?"

"If they had anything definitive, you'd still be inside," said Greta. "My guess? Those texts came from a burner. Cheap and common."

"But why would someone pretend to be me?"

"I guess someone doesn't like you," said Greta. "Which is, of course, a huge surprise." She sighed. "Look, the point of coming here was a clean break. If it's this messy already, you might as well be in New York. You can come home. Your mother wants you to know you've got options."

"She's a giver."

"She genuinely wants you to have whatever you need."

All Rook had needed for the last six years was a mom who cared she existed. "How's Caroline liking white-collar prison?" she asked, not quite able to hide her bitterness. "I hear they have yoga."

"You can go back to boarding at Saint Catherine's. You haven't lost your spot there. They understand the circumstances."

"Fuck Saint Catherine's."

"Brooklyn—"

"*Don't* call me that. I use a different name now, and I told you, I want that to be official."

"I'll start the paperwork." Greta tapped a cigarette from the pack and held it ready between two fingertips as she fished in her expensive handbag for a lighter.

"And I want to be emancipated," Rook said. "Let's do that paperwork too."

Greta gave her an arch look.

"Fine, then what do I need for a GED? I want to take the test and be done with high school."

"You're not getting a GED."

"That's not up to you! You can't tell me what to—"

"Your mother insists that you graduate."

"Why? Does she want me to go to Harvard, like her, so I can be as good a criminal?"

Greta gave a tight-lipped smile. "Tell me. If you were allowed to leave high school, what would you do?"

"Whatever I want."

"And that is?"

Rook couldn't fill in the blank. Nine months ago, the answer would have been easy. Since early childhood, she had wanted a life in elite athletics. The Olympics. But now, if she kept competing, the press would find her. They'd keep on hounding her. She'd never be left alone.

She would also have to work with a coach. The moment she thought it, Gabe's voice filled her head.

I've never seen anything like you, Brooklyn.

No. She had buried him.

"See?" Greta lit her cigarette and inhaled. "You don't know what you want. You're a child."

"I'm sixteen."

Greta gestured as if to say that this was exactly her point, and Rook paced several feet away to get clear of the secondhand smoke.

"I can't even go back to school, right?" she said. "They won't let me come back."

"They can't bar you from your classes. There's no evidence you've done anything wrong. You'll return on Monday. I'll see that it's handled."

Rook didn't want to return on Monday. Or ever. Nothing good would happen when she walked back onto that campus. Rumors would drown her.

"If you're set on staying in Cedar Point, you'll need

money." Greta dragged on the cigarette again. "I'll arrange an account for you—Caroline's legacy holdings are still intact, and I have access to what's legally clean."

"No. Tell Caroline to shove her money up her ass."

"Of course, I'll pass the message right along. But you'll need a gym membership at the very least, won't you?"

"I can lift at school." It was far from ideal, but still better than giving in.

"Clothing allowance?" Greta pressed. "Cell phone?"

Rook shook her head. She had clothes, and she could deal without a phone. She missed having one—she didn't have anybody to call, but it would have made evenings at Oscar's way less boring if she had internet access again. Oscar only had a landline and a cable subscription that he used to watch NASCAR races. That part blew.

"What about food? I assume you're still puritanical about what you eat. Public school lunches must be killing you."

Greta had that right—Rook did miss eating well. Her grandfather lived on canned soup and instant oatmeal, and frozen peas were his idea of vegetables. But the situation was temporary, and she didn't blame Oscar. He only had enough for one person to live on, and he hadn't planned to take on a teenager in his retirement.

He hadn't really wanted to, either. He wasn't unkind, but she knew he'd taken her in more out of duty than desire. He had only showed up at the police station tonight to sign a form and give the cops Greta's number—Rook had sat in the interview room alone for hours, waiting for Greta's plane to land.

It wasn't like Oscar could've helped, if he had stayed, she reasoned. He couldn't have defended her—that was Greta's job.

He could've sat with her, though. If he'd wanted to.

But he was her only family left, other than Caroline, and he was letting her stay with him. Because of him, she didn't have to go back to New York. That was enough.

"Take care of Oscar's rent," Rook said. "He had to move from a one bedroom into a two bedroom when I got here, and it costs him more."

"I've already done that." Greta looked critically at her. "What was it, by the way?"

"What?"

"The thing you remembered. Was something taken from AJ?"

"Maybe." Rook enjoyed the dissatisfied look that flickered across Greta's face. "But like you said, let's stick to facts."

Greta clicked her lighter shut and tucked it into her handbag as a town car pulled up. "I have a flight to catch. Call me when you realize that principles don't buy groceries."

She got into the town car and was gone.

EIGHT

Monday, before school, Theo faced Sareth Sok in the library, squinting down at his debate research. His head throbbed from terrible sleep. It didn't help that the other students in the library kept stopping to gawk.

"That's him—Theo. The one who found AJ."

He tried to ignore it. It was going to be like this all day. All week, maybe.

"That citation is lazy," said Sareth, in the condescending tone that Theo was sure he reserved exclusively for him. "I can't use that."

"It's a draft," said Theo.

"No, *this* is a draft," Sareth replied. He swept back the fall of dark hair that fell to his eyebrows and held up a card of his own. "Author name, title, source, date. Perhaps you'd like to keep it as a model? You know this is why I'm going to win."

"You didn't last time, but sure. Keep the dream alive." Theo pulled his notebook closer, trying to block out Sareth along with everybody else. "Don't interrupt me, I'm trying to think."

"Let me know if it happens."

"We cannot," Theo said to himself as he scribbled, "build moral policy on an immoral foundation."

Sareth yawned. "Abstract ethics. Waste of time."

"Even if the intention is decent... no." Theo tapped the pen to his mouth. "Because it's not. Locking up kids is immoral. The end."

"Soft. Also, *is* it? What if the children are murderers?"

"Human dignity... deserves better than a cage. Not quite. What am I trying to say?"

"Good thing you're pretty, Locke."

Theo shot him an irritated look. "The cage shouldn't exist. That's the point. If we build it, we *have* to use it. The premise gets accepted. And the premise is: someone belongs in the cage."

"For once, focus on something *concrete*," Sareth said wearily. "Crime reduction, measurable improvements to society—*facts*. Not this emotional tripe."

"It's not tripe," Theo snapped.

Sareth gave him a look of reproach.

They always needled each other. It was nothing new. Theo didn't know why he couldn't take it this time. Maybe the lack of sleep. Maybe the awfulness of Friday morning, and how dead AJ had looked, illuminated suddenly in front of him by that flashlight beam.

"I thought we agreed to push each other," said Sareth.

"We did."

"This is how we always work."

Theo sighed. "I know. Just been a rough couple days."

Sareth gave him a long, watchful look, opened his mouth like he might ask something, and then seemed to think better of it.

"Still debating philosophy, boys?" Delilah Prasad rolled

up to a nearby table in her wheelchair and took out her laptop. "When you're ready to level up, try physics."

"And a very good morning to you too," Theo muttered.

A voice he didn't know issued from behind the stacks.

"Does he *know* the girl who slept with AJ?"

"Rook? I think so. I saw the cops arrest her in his yard."

The speakers were quiet but energized. Theo looked toward the shelves. A group of students stood there, mostly out of view.

"The animals are bored," Delilah warned. "Don't feed them."

"Hey, Theo," called a girl he didn't know, stepping out from behind the bookshelves. "Were you there when she did it? Did you *see* it?"

Theo tapped his heel under the table. Rapid.

Sareth spoke up. "We have actual work to do," he snapped at the crowd behind the shelves. "If you could be quiet."

"Um, *hi*."

Colleen O'Hare appeared, red hair shining, phone in hand. She positioned herself between Theo and the cluster of gossiping students, but Theo didn't feel shielded. If anything, with Colleen involved, he was about to be even more exposed.

"Are you okay?" Colleen sat down at the table beside him. "I know you found AJ. What happened?"

She leaned in and waited.

Theo didn't reply. He had to be careful. Anything he said could and would be used against him.

"Locke is busy," said Sareth eventually. "He's attempting rational thought."

Colleen frowned at Sareth. "You got Chad banned from

the weight room," she said. "I heard you went to the principal."

"You did?" Theo glanced at Sareth. "What did he do?"

Sareth gave him a warning look, and Theo understood. Not in front of Colleen.

"So did you?" Colleen asked.

Sareth shrugged. "I made a report," he said. "And?"

"It's just, you know, some people feel like you snitched."

"Oh no, not that," Delilah deadpanned. "Anything but that."

Colleen peered toward Delilah's laptop screen, where the view was impossibly technical. Theo wasn't even sure what it was.

"What *is* that?" Colleen asked.

"It's a PID loop compensator for joint lag in powered orthotics," Delilah replied. "Want to check the math, or was that the info you needed?"

Colleen turned back to Theo. "AJ's in a coma," she said. "Can you believe that?"

A coma. Theo thought of AJ's white face, and the blood in his hair. He shuddered.

"People are saying you found her standing over him," Colleen added. "Did she freak out or something?"

Theo shook his head, barely, and started to say something. To defend Rook. Why was that his instinct? She had been on the scene, kneeling over AJ, holding a flashlight that could have been used as a club.

But the way she had looked... The way she had sat there, listless, staring, sucking for air. What had happened to her? Had AJ done something to her? Had she been defending herself?

"With a weapon," said Colleen. "Some people said a dumbbell."

"That's ridiculous," said Theo, unable to stop himself. "She didn't have a dumbbell."

"She was jealous," Colleen went on. "AJ was with Destiny, so I heard Rook texted him. Tricked him into meeting her."

Theo tried to process this. Rook had texted AJ to meet her? It didn't sound right. When she had walked away from AJ, she hadn't seemed uncertain, like somebody who might come back. And she had already known about Destiny—that information couldn't have triggered a blind rage. She had said as much to AJ. *Try that line on Destiny.*

Words that could have sounded jealous, maybe, but that hadn't been her tone. She hadn't sounded wounded, just worn down. Finished.

"We're up against a deadline," said Sareth, his voice clipped. "We need this time to prepare. Locke, should we look at Aff?"

"Uh—yeah." Theo refocused on his notebook, glad to have a task. "Aff."

Colleen got up and smoothed down her skirt. "We'll talk later," she said, with a knowing look at Theo. "Once I know more."

When she was gone, Theo tried to concentrate, but it was pointless. He couldn't sit still. He didn't want to stay here and wait for the next question or confrontation—he'd just go to class. Do his AP flashcards. Maybe Señora Delgado would have her door unlocked early, and he could get out of everyone's sight.

He swung his backpack onto his shoulder and grabbed the rest of his books in his arms. He checked Sareth. "Tomorrow?"

"I'll be here," Sareth replied, without looking up from his notes. "Before you."

Theo walked out, hugging his books like armor, weaving between groups of students who watched him, whispering. He pushed open the library door and went into the hall, where the situation was worse. People weren't just whispering now, they were pointing too—but not at him.

He didn't see Rook until he almost walked into her. She came around the corner so fast that she had to stop hard to keep from hitting him. She stood still for one moment, shoulders high and tense.

She met his eyes, and he saw her expression.

Hunted. Hurt. Theo drew a breath at the intensity of that stare.

Then, just as suddenly, her gaze was empty. Like she'd switched herself off. Exactly the way she'd looked when the police had arrested her behind his house—the way she had looked lying underneath AJ. Vacant. She kept moving, past him, heading in the direction of the gym, strides growing longer and quicker until she shoved open the door at the end of the hall.

Go. Talk to her.

Theo moved. His body acted before his brain caught up.

Why was he doing this? What was he going to do—interrogate her? He hated being questioned. Why would she be any different?

He didn't stop.

She was fast, cutting through the crowd. He trailed her at a distance. She ran up the weight room steps without looking back. Theo stopped at the bottom, uncertain.

He should walk away. This wasn't his business. The police were handling it. Curiosity wasn't worth the risk.

Goes by Rook Radcliffe.

What high school sophomore had an alias?

This wasn't just curiosity. It mattered. It was about truth. And if Mateo were alive, he wouldn't hesitate. He'd get it.

Go up there, said Mateo, in his mind. *What's the worst case?*

The worst case was she clubbed him in the head.

But the police hadn't kept her, which meant no charges. That didn't mean she was innocent. Just that they didn't have enough.

Gonna stand here all day, or what?

He remembered how easily she'd dropped him.

And how she'd looked behind his house—small. Shaking. Then silent and straight-backed in cuffs, like someone used to it.

Who was she?

Only one way to know.

Theo climbed the stairs.

NINE

Rook prayed the weight room was unlocked, because it was barely first period, and she was at capacity. If she had to listen to one more person say something about how she'd banged AJ and bashed him in the head with a dumbbell, she would hit someone in the face for real.

She needed her GED. She had to get out of this place. School always turned out like this—it didn't matter if she was somebody or nobody. She was a magnet for this crap.

Make bad choices, get bad consequences. Live and learn.

Just kidding. You'll never learn.

She reached the weight room. She didn't know why she had come here—it was probably locked. And if it was locked, she was skipping out for the rest of the day, and she didn't care if she got in trouble. If she couldn't lift right now, then she could not deal with this.

She reached for the door handle, praying for a miracle. She had only found it open once. Gonzalez almost always locked it after zero period.

She tested the handle.

It turned.

Relief surged. She stepped quickly inside before a teacher could spot her, and when she looked around and found herself alone, she slumped in the quiet, shut her eyes, and thanked the gym gods for cutting her a tiny break.

She could lift now. Really lift, exactly like she wanted, as hard as she wanted, heavy enough to push everything else out of her head. Nobody was here to stop her, or to start asking questions. For once, she was free. She needed it so bad she could have cried.

Deep breath. Release.

She opened her eyes and went to the floor barbell. She dropped her gym bag, knelt, and sat back on her heels, letting her hamstrings settle onto her calves. She leaned back until her shoulder blades touched the rubber floor, and she lay there, stretching her quads and breathing steadily, trying to find peace, her eyes wandering the familiar room.

It wasn't a great facility—like the rest of Lakeview, it was drab, dilapidated, and out of date—but weights didn't need any gloss. Heavy was all they had to be. This room had everything she needed to survive. She was even half glad to see the garish school-pride painting that covered most of one of the walls. *HOME OF THE SALMON*, it said in neon pink, and beneath that, the athletic motto *FEAR THE SALMON*. Beside this unlikely threat, someone had painted an anthropomorphic salmon, its teeth bared, its arms and legs bulging with bright pink muscles.

The Lakeview High School Salmon. Rook could've thought for a long time and not come up with a stupider mascot.

The door opened. Rook tensed with anger and disappointment—not only was she about to be sent back into the shitstorm of rumors, she was also getting cheated out of a lift—but the person who came into the room wasn't a teacher.

Theo Locke stopped just inside the weight room door, hugging an armful of textbooks. Rook had only learned his name the other day, but she had noticed him weeks ago, back at the start of school. Sitting alone. Looking, half the time, like he was trying not to cry. Plus, he had those eyes. Hard not to notice.

He fixed them on her now like he was trying to read her. Really see her.

She stared back and hardened herself up. She knew why he was here—he wanted answers. Everybody always did.

He wasn't getting anything.

"What?" she demanded.

The word landed hard in the silence. He jumped, barely.

"Can... we talk?" he ventured.

"What do you want?" she replied, getting to her feet. "Just say it."

He seemed to be trying to get up the guts. He opened his mouth and shut it a couple of times, and Rook studied his face. Pale, chiseled, golden-boy beauty—this guy was probably used to getting whatever he wanted from anyone he talked to. *Washington State Speech and Debate Tournament* was printed across his rumpled t-shirt. He had probably won every trophy just by walking into the room and looking sincere.

His expression wasn't aloof, though. She didn't see arrogance. He looked earnest. Nervous. An assignment of some kind stuck out of one of his textbooks with *100%* scrawled across the top.

"When I found you on the field, you were—" He stopped. "Were you—" He stopped again. "I don't want to assume."

"But you do," said Rook.

"No. I don't." He hugged his books tighter. "I know things. And I've heard things."

"You've heard things, huh?" She laughed, and she didn't mean to let it sound so bitter. She picked up a 45-pound plate and slid it onto one end of the barbell. "You should probably go, then."

"Why?"

She picked up the other 45 and stood. "Because I clubbed him, right?" she said. "That's why you're here. To see if I did it."

"I don't know if you did it." Theo looked pensively at her. "I want to know what happened."

"Join the fucking club."

"Then... you don't know either? You didn't see anything?"

Rook gave him a look that she hoped was maddening and turned away. She wasn't wasting this chance to lift. Let him watch. He wouldn't know how strong this was. She could still go heavy.

She loaded a barbell with enough weight to intimidate most high school guys, took a wide grip on the bar, and sprang, shrugging it high, lifting her hips and descending with expert speed into a deep squat, barbell overhead, arms locked out. She stood up and counted. One. Two. Three. She threw down the barbell, trembling a little, her heart thudding hard. That had felt good—light, for her, but it had been a minute, so it was good to start slow.

"You're strong," Theo said. It wasn't a compliment. "Really strong."

"Strong enough to bash a guy's skull in."

"Don't be flip."

"Flip?"

"You know—flippant. Glib, disrespectful, insincere."

She snorted. "Are you a multiple-choice question?"

"I just—" Theo exhaled. "Please."

He said it like he meant it. He sounded real. Her gut told her he was, but she knew better than to trust it. Anybody could sound like that. Look like that.

"Please what?" said Rook, almost enjoying herself now. He was easy to rile. She used her foot to roll the barbell back toward her and reached down to start her next snatch.

Theo's Converse-clad foot came down on top of the bar. She looked up.

"You sure you want to do that?"

"I want you to talk to me."

"What you want isn't my problem."

Theo's face settled into a frown. He moved his foot off the bar and stepped back out of her way. "Okay," he said. "Fair point. You don't owe me anything."

Rook hadn't expected him to acknowledge it, and now she didn't know what to make of him. She frowned back. Was he one of those guys who wanted points for being a feminist? Was this some kind of game?

"I don't know what you're playing." She locked eyes with him. "But you're not getting what you want out of me. You can go."

He swallowed. All of a sudden he looked sick—really sick, like he might throw up. What was wrong with him? Was he about to cry? Or make some kind of speech?

"You... don't owe me anything," he repeated, "but I owe you something."

So a speech, then.

"I... I did something," he went on. "No. I didn't." He winced. "I didn't do something."

"Then go do it," she said, "and leave me alone."

"You don't understand."

"No, *you* don't."

Rook stepped over the barbell and closed the distance between them. Theo drew a breath of alarm and backed up.

"What's wrong?" she said. "Scared?"

"Should I be?" He cringed when his voice cracked.

"If you think I assaulted somebody, then yeah."

His eyes darted to the door like he wanted to run. But he stood his ground, so either he was brave—or stupid.

"I don't think you did," he said. "I just don't *know*. I didn't see anything, but you were *there*, and—maybe there's another explanation."

Is there any other possible explanation, Ms. Chase? What time was it when you heard the gunshots? Where did you see your mother standing? Did you see the gun in her hand at that time? Did you hear anyone leave the property? Can you identify the men in this photograph? Just a few more questions, Ms. Chase—

The whine of the intercom made her jerk.

"Teachers and students, I need your attention for an important announcement." Principal Kim's voice was steady but urgent. "We are entering a lockdown. This is not a drill. Lock your doors, cover your windows, and remain silent. Students, if you are in the hallways or restrooms, enter the nearest classroom now."

The intercom clicked off.

TEN

Rook stood frozen. Theo looked toward the door.

He strode to it and turned the deadbolt, locking the two of them in.

Trapped. Rook worked to breathe.

Was she about to hear gunshots? She didn't want to hear gunshots. She fought the urge to go curl up in the corner; she couldn't let Theo see her freak out. She tried to breathe like they'd used to make her do in therapy. Smell the roses. Blow out the candles. In. Out. Repeat. Her eyes darted around the space.

"It's okay," said Theo, "don't be nervous."

"Isn't this what they do when there's a shooter on campus?" Rook asked, frustrated. Did she look nervous?

"Only in a worst-case scenario. That's never happened here. I guess there *was* a shooter last year," he added, "but not on campus. You know the hospital across the street? Somebody was on the roof with a gun." He studied her. "You didn't go here last year."

She shook her head.

"Where'd you move from?"

"Somewhere else," she said, in a tone that made it clear to Theo that there was no room for follow-up questions.

"Your old school never had a lockdown?"

Rook shook her head. Saint Catherine's Academy was East Coast old money, the elite of the elite, with all the security that bought. Lockdowns weren't part of the culture.

Theo took a seat on one of the weight benches and set his stuff down. "Guess we're stuck here."

"For how long?"

He shrugged. "Twenty minutes? Three hours?"

Rook didn't know if she could last three hours waiting to hear bullets. She went back to the barbell and briefly hesitated.

It would make a lot of noise if she started snatching weight and dropping it on the floor. If there was an intruder on campus, then she should be silent.

But if she couldn't lift, she might lose her shit.

She took some weight off the barbell. She'd do a complex. That way, she wouldn't have to drop it. Her feet would still slam the floor, but if she went light enough, she could tone that down.

She pulled the barbell off the floor and held it just above her knees, then snatched it from the hang position and locked it out overhead.

Silently, she lowered the weight. Reset it. Went again. And again.

The tension inside her slowly loosened.

Theo watched her. The push-up strength he had seen behind the graffiti wall was nothing compared with what he saw now. The barbell looked heavy, but it floated up over her head with efficient grace. He didn't know whether to admire or fear her.

Her physique belonged to an elite athlete—he had only seen bodies like hers in ads for expensive sneakers. Her muscles shifted under her skin as she worked. Her shirt rode up every time she raised her arms overhead, flashing abs that were... absurd. Unreal. Boss level. Nobody in real life was supposed to look like that.

She turned and caught him staring.

"Yeah?" she said.

"You're good at that. It's a little terrifying."

"So don't follow me places."

"I meant it as a compliment. You move it like it's weightless."

She tossed her ponytail.

"What was that lift?" he asked.

"What do you care?"

"There's one called a clean and jerk, right?" he said. "Is that it?"

"No, *this* is a clean and jerk."

Theo tried to observe the mechanics, but it happened too fast. One second, she set the weight gently on the floor; the next, she had somehow pulled it up to her chest, flipped her elbows underneath it, and squatted. She stood, bent her knees, jumped her feet apart, and shoved the barbell over her head. Then she lowered it to her shoulders with control and supported it in front of herself, elbows thrust forward under the bar, fingers pointed back toward her ears.

Theo tried to put his own elbows forward into that position and found it impossibly awkward. He couldn't imagine supporting heavy weight that way.

"That's so cool, honestly. How do you do that?"

Grueling, repetitive effort, Rook thought. *Years of focus and patience and painful grind. And it's all going to hell.*

"Practice," she said.

Theo was sure that was true. He could also tell there was more to the story. She said it like she was trying to be offhand—like she wanted him to think it was no big deal. But her eyes reminded him of Tuyet's. Grieved.

"What's the other one called?" he asked. "Where it goes straight up over your head?"

"The snatch," Rook said with crisp emphasis, enunciating it like she was daring him to laugh.

Theo didn't take the bait.

He watched her perform another snatch, and then another. Somehow, she was throwing it into the air. The movement was dramatic. Explosive.

"You're tall for weightlifting, right?"

She turned to him, surprised. "How would you know?"

"I did a project once on muscle growth in fourth grade, for science, and I read it somewhere. Weightlifters are short, I thought."

Rook carefully set down the barbell and rubbed a thumb over her calluses. They were fading. She couldn't remember the last time she'd torn one open.

He wasn't wrong—she was an outlier. The tallest girl at every meet. It was part of why she couldn't risk training or competing anymore; she was too recognizable within the sport. And although Olympic lifting had come quickly to her, her height had worked against her in a couple ways. In order to get really good, she had had to work harder on some things. Her front rack. Her leg drive. Her snatch was her favorite—her clean and jerk was better, but the snatch was her oxygen, because it had cost her so much to get good at it. Patience in the pull. Trust that she would get under it. Over and over and over and over.

"You remembered that from fourth grade?" she said.

"I remember most of what I read."

She looked at the stack of books by his foot. AP Lit. AP Spanish. AP European History. Precalculus.

"The police officer I talked to said that you go by Rook Radcliffe," he said, watching her eyes travel over his books. "What did he mean by that? Isn't it your name?"

A hit. Her stony expression cracked. "It's my name," she said, but something in her voice had changed. She went back to her barbell, and this time she turned her back on him.

For a couple of minutes he watched her work, trying to calculate his next move. She had told him that he wasn't getting anything out of her, and apparently she meant it—she had no intention of answering questions about AJ.

Maybe because she'd answered so many already, he realized. The police had taken her, and they'd interrogated her—probably not as nicely as they'd questioned him, either. She'd walked away in handcuffs, and the experience must've been terrible.

He could empathize. Not completely, but a little.

"The police questioned me at my house," he said. "I went my whole life without ever having to talk to the police, and now I've had to answer their questions twice in two months."

Rook couldn't quash her curiosity. "What happened two months ago?"

"My best friend died."

She set down the barbell and picked up her water.

"Anaphylactic shock, right?"

She had heard the story all over school at the start of the year. Mateo Salinas had died in August, and Lakeview High had mourned him all through September. She had seen a lot of people crying over him. Real crying, not the fake kind.

"Right." Theo looked at his hands and thought of how he'd stacked them on Mateo's motionless chest and pushed down, terrified. Talking to him, yelling, like if he was just loud enough, he'd break through.

Open your eyes. Come on, wake up, I know you're there—

Rook set down her water bottle. A short silence followed in which Theo braced himself for whatever question she was about to ask, wishing he hadn't said anything. It wasn't worth drawing her out, if he had to do it like this—he didn't want to talk about this.

When she didn't speak, he glanced up, and was surprised. For the first time, he saw compassion in her face.

"That sucks," she said quietly, and that was it.

No platitudes. No pity. No questions. Theo breathed out, relieved.

"Ten points for eloquence," he said.

She gave a ghost of a smile, like her mouth had forgotten how, but her eyes remembered. She went back to the barbell and kept on lifting.

"You must have to eat a ton to lift like that," Theo said eventually.

This got a nod of genuine approval out of her.

Hungry now himself, Theo dug into his backpack for his lunch, unzipped the cooler pouch, and rifled through the stuff his mother had thrown in there. He pulled out a Ziploc bag of broccoli and another one of snap peas. Baby carrots too.

"Good lord, no," he said, and he went to deposit the bags in the trash.

"What are you doing?"

Theo held up the bags. "Vegetables."

"You're throwing them away?"

"My mom knows I won't eat them, but she puts them in anyway. She thinks healthy food helps people cope with trauma. She's a psychologist—she gets ideas."

Rook's eyes were still on the vegetables. "Don't throw those out."

Theo realized his advantage. "You want them?"

She gave him a wary look and half a shrug.

He offered her the broccoli.

She snatched it, sat on the floor, and started eating.

He sat down on the floor with her. Far enough away that she wouldn't feel crowded—close enough for conversation.

"I know you said you don't want to talk," he said. "But it was rough, finding AJ like that. Can I just ask a couple questions? Not like an interrogation, just... I need to know."

Rook chomped another broccoli stalk and stole a quick look at him. She knew what it felt like. Needing to know. It could drive a person crazy.

"If I say no, are you going to keep following me around school?" she demanded.

He shook his head.

"Then no," said Rook.

Disappointment struck him, but there was nothing more to say. If she didn't want to talk, it wasn't like he could make her.

Theo pulled his backpack closer, unzipped it, and took out a test-prep book for history. He flipped it open to where he'd left off, dug out a pencil, and started working. Might as well make use of the time.

Rook watched him flip pages and mark answers for several minutes, eating slowly in the silence, wondering if this was a tactic. It was when he started outlining on scratch paper and muttering to himself that she decided he was actually studying and not just waiting to see if she'd crack.

"Liberty," he said under his breath. "Equality, fraternity..."

"Fine," said Rook, startling him. He looked up at her. "But I want the peas and the carrots—and the apple."

Theo sat still, processing. She would talk to him?

"Better ask your questions fast," she warned. "This offer is one-time only."

He closed his test book, dug into his lunch again, and offered her the carrots, which she took.

"When did you get to campus that morning?" he asked.

"Six a.m."

"Can anyone back up your story?"

"No."

"Your parents don't know where you go?"

"Oscar," said Rook, between bites, "doesn't care what I do."

"Who's Oscar?"

"My grandfather."

"And he doesn't know what time you left the house?"

"Apartment."

Theo ran a hand through his hair. "Okay, so what *did* happen?"

"I showed up and found AJ, and then you showed up."

"But why were you on campus so early?"

"Why were *you*?" Rook retorted.

"I was going to the library to prep for debate," said Theo.

"And I was warming up for zero period lifting."

Theo raised his eyebrows. "Warming up on the baseball field?"

"I walk. Then I jog. Then I go to the gym." Same lie she had told the cops. Neat and clean.

"Is that your routine?" he asked casually, popping the seal on the Ziploc that held his sandwich.

She nodded.

Theo's appetite vanished. He took a bite anyway and tried not to show his fear.

She was lying. He had crossed the baseball field early on many mornings—and he had never seen her there. Ever. She had no such routine.

"What is it?" she said.

He shrugged. If she had hurt AJ, he didn't want to corner her on a major inconsistency in her story. Not right now, alone with her, locked in. And if she was innocent, then whatever she had really been doing out there, she didn't want to tell him. Either way, pushing her on the matter wouldn't help.

"Hey."

Theo looked up.

"Your sister," she said. "Savannah, right?"

"Why?" he asked, immediately protective.

"Is she okay?" Rook looked down and rolled the last baby carrot in her fingers as she spoke. "Did she see anything bad? Like AJ? Any scary stuff?"

"No," said Theo, disarmed both by the questions and by Rook's tone of genuine concern. "It was too dark."

Rook's shoulders relaxed a little. "That's good," she said. She finished the carrot. Tossed him a look. "Peas."

He lobbed the bag of snap peas toward her. She caught them and started eating.

"So what did you hear about me?" she said, between bites. "You said you heard things."

Theo chewed a little more of his sandwich and considered his words before answering. She could throw him against a wall—he didn't want to set her off.

"I heard you were standing over AJ with a dumbbell," he said. "But I know that isn't true."

"*And?*"

Her tone made Theo tense. He kept his eyes on his sandwich and shrugged.

"Oh come on," she said acidly. "No other rumors you want to check?" She paused. "You're not gonna ask if I did it because I had sex with AJ behind the graffiti wall, and I'm jealous he's with somebody else?"

Theo's head snapped up. He flooded with uncomfortable warmth.

She snorted at his embarrassed expression. "You think I don't know what people are saying?" she said. "That's why you're here, right? That's the story everyone's after. So don't tiptoe. Ask."

"I don't have to ask." He couldn't look at her.

"Oh really?" She gave a humorless laugh. "You think you know?"

Theo managed to swallow the bite in his mouth but felt like it might come right back up. If he told her what he'd seen, and it upset her—he had no defense against her kind of strength.

Tell the truth.

The voice was clear. The path was not.

"I—saw you," he managed.

"*Saw* me?"

Rook didn't understand. He looked like he was going to puke again, and he didn't say anything else—what the hell was he talking about? What had he seen her do?

Burn her license. Bury her letter. Oh God. He knew who she was.

"Whatever you think you know," she said, her voice low and furious, "you better not say one fucking word to one *single* person or—"

"You and AJ," he blurted. "Behind the graffiti wall. I saw."

Rook's mouth opened. "Wait, you saw *us*?" she demanded. It was better than the alternative. But still. He had *watched* them?

"But we were by ourselves," she said. "We were alone. How—"

"I was on top of the wall. The whole time."

Rook's face went ruddy. "Perv!" she shouted, forgetting to be quiet for the lockdown. "What the fuck?"

"I didn't mean to," Theo swore. "It was a complete accident. I climbed up there to be by myself, and then you two came along and I was trapped, and I tried not to watch, but—"

She wouldn't look at him now. Her fingers picked at her leggings, agitated. "You could have said something. Jesus."

"I know. I'm sorry."

"You could have said, 'Hey, I'm up here.'"

"I know. I'm really sorry."

"Keep saying it," Rook muttered, "it'll help."

"I'm—"

"Really, *really* sorry?" she snapped. She stuck out her hand. "Apple. Now."

Theo fumbled to get it from his bag and tossed it to her.

She twisted the stem off too hard, peeled the sticker, and rolled it tight in her fingers, again and again as she backtracked in her head through everything that had happened behind the graffiti wall, and everything Theo had seen.

"I knew you didn't sleep with him," he said, his voice coming fast. Guilty. "I should've told people."

Rook chomped the apple and said nothing. Fuck this guy. She had known he couldn't be the angel he looked like. Everybody always had some sick secret.

"I'll tell my friends," he said. "I'll fix it."

"You can't fix it," said Rook. "It won't change anything." She looked resentfully at him, thought about throwing the apple at him, and only resisted because she wanted to eat it. "Creeper," she said, and his white, chiseled, model-boy face got so red he looked like he might pass out.

Good.

"Can I ask you one more thing?" he asked. His voice was quiet, like he knew he was out of line even speaking.

"Oh sure, ask anything," said Rook angrily. "I can't wait to tell you whatever you want to know, Officer Cheekbones."

"What?"

"Nothing. Fuck off."

"Did he hurt you?"

Rook made an impatient noise. "What are you talking about?"

"AJ. The way he—" His voice cracked again, but he fought through it. "Flipped you over. And what he said, when you left."

"What about it?"

"The other morning, when I found you—did he try to hurt you, out there? Did you have to defend yourself?"

She got to her feet and looked down at him. Tall. Powerful. Flinty-eyed.

"I was fine," she said. "He didn't scare me. I wasn't jealous. I didn't hurt him. End of story."

She polished off the apple, chucked the core in the trash, and went back to the barbell.

The lockdown continued; the conversation was done.

Theo took out his European History flashcards and was halfway through them when the intercom came to life with a whine of feedback.

"Teachers and students, the lockdown has ended. Please proceed to your second period classes."

Rook grabbed her gym bag, unbolted the door, and left.

ELEVEN

Rook moved toward her second period class with her hood up and her head down, checking back over her shoulder just once to see whether Theo was anywhere near her. It didn't look like he was following her this time.

Lifting had given her back just enough grip that she thought she might make it through the rest of her classes—but it was going to be tight. She walked toward the tech building, trying to pretend she couldn't hear people saying her name. Trying not to react to the bursts of laughter. The whispers.

I've survived worse, assholes, she thought, *but thanks for playing*.

She reached Mr. Magnusson's second period computer fundamentals class and hung back by the door, hoping not to get noticed. It was easy with Colleen O'Hare standing in the middle of the room, holding court.

"Sareth Sok got *arrested*," said Colleen. She sipped from her giant water tumbler, clearly enjoying the pause while everyone leaned in. "That's why there was a lockdown. The police walked him right out of AP Spanish. I was there."

Rook was surprised. Sareth, from the weight room? Arrested? That kid hadn't looked like the type to get himself handcuffed. But you never knew.

"Sareth?" Angelina Bradshaw said, looking unconvinced. "For what, studying too hard?"

"It's true." Colleen produced her phone. "I have video."

Most of the class got closer to Colleen as she pressed play.

Rook used their distraction as an opportunity to slip silently to her computer station and sit. So far, so good—nobody was paying attention to her.

"Colleen on the *scene*." Fernando Valencia removed his Lakeview baseball cap to smooth back his dark hair. He replaced the cap on his head. "So did Sareth..."

"Attack AJ?" said Colleen. "The cops must think so. Why else would they literally lock down the school? They obviously think he's dangerous."

"No way." Nolan Becker's voice was resolute. He pulled his thumb, and his knuckle cracked, loud. "No *way* that kid took AJ. Look at him, he couldn't knock somebody out. You should see him in weight training, he can barely lift fifty pounds."

Rook agreed. Unless Sareth had been pretending to be weak—and she didn't think so—then it was difficult to imagine.

"They didn't seriously arrest him." Nolan passed a hand over his auburn buzz cut. "Maybe they're just questioning him."

"No, the cops outside had evidence," said Colleen. "I filmed through the window—see the bag they're holding?"

"What's in it?" Fernando squinted at the screen. "I can't see."

"I know," Colleen scowled. "It's too small, even if I zoom, look."

In Rook's mind, two dots connected. Small evidence? AJ's chain with the baseball ring was small. Had Sareth hit him and then taken it off him? Why? Keeping evidence like that was a stupid thing to do...

Unless it meant something.

She suddenly wished she could go stand with everybody else and look at Colleen's video. Even if the evidence was too small to see clearly, maybe she'd be able to catch a glint of metal.

"Oh, *and*—" Colleen looked over at Fernando, "did you know that Keanu's your quarterback now? He found out this morning. Jill told me."

"Faletogo's our QB?" Fernando played with his own championship baseball ring, which he wore on his finger. "First Crusenberry gets injured, then AJ gets knocked out... kind of makes you wonder."

"Wonder what?" said Colleen.

"I'm not saying anything," said Fernando. "But Crusenberry popped his ankle on Keanu's trampoline. And now AJ's in a coma, and Keanu is QB."

Colleen's mouth fell open. She gave a shocked, delighted laugh. "Oh my *God*. Fernando, you are *messy*. But you don't think Keanu would really attack AJ, do you?"

"It makes more sense than Sareth," muttered Nolan. "No—Keanu didn't. He wouldn't."

Rook hadn't considered that the attack on AJ might be related to football. She hadn't considered much at all, beyond covering for herself. But she couldn't deny that the idea was interesting. She gave Fernando a sidelong glance—

And froze. He was looking right at her.

"I thought she did it," Fernando said, nodding toward Rook.

Her classmates fixed her with their many-headed stare. The whole classroom was silent. Waiting. She looked back at her computer as her pulse sped up.

Colleen approached.

"You got arrested," she said. "People saw you coming out of Theo Locke's backyard. He found you by AJ on the baseball field, and the cops took you. True?"

The gun was in your mother's hand, Ms. Chase. You saw it, true?

Rook's breathing became uneven. Her hands tingled. She saw the door, all the way across the room, behind everybody else. Too far away.

"You told AJ to meet you at the wall," Colleen went on. "What happened? Did he break up with you? Was it because of Destiny?"

Did your mother intend to break it off with Klaus Dekker? Did you ever hear her say that the engagement was ending?

Blood thudded behind Rook's eardrums as her vision narrowed until she only saw the door. She should run. But then they'd know she had flipped out. She couldn't have a panic attack here, in front of the whole class—she didn't want them to see that.

She opened her mouth. Tried to sound like she was bored.

"Why ask me?" she said. Her voice came out dry—she could barely hear it, even in her head. "You already know."

"Students, take your seats." Mr. Magnusson strode into the room, brusque as usual. "We've already lost half our class time to the lockdown. Open your assignments and update your progress logs."

Rook gazed at her screen, lightheaded, staring at her blank password field and willing herself to maintain composure. She would not end up getting walked down to the nurse's office.

"Ms. Radcliffe," Mr. Magnusson's voice cut sternly through the fog, "log in and open your slides."

"Damn, Mr. M." Elijah Jones kicked back his chair until two legs were off the ground. "We already know how to make slideshows, come on. We've been doing this since second grade. Let us do something interesting, *please*."

"Put your chair legs on the floor, Mr. Jones. This is a computer fundamentals course. If you wanted another elective, you should have registered for one."

"Didn't this class used to be A/V? Didn't you do films and stuff? How come we can't register for that anymore?"

"Film would be better than this," Colleen agreed.

"The cameras are in storage," said Mr. Magnusson.

Blaine Bonderman pointed to a dark, disused portion of the classroom. "You mean in there?"

The tech classroom was three times larger than a normal one. Housed within it was a separate, windowed space with a door of its own. The lights were out, and the blinds were drawn.

Colleen got up and peered through a crack in the blinds, then tried the door handle. She opened it.

"Ms. O'Hare, close the door."

"Is that a news desk?" Colleen replied.

"It was," said Mr. Magnusson. "We used to do a news show here, many years ago, but the class was eliminated from the course catalog—"

"A news show?" said Blaine and Elijah together, with enthusiasm.

"That would rule," said Tapeesa Bear from her corner

of the room. "Let's do it. I'll be like—" She spoke in a low, formal tone. "I'm Tapeesa Bear, and this is the news."

"I haven't taught film for a decade."

"If we had a news show," said Colleen, "we could do stories on everything that happens at this school."

"We could do comedy," said Blaine.

Fernando sat forward. "And sports."

"Can we at least learn the cameras?" Elijah begged. "Come on, Mr. M."

Mr. Magnusson inclined his bald head and rubbed the bridge of his nose as though he had a headache. "Proceed with your assignment. Ms. O'Hare, I believe I told you to close the door."

Colleen sat down. The class wilted and went back to their slideshows.

When the bell rang, Mr. Magnusson asked Rook to stay behind. She waited by his desk as the other students filed out, afraid he was going to ask her about AJ. But he only offered her a blue slip.

"The counselor wants to see you."

"I don't need a counselor."

"Take the pass."

Rook reached for it—and paused. A sticky note sat on his desk: *Thurs. Campus security mtg. w/ RK, 401.*

Regina Kim. Was this about AJ?

"You're talking to the principal?" she asked.

"Take the pass," said Mr. Magnusson.

Rook scowled and left.

There had been counselors back East, too. Lots of them. Over the years, Rook had learned that the best way to beat them was to go without resistance, say as little as possible, and give them absolutely nothing to latch onto.

She showed her pass in the front office and was directed

to a chair outside a door. The window in the door was covered with an opaque curtain. From within came the sound of crying, and a soothing, indecipherable voice.

Fucking counselors.

Across from Rook, a different door opened—one marked Family Services. Destiny Bray from zero period stepped out, expression tense, followed by a thick-set woman who said something to her that Rook couldn't hear.

"I told you," Destiny snapped, "Faith's at school. I'm at school. We're both showing up, and we're *fine*, you can stop checking—"

"Rook?"

The school counselor had opened her door.

Destiny's head turned. Color rose in her face. She gave Rook a hard, none-of-your-damn-business look, and she walked out of the office.

"I'm Ms. Winter," said the counselor. "It's good to meet you. Come on in."

She was on the young side, but she already had the practiced sympathetic expression of a professional. Rook got up and followed her into the office, where dark blue curtains and dim, warm-bulbed lamps created an atmosphere of calm privacy. Framed diplomas hung on the walls; photos and affirmations littered the corkboard; pamphlets covering everything from pregnancy to suicide peeked out of a wall file organizer, easy for kids to grab without having to admit anything.

On the wall hung a framed picture of Ms. Winter in gym clothes, her light hair pulled back in a sweaty knot, her arms around the shoulders of two teammates, all of them wearing silver medals, glowing with pride in front of a giant sign that read *GALA GAMES*.

Rook looked at that one a little longer. The Gala Games

was a national-level functional fitness competition—a serious one, for people who made it past the local qualifiers. And it looked like Ms. Winter had.

That was cool.

"You can sit if you like," said Ms. Winter. "Up to you."

Rook sat on the sofa, which was a mess of throw pillows and blankets. The small coffee table between them was cluttered with college brochures and fidget toys. The whole place was designed to feel safe and cozy. It made Rook itch.

Ms. Winter sat in her desk chair, a cushy, upholstered swivel that didn't look like school furniture—the counselor must have bought it herself.

"I thought I'd check in. Last Friday, you found AJ unconscious—are you okay?"

Short answers, calm demeanor. That was the way forward.

"It was a shock, but I'm fine."

"Good. I'm glad."

Silence. This was the part where counselors played chicken to see who would crack first and start talking. Rook picked up one of the fidget toys, a small sand timer, and flipped it in her fingers, making the black sand fall through. She could wait all day.

"The police spoke with you," said Ms. Winter. "How was that?"

Rook shrugged. "It's their job."

"Do you need legal support? I can connect you with a free defense attorney."

"I'm good."

Silence again. *Tick tock,* Rook thought, and she flipped the sand timer. *Ask all the questions you want, lady. I bet I've been playing this game longer than you.*

Ms. Winter gestured to the door. "You don't have to

stay. Stop by when you want to talk about college pathways, okay? I hear you're an athlete, so there might be scholarships out there for you."

"Who said I was an athlete?"

Rook instantly regretted her response, which was both too quick and too interested. The shine in Ms. Winter's eye told her the counselor knew she'd found her angle.

Fucking counselors.

"Let's just say your name has come up, and I'd love to help."

Ms. Winter stood up, signaling the end of the conversation, and Rook stood too, irritated that she hadn't done it first. She went to the door, catching sight once again of the photo of Ms. Winter with her Gala Games teammates.

"You medaled?" Rook asked, in spite of herself. She nodded toward the picture. "Did you go to Nationals?"

"I was supposed to. One of my teammates sprained her wrist." Ms. Winter sounded like she was trying to be a good sport about it. "But hey, it's just for fun, right?"

"No. That sucks. You're legit."

Ms. Winter smiled. Not a therapy smile—a real one. "Thanks, Rook. Glad we had a chance to talk. If you ever need anything, my door is open."

TWELVE

"A lockdown?" Theo's mother didn't hide her dismay. She cupped his face in her freckled hands. "And an arrest? Honey, what happened to Sareth? What is going *on* around here lately—are you okay?"

Theo nodded. "I'm fine."

But he wasn't. He was back in shock, where apparently he was going to spend the rest of his high school life.

Sareth, arrested.

The idea was absurd. Sareth wasn't arrested—Sareth was going to meet him in the morning to prepare for debate, because Sareth was reliable. Trustworthy. Not a criminal.

How could anyone with half a brain think that Sareth would attack AJ? Were the police completely out of their minds?

Theo imagined Sareth in juvenile detention, surrounded by real criminals, and his stomach clenched. That wasn't acceptable. He couldn't let that happen.

But what was he supposed to do about it?

The question rooted in him, thorny and uncomfortable. He hadn't done anything about Rook. He'd stayed silent on the wall. He'd kept his mouth shut at school. Her face flashed into his mind, the way she'd looked in the weight room, at the moment he'd confessed to her what he had seen.

Humiliated. He had let that happen.

Was he a good person? Or did he just sound like one in debate?

His mother turned her attention to his backpack, which she opened and began to unpack as though he were in the second grade. She yanked the cooler bag out from where it was wedged between two giant textbooks and started organizing his folders, grumbling about the lack of mental health services in the community and the consequences for young people who were left to fend for themselves.

"But this is the world we live in." She finished with his papers and unzipped his cooler pouch. "Plenty of money for sports, but if children need mental healthcare, parents are supposed to go into hock. It should be the other way around. Buy your own damn footballs."

Theo barely listened to her.

What *could* he do about Sareth? Even if he wanted to help, did he have any power here? He was a sophomore. He couldn't even drive.

Could he go to court? Make some sort of character statement?

Officer Petros had left his contact information. Theo imagined, for a moment, calling the station and telling the detective that he had the wrong guy—that Sareth was full of himself, but he was innocent of everything else, and that they had to let him go.

What good would that do? The police wouldn't listen to some speech. He could make the best, most emotionally loaded argument he'd ever made in his life, and it would do nothing unless he had hard evidence.

How was he supposed to get that? Was there *anything* he had noticed on that baseball field that could point the cops away from Sareth?

No...

But he knew that Rook was lying about her warm-up. He knew she didn't have a routine, and that she'd been out on that field for some other reason.

Was he supposed to call the cops and tell them that?

You know the answer, amigo.

Theo hated what he had to do. He had already hurt her, he didn't want to do it again.

Why not? Why protect her? You don't know her—maybe she did it.

But he didn't think so, and he couldn't quite place why.

"Hey there, Theodore James." His dad came into the kitchen and slung an arm around his shoulders. "Did you take your meds today?"

He hadn't. He usually did it on his way in the door, but he'd been distracted. Theo grabbed the bottle from the cabinet by the fridge and popped his anti-seizure meds.

"Is Ana taking you to counseling," his dad asked him, "or am I?"

"Ana. If I still have to go."

Kurt Locke pushed up his glasses. He looked like Theo's future self, slender and fine boned with Nordic coloring. His thinning blond hair made the gray hard to spot.

"You don't want to go?"

Theo shook his head. He had seen the grief counselor every week for two months, and there was nothing left to say. Mateo was dead. If he had started walking six minutes sooner, Mateo would be alive. Discussion complete.

"What happened to AJ is traumatic," said his mother. "Coping with the arrest of a friend is difficult."

"And it might be bringing up other feelings," said his father.

"You can just say Mateo," Theo snapped.

His parents made no reply to this, and Theo felt ashamed of himself. His mom and dad were loving, supportive people—but they were also really forcing it. The two of them had paid him more attention since Mateo's death than they had paid him since early childhood. Not that they had ever neglected him—they took him to get his labs drawn and came to all his events—but he'd been young when they'd realized he was smart and trustworthy enough to handle most day-to-day stuff by himself. As long as he kept his grades up and took his meds, they left him to his own devices. He liked it that way.

"Go to the session," his dad said. "You might get more out of it than you think."

Theo doubted it. Living with two psychologists had honed his self-awareness to a fine point—he knew what he felt, and he usually knew why he felt it. For example, right now, he felt irritated, because the two of them were getting on his nerves.

Two short car-horn beeps sounded from outside.

"Say hi to Ana for us," said his mom.

Theo headed outside. Ana was already out of the car and coming up the walkway, dark curls still in her cheer practice ponytail. She threw her arms around him and hugged him tight, and he slumped into the embrace, grateful.

She always smelled like flowers. He didn't know what kind, but he liked it.

"Hi," he mumbled.

"Theo," she said quietly. "Teo, mi querido." She always made his name sound like the best word in any language. "All this stuff keeps happening to you, and I never know what to say. Are you okay?"

Theo kissed her. She didn't have to say anything. This was all he needed.

Before the kiss could deepen, Ana turned her face away.

"We can't make out right in front of your house, with your family at home."

"So where should we go?"

"You have counseling."

He sighed.

Ana drew back just enough to hold up the little figurine of Akari, her favorite *Death Kingdom* character, which Theo had given to her for her keychain. "This blade is a light in the darkness," she quoted, moving the figurine back and forth like it was talking to him. "Come, follow me into the night." She tugged him by the hand toward her car.

Theo got into the passenger seat, wondering for the thousandth time how he had lucked out so profoundly. He didn't lack confidence—he knew he was attractive—but Ana still should have been out of his league. She was beyond him in every way, right down to winning Homecoming Queen at her school's dance two weeks ago.

He knew that her friend circle at Highland High didn't understand why a person of Ana Castillo's elite social status was dating a random sophomore from the local public school. Luckily for him, she didn't care.

"How did I end up with you again?" he said, as she started the car.

She shot him a grin. "Because you're hot like an anime character," she said.

"So it's just my face."

"Yep." She snickered. "Okay, and maybe your hair a little bit."

He pretended to be wounded.

She slapped his knee. Light. Teasing. "You want me to tell you all the reasons I really like you?"

"I want a full breakdown of your reasoning," said Theo. "Organized and defended by category, with evidence. Essay on my desk in the morning."

She laughed. "Do I get one too?"

"I could write it in my sleep. You're..." He stopped. Every word he could think of sounded corny in his head. "I don't know."

"I'm super flattered."

"I seriously don't know," he said. "I don't know how to say it without sounding dumb."

"I thought you could write it in your sleep," she teased. "Just pretend it's a debate. Then you'll know what to say."

"Fine. You're incredible."

"Specificity, please. I want three pieces of solid, irrefutable evidence."

"One," said Theo, warming at once to the challenge. "You basically de facto took over for the cheer coach when she was on maternity leave and you got the JV team ready for competition all by yourself."

"Yes," Ana said, turning left at the next light. "Yes I did. And they won," she added. "I am awesome."

"Two. You always invite me over when there's pozole."

"That's accurate, but less complimentary, since my mom makes the pozole."

"Three." Theo glanced at her profile as she drove. "You're the only reason I haven't completely fallen apart since August."

She paused at a stop sign. Looked at him, dark eyes eloquent. "If I could do more, I would," she said. "I wish I could."

Ten minutes later, Ana pulled up in front of the tall, brick building that housed the grief counselor's office. Theo looked up at the lit windows, unwilling to go in. An hour of emotional reflection stretched unhappily before him. He didn't want to talk about Mateo anymore. He couldn't change what had happened, and he was tired of rehashing it.

What he wanted to talk about was Sareth. Someone he might actually be able to help.

He looked over at Ana, who had already moved her seat back to make room for the homework in her lap.

"My friend Sareth," he said. "The one who got arrested today."

Ana glanced at him.

"He didn't do it," said Theo. "He's not a criminal. I can't understand what happened."

Ana's fingers tightened on her pen. She looked back down at her homework. "The police must have their reasons," she said, and went back to writing.

"Maybe, but whatever they think they know, they're wrong. They have to be."

"Won't you be late?"

"Yeah, but listen," said Theo. "I know Sareth. I know him well, and he can be a pain, but he would never break the law."

"I thought the police arrested that girl from the baseball field," Ana replied, as she took notes from her textbook.

"That's strange too. Today, during the lockdown, I was alone in the weight room with her—"

"Alone?" Ana blinked, sitting up straighter. "Wait—are you okay? Why were you in the weight room?"

Theo fidgeted.

"I was asking her what really happened."

Ana's eyes widened. "You mean you followed her on purpose? Why? You saw what she's capable of—"

"I saw nothing conclusive."

"Conclusive?" Ana repeated, with a dismayed shake of her head.

"It's true. I didn't see her hurt AJ—the circumstances are admittedly pretty damning, but—"

"I just don't want her to hurt *you*," Ana said. "I know you want answers—I would too—but you should stay away from her. Even if she didn't do it. Just in case."

"I'll be careful," he said. "I promise."

And he would be careful, he thought, as he got out of Ana's car and walked toward the counselor's office. But careful didn't have to mean passive.

He thought of Sareth sitting in the library with him, joking at him, needling him, pushing him to push, to think clearly, to be rational. He thought of him on the debate stage, crackling with certainty and relentless citations. Sareth was annoying. He was brilliant. He didn't belong behind bars.

Theo made up his mind.

He would tell the police about what he knew. He would look around at school and find out if there was anything he'd forgotten. Maybe he couldn't do anything to help—maybe, if he got involved, he'd screw it up and make it worse.

But he had never missed an opportunity to solve for X. And this time, the answer mattered.

THIRTEEN

Rook got back to Oscar's after school that afternoon, feeling grouchy and overexposed.

She had talked to Theo way too much. Why had she told him her grandfather's name? Or anything at all? Was she actually stupid?

No, she was weak. Crappy school food and microwavable burritos from Oscar's freezer had made her weak, and now she was spilling her secrets for broccoli and an apple.

She needed a job. Her own money.

She drove to downtown Cedar Point. She thought it was funny that a few blocks of mediocre restaurants and shops qualified as "downtown" anywhere, but her new home wasn't exactly a metropolis.

She didn't mind the weather, though. She had grown up in places where it fluctuated between muggy and freezing, and when it rained, it *rained*. Intense, soaking downpours. In Cedar Point, it was mostly drizzle and mist—and she weirdly liked it. It hung around the buildings and the evergreens as she headed toward the first shop she saw: a Dollar Tree.

They weren't hiring. Neither was the bookstore. She went into each business in the order she came to them, because she didn't really care where she worked. She only skipped the marijuana shop because she wasn't old enough to work there.

She almost skipped The Lighthouse, too.

It was a diner with a busted neon sign out front. Sticking off the roof was a fake lighthouse tower that belonged on a mini-golf course. It also had a *Help Wanted* sign in the window.

Rook went in. The cacophony that greeted her was almost like the school cafeteria, and so was the stink of cheap, greasy food. Nostalgic diner music mingled with loud chatter, and two old Skee-Ball lanes in the back of the restaurant rattled away as people played.

The place was packed full of Lakeview kids, she realized, glancing around—and they were already watching her. Nudging each other.

She did not want to work here.

But she couldn't ask Oscar for anything else. Not protein powder, not chalk, nothing. He let her stay. That was enough. If she wanted more, she would have to earn it.

"It's at least a thirty-minute wait," said a scruffy-bearded white man wearing a cheap, party-store ship captain's hat. He stood at the host stand, counting out change for a girl who wanted to play Skee-Ball.

Rook nearly turned and walked out. If she hadn't still been able to taste the microwave burrito in the back of her throat, she would have done it.

Fish and chicken. Vegetables and rice. A gym membership so you don't have to lift at school.

Suck it up, Radcliffe.

"You're hiring, right?" she asked.

The man in the hat looked hopefully at her. "You want a job? You can start right now."

"You... don't want to interview me?"

"Sure, okay—you have a name?"

"Rook Radcliffe."

"Great, I'm Barney Little. Drugs? Felony?"

Rook raised an eyebrow. "No."

"Then ahoy, matey. Welcome to The Lighthouse."

Barney showed her to the back of the restaurant.

"Here we go—one Lighthouse staff t-shirt. Sorry about the size—it's the only one I've got on hand. Wear it when you're working for now, if you can. Ever been a waitress before?"

"No."

"Well, you'll learn fast, or they won't tip you. Aprons are there, tablets there. You can change in the employee bathroom."

In the bathroom, Rook wriggled into the t-shirt, which was an extra small. She was lean enough to squeeze into it, but the fabric strained against her shoulders and upper arms —and because she was tall, it exposed a slice of midriff. She tied a half-apron around her hips, grabbed a tablet, and made her way out to the front.

"Here's how you put in orders for the kitchen." Barney swiped her tablet screen and gave her a tutorial. "Pick up food and drinks over there. Then it's just a matter of putting the right plate in front of the right person. Think you can handle it?"

Rook wasn't sure, but she nodded.

For the first couple of hours, she regretted taking the job. Putting the right plate in front of the right person was tricky. Most of the people in the restaurant wanted to make changes to the menu or split the bill, which Rook had no idea how to do. The tablet looked simple enough, but she kept screwing up, and when she tried to go back a step, the whole order would get wiped out. People got impatient when they had to tell her everything again.

But the worst part, by far, was being steeped in Lakeview drama—especially since most of it was targeted at her.

"Hey, headbasher," said Adel Juárez from zero period, when Rook approached to take her order. Her short hair was pushed back by aviator sunglasses, and her arm was slung around a girl's shoulders. She surveyed Rook like she was a fan. "You work here now?"

"What do you want?" Rook replied without feeling.

"The Starboard Salad," said Adel, tipping her head toward her girlfriend. "And the First-Mate's Fries. You texted AJ, right? To meet you at the wall?" She glanced at Rook's arms. "Always knew that fuckboy would make the wrong girl mad one day."

"So that's a salad and fries," said Rook, moving on to the next table, where a dark-haired girl in a wheelchair sat alone, working on her laptop.

"Order?"

"Coffee. Black."

"Nothing to eat?"

"Do I look like I have a *speaking* problem?" the girl replied tartly, looking over her shoulder at Rook. "Oh," she said, pursing her red-painted lips in disapproval, "*you*. How is Sareth arrested, and you're not?"

Rook moved on toward the next booth, saw the back of Colleen O'Hare's red head, and stopped walking. She didn't have it in her to talk to that girl again. She couldn't risk freaking out in public.

She had to walk over there. It was her job.

Maybe it wasn't worth it. She could find something else.

Like what? You want to eat frozen peas out of the bag and lift at Lakeview like an amateur for the next three years? Don't be a fucking baby.

"Don't listen to Fernando, it wasn't Keanu," Colleen was saying. "Keanu went home, he couldn't have attacked AJ."

The girl across from her looked up from her phone. She had a startlingly beautiful face and sheet-straight dark hair that hung to her waist, and Rook knew her name because everyone at Lakeview did. Tuyet.

"Keanu didn't go home," said Tuyet. "I saw him at Shakemaster."

"Oooh, you did?" Colleen bounced a little. "What was he doing?"

"He was in the parking lot." Tuyet looked back down at her phone. "He got into somebody's car."

"Whose?"

Tuyet shrugged.

"You guys, don't," said a girl with brown skin and big, shiny dark curls, who wore a look of sorrow on her face. "We don't know who did what."

"We don't?" said Colleen, with a laugh. "It was obviously Rook. Can you believe she's waitressing here now? Where'd she go, anyway?" She looked around. "She is so weird—she barely talks and I heard she can lift like, hundreds of pounds—"

Colleen caught sight of Rook and froze. Colored.

The girl next to her with the big shiny curls turned and saw Rook—and smiled.

"Hi," she said warmly. "I'm Marna Hauterman. I know you're new, and we haven't met, and I'm sorry, I normally would have said hi by now, but this year has just been so awful, I haven't been myself. Can we order now, do you have time? Or do you need to come back to us?"

Rook approached.

"This is Tuyet Pham," said Marna, gesturing, "and this is Colleen O'Hare. Don't mind her, she just likes to talk. A lot," she added ruefully.

"She might actually have a disorder," said Tuyet.

Colleen scowled.

"And we all want the same thing, so it's really easy," said Marna. "We just want the Anchors Aweigh app platter and three Sprites, okay?"

Rook wrote this down.

"Thank you," said Marna. "Is this your first day?"

"Yeah."

"You're doing *so* great," said Marna, and Rook couldn't catch even a faint trace of mockery in the statement. Marna seemed to mean it—she beamed at Rook so sunnily that Rook had to walk away to get out of the heat.

A group of Lakeview boys came crashing through the door, laughing raucously. One of them was Chad Perkins. Rook recoiled in distaste. She did not want to serve that guy fries.

Chad and his boys settled down at table five, smack in the middle of the restaurant. He balanced his phone against the napkin holder so he could see himself and push up his pomaded brown hair, making it stand even taller.

"Look at it," said Quinn, an overeager guy with chin-length waves who was trying to stick a piece of paper under Chad's nose. "It's good, right?"

Chad ignored him. "I heard there's a UW scout coming to the game on Friday," he said to Keanu. "Better not choke."

"Great pep talk," Keanu replied, giving Chad a narrow

look as he retied his dark topknot. He held up the menu and blocked Chad out.

"*Look* at it," Quinn insisted. He stuck a Sharpie on the table. "I need to ask her tonight, man, just tell me if it sucks."

"Why are you asking Lola? I thought you were going with Colleen," said Demetrius Washington, a giant nearly twice the size of the other guys, who already had a beard coming in.

"Colleen rejected his ass," said Chad, laughing. "Bro cried."

"I didn't *cry*, screw you."

Quinn moved to take back the paper and Sharpie, but Chad was quicker. He snatched the paper and uncapped the Sharpie.

"You just need to fix one thing," he said.

Then he scrawled *PERKINS #1* across Quinn's paper in giant, unrepentant letters.

"Asshat!" Quinn cried. "That's for Lola!"

Chad capped the Sharpie and tossed it on the table. He pulled Keanu's menu down to look at him.

"You should quit the team," he said. "Three quarterbacks in two weeks? Cursed. First Crusenberry got wrecked, then AJ got his head smashed, now you're gonna get stabbed or some shit."

"Wow, thanks," said Keanu.

"I'm just saying," said Chad. "Be like me—baseball or nothing." He caught sight of Rook, grinned, and waggled his eyebrows at her. "Rookie looking *hot*," he proclaimed, and he patted his lap. "Come here. Take my order."

"You have a girlfriend," Keanu muttered.

"Jill's not here," said Chad.

Rook walked to the side of the table farthest from Chad

and pulled up the menu on her tablet. "What do you want?" she asked tonelessly.

"For all your shirts to be that tight."

Rook turned her attention to Quinn. "You?" she said.

"Deckhand burger," he replied. "Mariners mocha."

She got everyone's order except for Douchebag Perkins, and she walked away.

"Hold up," he called after her, "I never told you what I wanted."

She kept working and ignored the douche's increasingly boisterous bids for attention. Only when everyone else's food was ready did she head back to table five. She set down the burgers and drinks for everyone except Chad.

"Seriously?" he complained. "Not cool, waitress. I want pancakes."

A girl at the nearest table pushed back her chair, almost knocking the empty tray out of Rook's hands. On instinct, she lifted it up and out of the way.

Instantly, Chad scooped an ice cube out of Keanu's water.

"Snowball challenge," he cried. "You flinch, you lose."

He flicked the ice cube at her bare stomach, and it hit her in the navel. She gasped and dropped the empty tray on the floor as every muscle in her body clenched.

Quinn cackled.

"Bro," said Demetrius, "don't."

Rook picked up Keanu's full water glass and dumped the entire contents over Chad's head.

"Suck it," she shouted, as he spluttered and his friends howled with laughter.

Chad stood and faced her. Rook stepped up to him. And now the whole restaurant was paying attention.

"You *did* hit AJ," he accused. "I saw those texts, he showed me."

Rook opened her mouth to protest. She hadn't sent the texts. She didn't have a phone. She hadn't slept with AJ—everybody had everything wrong, they didn't know shit about her, but saying the truth wouldn't fix it. It never did. She gritted her teeth.

"You're a psycho," Chad went on, "and if I don't have my best shortstop this spring, I will make you regret it."

"If you touch me, douche? I'll break you."

Chad replied by shaking his wet head like a dog and making water rain all over her. He walked out of The Lighthouse with his friends behind him. All over the restaurant, people stared at Rook, who still clutched the empty water glass in her hand.

Barney approached, looking angry. "Thought you said you weren't a felon."

Rook gave him a dark look. "So fire me."

"I need a waitress," said Barney, "but I'm not that desperate. If you're gonna threaten my customers, then this won't work out—"

"Those customers were harassing her," said the dark-haired girl in the wheelchair, without turning away from her laptop. Her fingers continued to click on her keyboard. "One of them wanted her to sit in his lap, and then he threw ice at her stomach."

Barney's face fell.

"And I bet if you look around," the girl continued, "you'll see that someone has video of everything. They didn't *help*, of course. Just videoed like creeps."

Across the diner, Colleen lowered her phone.

Rook looked at the dark-haired girl in complete surprise

—and gratitude. The girl tossed a couple dollars on her table, picked up her laptop, and rolled out of the diner.

Barney had turned pink behind his beard. "Oh, well then, that's different." He looked down at Rook. "Why didn't you say that?"

"Might have," Rook replied, wiping water droplets off her face with her arm, "if you'd asked me."

Barney put up his hands. "Understood," he said. "We okay?"

Rook shrugged. "Do I still have a job?"

"Sure. Yeah, you have a job."

Barney hurried back up front to make change, and Rook started to mop up the water, surprised anyone had her back, and wishing the diner would go back to being loud. The silence was worse. She could hear every faint titter, and a voice saying, "Chad barely even touched her."

Her jaw tightened. She wasn't sorry at all for what she'd done. Colleen's video would probably be all over school tomorrow, but she didn't care. If the douche was dumb enough to fuck with her, he was going to keep finding out.

FOURTEEN

The next morning, Theo sat in Lakeview's library across from the seat where Sareth should have been, his phone on the table in front of him. He'd edited the text five times. It was good now. He could send it.

> [THEO] Hi, Officer Petros. It's Theo Locke. You said I could get in touch if I thought of anything. Can we talk?

It was worth sending, he told himself. Even if all he had to offer was something small.

Maybe then you won't feel so guilty.

He turned off his screen and put his head down on his folded arms.

Was that what this was? Not helping Sareth, not finding the truth, just... trying to feel better? Like one tiny gesture could make up for Mateo's death?

No. He wasn't responsible for Mateo's death.

He wished he could crack open his brain. Root out the liar inside that whispered, *But you are responsible. Hit rewind, go back, start walking sooner, and he's not dead.*

That's the truth.

Shut up.

He had been over this with the grief counselor again just last night. Step by step. Facts first.

Mateo had been late coming over. That was normal. There was no reason—*none*—for Theo to have assumed the worst. So he had kept gaming, expecting Mateo to walk in and pick up the other controller, as usual.

Mateo hadn't walked in. Theo had texted him.

Mateo hadn't replied. Theo had started walking, figuring they'd meet up.

Instead, he had found his body.

It wasn't guilt, or fault. Just random, brutal timing. If he had known about the bee sting, he would have sprinted to help. He would have done everything in his power.

You still could've put down the controller sooner. Started walking sooner.

Couldn't you?

Theo didn't mean to make a sound, but it escaped him anyway. A low noise of pain. Was it ever going to stop?

"Are you all right?" the librarian asked, pausing beside his table. "Theo?"

Theo made himself sit up. "Yeah, I'm okay—just tired."

The librarian frowned. "Do you need to see the nurse?" he asked. "The counselor?"

Theo shook his head and waited to be left alone.

The second he was by himself again, he picked up his phone. Screw his brain. It could lie all it wanted. He would learn to ignore it.

Theo sent the text. At once, he felt lighter inside. This was the right move, he was sure of it. He moved to put the phone in his pocket.

Three dots appeared below his text, moving. Promising. The officer was texting back.

The dots stopped. No text came.

Theo deflated. Maybe Petros wouldn't even reply. Maybe he thought there was no point, now that they had Sareth. They also had evidence of some kind, or so he'd heard. He had no idea what it was.

He got to AP Spanish early and found Colleen near the whiteboard with half a dozen students, telling them everything she knew. Theo joined the crowd and listened.

"And then she dumped the water over his head."

"Who?" said Theo.

"Rook Radcliffe," said Colleen. "I have second period with her. She's a waitress at The Lighthouse now, and she drenched Chad in the diner last night."

Theo wished he had seen it—Chad was an imbecile.

"Chad put ice on her stomach, so she flipped out," Colleen went on.

"En español, por favor," called Señora Delgado from her desk.

Theo switched instantly. "¿Qué hizo?" he said. "¿Por qué?"

Colleen kept speaking in English, but she lowered her voice. "You know how Chad is," she said.

They all knew. Chad was one of the best high school pitchers in the state, so he treated the world like it was already his footrest.

Theo fumed inwardly. Another guy, crossing the line with Rook. And here *he* was, going behind her back and reporting her to Petros. For what? Walking around in the dark?

His certainty vanished. Maybe he'd been wrong. What had made him think he should text the police? Ana had told him not to get involved. Rook wouldn't have wanted him involved. He was making it worse.

He wished he could unsend the text.

No. Even if everything is confusing, truth is truth.

But he couldn't trust anything his brain told him.

Colleen showed them all a video on her phone. Her angle was blocked, and she only had half the shouting match, but Theo heard Rook's voice, low and cool and unmistakable.

"I'll break you."

She was brave. Chad wouldn't take well to being publicly shamed, Theo was certain. He'd want to hit back.

"And guess what?" said Colleen, pocketing her phone. "I heard from AJ's cousin Grant that the evidence they found, they got from Sareth's locker."

Theo stared at Colleen and replied in incredulous, rapid Spanish.

"Oh my God," said Colleen, rolling her eyes at him. "Calm down, Duolingo."

Theo exhaled in frustration and switched to English, casting a quick look at the teacher to make sure she wasn't listening. "They think Sareth would put evidence in his own locker?" he repeated in a low voice, incensed. "Why did the police even search it?"

"Cameras," said Colleen, like it was obvious. "Campus security must have seen him stash whatever it was."

"You don't know what it was?"

"I have checked every picture I can find." Colleen gave a sigh of defeat. "*Nobody* has a good one."

After Spanish, Theo walked past Sareth's locker on his way to precalculus. He stopped in the hall and studied the ceiling until he found the security camera. He had never paid attention to the cameras before, because he had never tried to get away with anything. Now he saw that there was only one in this area, and Sareth's locker wasn't in its sight.

And if that was true...

Then someone must have told the police to search his locker. They'd pointed the cops to Sareth on purpose.

They'd framed him.

A thrill raced through Theo. Fear and excitement. Who would frame Sareth? And why?

He remembered what Colleen had said in the library on Monday morning. Sareth had reported Chad Perkins to the principal and gotten him suspended from the weight room. What had happened?

He knew exactly who to ask.

Theo passed his precalculus classroom, mind buzzing, and did something he'd never done before—skipped math and went home.

His heart raced as he crossed the baseball field. He kept checking behind him, waiting for an adult to catch him. Stop him. They'd ask him what he thought he was doing. And he'd say...

What would he say?

I had to go home, because Sareth is being framed, and I need to bribe a weightlifter who barely knows me into solving a felony with me.

He was out of his mind. But he felt lighter with every step.

Theo threw his backpack onto the dining room table, took out his laptop, and did a minute's research. He went into the kitchen and opened the fridge. His mom ate pretty healthy. He found a glass bowl full of leftover Brussels sprouts and another full of brown rice. He rummaged for protein—he needed lots of it—and found half a grocery-store rotisserie chicken, which he cut into pieces before taking out a Tupperware container that was big enough to hold four lunches.

He filled it to the top with chicken, vegetables, and rice. He threw a fork in, snapped it shut, and wedged the thing halfway into his cooler pouch. Good enough. Almost. He snagged a protein breakfast bar from his mom's stash, shoved it in his pocket, and marched back to Lakeview, determined.

FIFTEEN

After her run-in with Douchebag Perkins, Rook slept like garbage, dreamed she was suffocating under a weight that she couldn't move no matter how hard she pushed, and woke up feeling both fragile and furious.

She saw Chad at lunch, sitting next to his girlfriend, Jill Zeller—the softball pitcher. She wore a letterman's jacket with her own last name emblazoned on the back, and she examined the end of her black braid, which hung over her shoulder like a whip. She seemed to be barely tolerating the douche. He hung an arm around her shoulders like she was his territory, and Rook saw the look she shot him. Irritated. Over it. Then her eyes slid to Rook, and her expression turned frosty.

So she'd heard about The Lighthouse. Probably knew that Chad had flicked ice at Rook. Probably didn't care. More likely, she was mad because Rook had dumped water on her boyfriend. Or maybe it was option C: Jill knew that Chad had called Rook hot in front of everybody, and now she wanted blood.

Well, what had she expected? Date a douche, get douched.

Rook turned her back on the rest of the cafeteria, sat down with her disgusting school lunch, and hoped nobody would come near her.

That hope was dashed in under ten seconds, when Theo sat down next to her in a faded Super Mario t-shirt and started talking to the side of her head.

"I have a question. It's about the weight room."

Rook scraped a thick coat of greasy breading and a square of orange cheese off the rubbery chicken patty that Lakeview considered an appropriate protein source.

"Don't eat that," Theo said. "I brought you a present."

She narrowed her eyes, suspicious. "What? Why?"

He handed her a giant Tupperware container, and when Rook opened it, her insides melted. Just a little bit. Just enough.

She glanced up at him. "How did you know?"

"I googled to see what Captain America eats."

Her mouth twitched.

"Can we talk?" he insisted. "Just for ten minutes?"

Don't laugh at his jokes. Don't eat his food. Don't go with him.

Do not be a dumbass.

"This doesn't make up for what you did," she said.

"I know. But I have an idea about AJ, and I need to know what you know."

"I told you already."

"I mean about Chad," said Theo, lowering his voice and glancing toward the table where Chad sat with all his friends. "You have to tell me what happened with Sareth. Because I think—I don't want to say it here. Come with me. Please."

He looked earnest. Honest. And the chicken smelled amazing.

Rook caved.

"You're not about to poison me, are you?" She sniffed the chicken again.

"It's tactically sound," he replied cheerfully. "I could never take you in a fist fight. Let's go."

She flung the terrible chicken patty into the garbage where it belonged and walked through Lakeview's downstairs halls with Theo, passing Nolan and Destiny, who stood together against the lockers. Destiny played with his varsity collar, smiling up at him. Nolan brushed a blonde wave from her face.

Then he noticed Rook. His eyes lingered on her as she and Theo passed.

Destiny's smile stayed fixed in place, but her hand moved. She released Nolan's collar, ran her pink fingernails gently along the back of his buzz-cut scalp, then guided his face with her fingers until he was looking at her again.

When they came to the end of the hallway, Theo pointed to locker 702.

"That's Sareth's. Look around. Are we on a security camera?"

Rook could only find one camera, which pointed the other way, toward the doors at the end of the hallway.

"You think that matters?" she asked.

"The cops had an evidence bag when they arrested Sareth, right?"

"And?"

"Whatever the police put in that bag, they took it out of Sareth's locker during the lockdown. But he would never, *ever* put evidence in his own locker. I think the evidence was planted there because it's off-camera and it can't be traced back to the real criminal."

"So Sareth's just the fall guy?" Rook said. "Because his locker's convenient?"

"And maybe also because someone has a grudge against him."

Rook shook her head. "He doesn't seem like grudge material. Have you met him?"

"I know him," said Theo. "He's my friend. And he got Chad suspended from the weight room."

Rook's mouth opened. "You're saying Perkins did this?"

"I'm saying the facts fit. What happened in the weight room? Why'd he report Chad?"

"Where are we eating?"

"What?"

"I want to eat this," said Rook, holding up the Tupperware. "While we talk. Are we going outside?"

"In here." Theo led the way into his AP European History classroom, which was open but dark and empty. Mr. Ramesh never minded his students coming in here at lunch.

They sat at one of the classroom tables, and Rook dug in. It was, hands down, the best meal she'd had since coming to Cedar Point. She shut her eyes for the first few bites, and she didn't care if Officer Cheekbones thought she looked weird doing it. She chewed and swallowed in total bliss.

Jesus, that was good.

She didn't speak right away, and only after she had ingested a substantial amount of food did she look up.

"He changed his weights," she said. "Perkins did. Sareth was benching, and Chad added ten pounds without telling him. It was more than Sareth could handle."

"He could have really hurt him," Theo said angrily. "Who does that?"

"Maybe someone who clubs his friend in the head," said Rook, almost hopefully. If Chad Perkins were arrested for assault, it would be a great day.

"And then what happened?"

"Me and Nolan got the barbell off Sareth," said Rook, "and Nolan went at Perkins hard. Threw him against the wall." She smirked, remembering. "Then AJ got in the middle and told Perkins to apologize."

"AJ stood up for Sareth?" Theo frowned. "Why?"

Rook flushed. "Who knows?" she said. "Anyway, that's what happened." She took another bite of chicken. "I wonder where Chad was that night," she mused.

"You mean that morning."

"No, it happened around midnight," said Rook. "When the cops interviewed me, they wanted to know where I was at midnight."

"Where were you?"

"Sleeping. But AJ got some texts that night, and I guess it looks like they're from me. So he went out to the wall to meet me. But somebody else was there."

"You're saying someone lured him there."

Rook nodded and polished off the rice. "Maybe Chad," she said. "Maybe Keanu."

"Keanu?"

"He's the QB now, right?" said Rook.

"Yeah..." Theo shook his head. "Wow. Okay, but here's my question. Since Sareth's locker isn't on camera, how did the police know to search it?"

"Huh." Rook stabbed the last Brussels sprout. "Good point."

She finished the last bite of food with a sigh of contentment and pushed the empty Tupperware toward him.

"Think fast."

Rook held up her hands just in time to catch the protein bar he lobbed at her.

"Down payment," he said, "for next time."

"What next time?" she said, but the bar went in her backpack anyway. She headed into the hall, and Theo followed.

"I bet they increase school security now," he said. "They'll probably put a camera out by the baseball field, and I bet they add another one in this hallway."

This gave Rook an idea. Mr. Magnusson was supposed to have a meeting with Principal Kim about school security, and whatever they discussed might be worth knowing. A plan began to form in her mind—risky, but possible. She glanced at locker 702. She had never noticed it was Sareth's. She tapped 703 with the toe of her sneaker.

"Close call," she said.

"Meaning?"

"That one's mine. If someone had thrown the evidence in there instead, I'd be screwed."

Theo turned his green-yellow eyes on her, alert.

"That's your locker? Right next to Sareth's?"

"So?"

"Rook." Theo's voice dropped. "What if someone was trying to frame *you*?"

SIXTEEN

"*Me.*"

The gut check was instant. He was right. It made sense.

"Someone's pretending to be you," said Theo, holding up one finger, his voice tense and rapid. "Texting AJ, luring him out there. And they chose the graffiti wall," he said, holding up a second finger, "because everybody knows you were out there with him, and everybody *thinks* you were *with* him with him, and that you're jealous because he's a player." He held up a third finger. "And now Sareth gets arrested, with evidence in his locker, which makes no sense because it makes *no sense*, because it wasn't supposed to be *his* locker, it was supposed to be *yours*."

"Fuck," said Rook quietly, her mind racing. Did somebody know who she was?

The bell rang to end lunch.

"We can keep talking," said Theo. "After school, you can come to my house. We can track everything we both know, and then figure out what to do next. Do you want to meet up after sixth?"

She did want to. More than she should have wanted to.

She couldn't go to his house. That was way too real.

"I'm busy," she lied.

She turned and walked away from him, striding fast toward her fourth period class—leaving Theo stranded before he could say another word.

THE NEXT MORNING, before school, Rook prepared to be truly stupid.

She stuffed a bunch of rations into her backpack. An expired granola bar, two hard-boiled eggs, a pull-top can of green beans, and her water bottle. She wouldn't get her first paycheck from The Lighthouse for a while, and it was the best she could scrounge up in Oscar's kitchen.

She had already taken most of her school supplies out of her bag. She stuffed in a pillow instead, zipped the bag shut, and went to school like she was a normal person who wasn't planning to spy on her teacher.

Rook parked off campus, went to her first period class, and tried to stay calm even though she was starting to sweat it, wondering if she should change her mind. Before second period, she used the bathroom—she wasn't going to have another chance for a while—and she went to Mr. Magnusson's class, where she worked on her slides, hoping no one could see how anxious she felt as she waited for her opportunity.

About twenty minutes into class, Mr. Magnusson asked them to do peer review of each other's presentations. Half the class got up and went to sit with their partners. Rook used this chance to move her backpack over toward the door of the newsroom where the old camera equipment was stored. She pretended to care about peer review for the next twenty minutes, jumpy inside the whole time.

This idea was dumb. Really dumb. Epic dumbassery. If she got caught, she was going to need a lawyer again. Greta would fucking throttle her. But if she wanted inside information on what had happened to AJ, then this might be a way to get it.

A few minutes before class ended, Rook logged out of her computer early and pretended to need a tissue. She stood near the wastebasket at the newsroom door, her backpack at her feet, aware of the room around her.

"Please log out," said Mr. Magnusson, tapping the smart board. The bell hadn't rung yet, but kids were already packing up.

Rook turned the unlocked knob of the newsroom door, used her foot to push her backpack in, and slipped into the dark room. Heart beating wildly, she closed the door behind her and dropped down on all fours so she couldn't be seen through the windows. She crawled to the back corner behind all the camera equipment, bringing her backpack with her. When she was tucked against the wall, she took out her pillow, lay down on her back, and went still among the tripods and the stacks of storage boxes.

She would wait here until the end of the school day and listen in on Mr. Magnusson's campus safety meeting with the principal. When they were done, she'd sneak out—hopefully knowing more than she did now.

Third period passed quickly. Fourth felt longer. For one thing, lunch happened before fourth, and Rook's body became ravenous on schedule. She waited for some noise in the classroom before unzipping her bag to eat a couple of her snacks—she horked down the hard-boiled eggs, because they'd be disgusting if she waited too long, and she also ate the canned green beans. She didn't drink any water—her bladder would betray her in an hour if she did—so she lay there with a dry mouth and a rising headache.

"No, not the basic interface," she heard someone say. A girl. She sounded frustrated. "I mean an adaptive sensor array. If I can calibrate it to respond to subtle fluctuations in motion, like grip strength, I could code it to assist users with impaired muscle control."

"Delilah, bring it down a notch," someone else complained. "This is high school robotics, not freaking M.I.T."

"This is my life, actually," Delilah snapped back. "So I'll keep the dial on ten, thanks."

Fifth and sixth periods felt endless. Rook thought about napping but worried she'd end up sleeping through the meeting she was there to spy on. She got hungry again, but she tried to make herself wait. She didn't know when Mr. Magnusson left campus, and if she ended up having to stay here until late, she'd regret eating all of her snacks before school was even out.

She caved before sixth period was over and ate the granola bar, which was a terrible idea because it was full of sugar, and now she was hungrier than before.

When the final bell rang, Rook lay in the newsroom fantasizing about the food that Theo had brought her yesterday. When she got to the point where she couldn't stand it, she rifled through her backpack for the tuna. To her surprise and elation, her hand closed around a bonus snack.

The protein bar from Theo. She had forgotten about it.

Rook unwrapped it, grateful, wondering if Theo had actually researched the food she might eat. She bet he had. He was that kind of guy. He had gone on his computer, searched weightlifting nutrition, and brought her the perfect thing. It was a lot of effort to get her to talk to him for ten minutes...

Which probably meant he was into her.

She smirked as she chewed. Of course he was into her. Well, he could dream the dream. She was done with all of that. She had made her last mistake, and it had been a doozy. AJ was terrible, and comatose, and people thought it was her fault. If there was a time to swear off guys forever, it was now.

She took another bite of the bar, wondering what Theo would say if he knew she was lurking on the floor in the tech room right now. He'd probably think she was a complete head case.

He'd be right.

She stopped mid-chew when Mr. Magnusson's footsteps moved closer to the newsroom. He opened the door.

Rook lay stock-still on the floor, praying he wouldn't flip on the lights and find her. It wouldn't matter how she explained herself—she would still look guilty.

A flash of blue light flickered between the stacks of storage boxes—Mr. Magnusson's phone. For one second, the glow lit his face. Rook saw his eyes.

"Oliver?"

Mr. Magnusson turned away without seeing her.

"Come on in," he called. High-heeled shoes clicked against the linoleum outside as Mr. Magnusson closed the newsroom door.

"I know we scheduled half an hour, but they've called me to a district meeting," said Principal Kim. "If you want to reschedule—"

"No, I'll keep it brief," said Mr. Magnusson. "I want to speak with the district about security, and I don't want to undermine you, but there are areas on campus that need cameras. We're at the bare minimum. What can we do?"

"You want this school to be a police state?"

"I have a security keypad by my door. I can alarm this building every night when I leave. My computers are safer than my students—that's backwards. We need to fix it."

Rook tensed. She had never noticed the security keypad. If he alarmed this room, she'd be trapped here all night—with no bathroom.

Slowly, silently, controlling every muscle, she knelt up. She tilted one slat of the blinds and created a tiny space to peek through. From here, she couldn't see Principal Kim or Mr. Magnusson, but she *could* see the illuminated security pad by the front door—the numbers were clear. Maybe, if she watched Mr. Magnusson key out, she'd be able to copy his movements.

It was a big maybe.

"If there had been a camera out there on the baseball field," Mr. Magnusson continued, "that assault might not have happened. Our students are savvy, Regina. They know where the cameras are, and where they're not."

"Given the budget cuts, what do you want me to do?"

"We need eyes where we know students congregate. Like the graffiti wall. Also, how is there no footage of Sareth Sok stashing that necklace in his locker? Isn't there a camera at that end of the hall?"

The evidence *was* AJ's necklace. Rook pumped one fist. She'd been right.

"It was vandalized last year," said the principal. "If a concerned student athlete hadn't emailed us a tip, we wouldn't have had any idea that Sareth was holding onto evidence."

Mr. Magnusson snorted richly. "The fact that Chad

Perkins, of all people, showed that level of school citizenship is, frankly, miraculous—but we can't rely on student tips. We have to do more. Some of our students have seen too much, and they're carrying histories that should scare us a little."

Rook listened, surprised. She'd never heard a teacher say something like that. He wasn't wrong.

Was he talking about *her*?

She swallowed, her throat dry from lack of water. No—he had no idea who she was, she was being paranoid.

Probably.

"Cameras won't solve the problem," said Principal Kim. "What we need is to inspire students. We need to teach them to take ownership of this school. We need to build *culture*."

"I agree. But culture takes time. Right now, we need coverage."

"I know."

They were quiet for a moment.

"This school is upside-down," said Principal Kim. "Sometimes, that's how it feels. I thought I could do something here. Maybe I'm not the right person."

"That's just time catching up with you. You've been here ten years now, and it's taking its toll. I've been here thirty, and I've been through eight principals. You've lasted longer than any of them."

She laughed wearily.

"I think we should revisit something," said Mr. Magnusson. "You made a choice, when you got here, and I didn't push back, but we're in a different place now. Students need to see each other—really see each other. I'll come by your office in the morning with a plan. Something student-led. No budget needed. All about building culture."

"Yes. All right."

Rook heard the scrape of a chair, and high-heeled footsteps, and then the classroom door opened and shut. The lights in the tech room went out. Mr. Magnusson's footsteps traveled toward the security keypad. She stayed still and peered through the small crack she'd created in the blinds. Mr. Magnusson had his back to her. He opened the classroom door and held it with his foot, then shifted his bag into his left hand and raised his right to the keypad. Its numbered keys glowed green in the darkness.

He moved his thumb across the pad. As he keyed in the numbers, they appeared on the illuminated screen above the keys, making the code easier for Rook to see. She mouthed the numbers silently, hoping she could memorize them.

Nine, five, eight, six, four—enter.

The keys on the pad turned red. Mr. Magnusson walked through the door and let it fall shut.

"Nine five eight six four," Rook whispered, before she could forget. "Nine five eight six four, nine five eight six four..."

Still whispering, she stuffed her snack wrappers into her backpack along with her pillow, and she hurried to the keypad with her bag. Then entered the code, just as she had seen Mr. Magnusson do.

When she pressed *Enter*, the alarm screen started blinking—was that supposed to happen, or was she about to get arrested?—and then the system gave a long *beep* of confirmation, and the red keys turned green.

Rook pulled up her hood, slipped out of the classroom, and sneaked around behind the tech building to shimmy along a narrow, weedy path between the wall and the fence to avoid being seen by a security camera.

When she reached the back steps to the parking lot, she broke into a run. She ran full-out, up the stairs, across the lot, off campus, and down the block to where she had parked her car.

That had been worth it. Not only did she know now, for sure, that the evidence in Sareth's locker was AJ's gold chain, but she knew that Chad had sent in the tip. Why had he done it? How had he known what was in Sareth's locker? Had he seen Sareth put it in there? Had he seen somebody else do it? Had he put the evidence in there himself?

Had Chad attacked AJ?

Rook couldn't believe what she wanted to do next, but she knew she would.

Tomorrow, she was going to find Theo and tell him everything.

SEVENTEEN

In the morning, Ms. Winter came to AP Spanish and asked Theo to come with her to the counseling office. Colleen watched him leave, phone poised under the table, looking desperately curious. But even if he had wanted to tell her what was going on, he couldn't have. He didn't know.

"Am I in trouble?" he asked, once he was in the hall, walking with Ms. Winter toward her office. Was this about cutting class yesterday?

"You're not in any trouble," said Ms. Winter. "There's a police officer here who wants to speak with you."

Officer Petros.

Theo froze.

Ready to snitch on Rook?

But it wasn't snitching. It was the truth.

Right. Just the truth. Just ratting her out to the cops so you can feel like a good guy, because you know you're not.

No. That wasn't what this was. Sareth was in trouble, and this was how justice worked.

Wasn't it?

Ms. Winter waited next to him. "Officer Petros said you

contacted him. I came to walk you down in case you want support before meeting with him. Do you want to sit somewhere? Take a moment, talk it through?"

Theo shook his head, slow.

"I know what I want to say. I'm okay."

But when he entered Ms. Winter's dim, quiet office and saw Officer Petros in his uniform, official and badged, Theo felt the weights of doubt and guilt come down hard on his shoulders.

He was screwing Rook over.

Officer Petros ran a hand over his mustache, and Theo's heart beat harder.

Trust yourself, you got this. For Sareth, right?

"Hey, Theo. Have a seat."

Theo sat on the sofa and picked up a stress ball. He squeezed it six times.

Six minutes.

Things he couldn't change. Things he could.

"You wanted to tell me something," said Petros. "Go ahead, I'm listening."

Theo worked his throat in the quiet.

"I don't know if it's anything," he said. "It's not big."

"That's okay." Petros's tone was warm. "Small stuff counts more than you think. All the little pieces help with the whole picture. Did you see something you forgot to tell me about?"

"No, I... I talked to Rook."

"Yeah?" Petros flipped open his small notepad. "When?"

"We were locked down in the same place," said Theo. "The other day, when Sareth was arrested. So I asked her why she was out on the field so early, the day we found AJ. I was just curious."

"Sure. I would be too." Petros glanced up at him. "Did she answer?"

The officer's tone was still warm. Encouraging. He seemed like a good cop.

But everything Theo said was going right into that notebook.

"Yes," Theo answered, watching Petros's pencil move. "She said she was warming up for the gym."

"Right, okay—that everything?"

Theo almost said yes. If he said yes, it would be over. No betrayal.

Was it betrayal? She was lying about something. Sareth was wrongly accused.

It was betrayal to hold back.

"No." Theo squeezed the stress ball again, harder. Like he could press his guilt right into it. "I asked her if that was her routine. And she said yes."

Petros's pencil kept moving. "You sound like you think that's meaningful," he said. "Why?"

"Because I walk across that field in the morning all the time," said Theo, "and I've never seen her there warming up. I go the same way every day. If she were out there, I'd have seen her."

Great job, said his brain. *Feel better about yourself now? Feel like you made up for Mateo?*

"You're a good kid, you know that?" said Petros. "You were right to get in touch. You're helping."

Theo didn't feel like a good kid. He felt like a traitor. He squeezed the stress ball so hard he was surprised it didn't burst.

"You're doing great," said Ms. Winter quietly. "Do you want to take a break?"

Theo shook his head.

"I have a question for you," said Petros. "The morning you found her on the baseball field, did you notice if she was carrying anything?"

"She had a flashlight. I think I told you last time."

"Just double-checking. When did you notice the flashlight?"

AJ's face, suddenly lit at his feet. Dead white. Mouth open.

"I was almost on top of them," said Theo. "I was walking across the field, and the light switched on, and I saw AJ's face—they were two feet away."

"You're sure about that? You didn't see the light before that?"

"No."

"She wasn't using it to find her way across the field?"

Theo shook his head.

"Okay," said Petros, getting to his feet. "If anything else comes to mind, don't hesitate."

"Wait." Theo dropped the stress ball and stood too. "Sareth Sok. Is he in juvie?"

"I can't share that."

"What evidence do you have on him?"

"A smart kid like you probably knows I can't share that either."

"He didn't do it," said Theo. "I don't have evidence, but I know him. And for the record, I don't think Rook did it either. I think someone's trying to frame her, and they ended up accidentally framing Sareth. Their lockers are right next to each other's, and there's no security camera on those lockers. I think somebody tried to put the evidence in Rook's locker, and they missed and got Sareth's instead—check that hallway. You'll see."

Petros glanced at Ms. Winter. "Right next to each other? That true?"

"I can take you," she said, "if you'd like to see what he's talking about."

"I would." Petros flipped his notebook open, wrote a few more strokes, and gave Theo a keen look. "You think Rook's being framed. Any reason someone would want to do that?"

Theo shook his head. He didn't know.

"Has anybody mentioned anything about her? Any... unusual rumors, any stories? I don't mean the stuff with AJ."

Theo shook his head again, perplexed.

And then, for the first time, he really thought about what Rook had said in the weight room. Right before he had told her that he'd been up on the graffiti wall. She'd said something, and it had gone right past him, because he'd been so deep in his own discomfort. What exactly had she said?

Whatever you think you know, you better not say one fucking word to one single person.

What did she think he knew? What was there to know?

What had she been doing out there on that field?

Goes by Rook Radcliffe.

Theo nearly repeated it out loud. He wanted to ask Petros if Rook's name was an alias—because it had to be. Otherwise, the officer wouldn't have phrased it that way.

But maybe Ms. Winter didn't know about that.

He'd already done enough damage. If Rook didn't want attention, he wouldn't add more—so he kept his mouth shut.

Petros tucked the notebook into his pocket. "Ms. Winter, can you show me those lockers?"

Ms. Winter opened her door and led Petros out.

Theo headed to his locker to grab his stuff for precalculus, questions digging at him. First an alias, now unusual rumors. What *kind* of unusual?

"She's one of those girls," he heard someone say. "Goes after people's boyfriends. First she took AJ from Destiny, now she's trying to take Chad away from Jill."

He looked over and saw two girls he didn't know—and Rook. She stood a few paces away at the water fountain, screwing the cap onto her bottle, her back to the hallway. Close enough to hear every word.

"Like she can get Chad," the other girl scoffed.

"Maybe if she does him on campus," said the first girl, laughing. "So gross."

Rook turned. She didn't see Theo—she didn't seem to see anything at all. She walked out of the building without looking up.

"Hey, debate boy," said Adel Juárez, as she passed him. She adjusted her aviators. "Did I just see you with the cops again? You trying to get the headbasher put back in jail?"

"No," said Theo. The word came out of him hot and fast. "And she didn't hurt anyone."

"Damn, okay," said Adel, dark eyebrows up. "Not trying to make you mad." She paused. "You sure she didn't bash the shortstop, though? Because everyone's saying—"

"Everyone's wrong." Theo turned on the girls who had been gossiping. "Including you," he said, with the same angry heat. "She didn't *take* AJ, and she doesn't want anything to do with Chad."

The two girls stared at him.

"That's what Colleen said," one replied.

Theo drew a deep breath. He knew what he had to do next, and he dreaded every second of it. He didn't even know if it was possible.

But he had to stop Colleen.

IN SECOND PERIOD, Rook walked into Mr. Magnusson's classroom to find it transformed. The newsroom was open, clean, and lit. The blinds had all been raised, and the storage boxes were gone. A camera on a tripod pointed at a long, curving news reporting desk, which stood empty except for two microphones.

Rook's heart did flips of alarm. Mr. Magnusson must have done all this last night. Why had he cleaned it out? Had he realized someone had been hiding in there? Did he know it was her?

"Class." Mr. Magnusson sat on his desk and folded his powerful arms. "Sit down. Don't bother with the computers today, leave them off. We've got something else to do."

Intrigued by this break in routine, the class took their seats with unusual speed and listened with uncharacteristic focus.

"You know I'm retiring at the end of this year. Or maybe you don't know," Mr. Magnusson added, with a laugh. "Why would you? But I am, after thirty years," he said. "Thirty. You're so young, you can't understand what that means. You have no idea what I've had to witness. This school used to be something special, but bit by bit, it's all been stripped away. Everything I used to love about my job has been erased. Tests, standards, funding—blame what you want. I blame myself."

If there had been crickets, their song would have been loud and clear. It was so rare to hear an adult being candid like this. Rook found herself caught up in the energy, leaning forward in her seat.

"Tradition," he said. "That's what I want to leave here,

when I go. A tradition worth keeping." He pointed to the newsroom. "We used to do a show in there," he said. "Every day, my second period class did a show, a live TV show, broadcasted to the entire school, for five minutes at the end of class. It was a bit of everything–school announcements, sports, local news, comedy, blameless gossip. *The Wolf Howls*, that's what we called it, back when we were the Lakeview Wolves, of course." He got up. "This school is in the middle of a crisis. And not just because of the violence on campus. We have a morale problem. Nobody wants to be here."

"Facts," muttered Fernando, from the back of the room.

"Ten years ago, I was told I couldn't do *The Wolf Howls* anymore, because it cut into important instructional time. And I was so beaten down, I didn't fight."

"I'm sensing a but," said Elijah, rubbing his hands together. "Come on, Mr. M., tell me there's a but."

"Elijah's a butt man," said Blaine soberly, and the whole room, including Mr. Magnusson, laughed.

"*But*–" said Mr. Magnusson, "I went to Principal Kim this morning and told her we're starting the program again. I told her it was necessary to build the culture we want in this building, and she agreed. So as of today, for the rest of the year, computer fundamentals is suspended. This class will produce *The Wolf Howls*."

The students shrieked with excitement. Several shouted ideas at once.

"We can't call it *The Wolf Howls*," said Colleen. "That's just stupid."

"The Tea," suggested Tapeesa, slapping the table.

"Ace of Swords," said Ursula, glancing up from her tarot deck.

"FEAR THE SALMON," shouted Blaine and Elijah together.

"Naw, man. It's the *Seventh-Inning Stretch*," said Fernando, holding up his fist to show his state championship baseball ring. "We're a baseball school."

It was a solid idea, and consensus was reached. On the whiteboard, Mr. Magnusson listed jobs that would need to be done and asked the students to choose their initial roles. Rook read over the various responsibilities, considering how involved she wanted to be. Her first instinct was to run the camera—an offscreen role would be good.

Then it struck her. If she played it right, this was her excuse to ask questions.

She headed up to the whiteboard and grabbed an erasable marker. Next to Investigative Journalist, she wrote *Rook Radcliffe*.

EIGHTEEN

At lunch, for the first time since the beginning of the school year, Theo sat at the table where Mateo no longer was. The only person there so far was Tuyet, so he set down his tray across from hers and glanced briefly at the book she was reading—*Tess of the d'Urbervilles*.

"I haven't read that," he said. "Any good?"

Tuyet's gaze rose to meet his, and her expression chilled him. Her face had changed, since the funeral. The beauty was still there, still perfect, but it had hardened like a mask.

"Look who's graced us with his presence," she said softly. "I'm honored."

Theo's teeth came together.

"It must be so hard." Tuyet's eyes dropped to her book. "Being the only one who *really* misses him."

"That's not fair," he said.

"Nothing's fair," Tuyet replied, without looking up. "Thought you'd heard."

"Oh. Theo."

Marna approached with her lunch tray and Alejandro

in tow, clearly not thrilled to see him. No wonder, since the last time he'd talked to her, he'd snapped.

"Um... are you actually sitting here?" she asked him.

"I don't know," he said, still angry at Tuyet and her spite, and feeling like he might snap again.

Marna sighed and sat next to him. Her glossy brown curls smelled like vanilla coffee. Alejandro sat on her other side.

"You don't have to sit with us if you don't want to," she said.

"Oof," Alejandro said quietly.

Theo had known Marna for a long time. He knew she was incapable of rudeness. He understood, as Alejandro did, that this was her way of telling Theo she wanted him to go away.

He didn't. He waited for the person he wanted to speak to, and he didn't have to wait long. When Colleen spotted him from across the cafeteria, she moved toward him fast and plunked down beside Tuyet.

"Theo, I heard the police were here," she said breathlessly. "To talk to you, right? About Rook?"

He met her gaze and didn't answer.

Colleen sipped from her tumbler. "Do you think they'll arrest her again?" she asked. "Do you know something?"

"Do *you*?" Theo replied, his jaw tight. He had expected this confrontation to be difficult, but anger made it easier. "Do you actually *know* anything?"

Tuyet turned her book over on the table and pinned her eyes on him.

Colleen tossed back her red waves. "Oh, I know tons," she said, "but you've probably heard most of it by now—if you saw my socials last night, I pulled most of the proof together. Rook texted AJ and lured him out to the graffiti wall—"

"That's hearsay."

"Nope. Chad and Keanu both saw the texts," said Colleen. "Here's the timeline. Two days before the attack, Destiny said Rook was showing off for all the guys in the weight room, trying to get AJ's attention. Then, after school, we all know what happened."

"Do we?" Theo shot back. "Do we *know*? Or do we just know what AJ wanted everyone to think?"

"She didn't deny it when I asked her," said Colleen with a shrug. "They had sex behind the wall. And then she found out AJ was still with Destiny, so she decided to get back at him. Plus she was mad that he told all the guys they did it. I don't blame her for being mad, AJ's the worst about that stuff." Colleen laughed. "But I should be nicer. He's in a coma. And *then*—this is just a guess, but some people are saying it, and it makes so much sense—she put evidence in Sareth's locker so that he'd get in trouble instead of her, because I don't know if you know this? But her locker is *right* next to his."

"You have no idea what you're talking about," Theo said coldly. "You should shut up."

Colleen's mouth opened, indignant. "Excuse me?" she said loudly. "You ignore us for weeks, and now you think you can just—"

"You. Don't. Know," said Theo. "Rook didn't have sex with AJ—she doesn't even *like* him, he asked her to Homecoming and she said no. He wanted to see her again, and she said *no*. You have no idea what happened behind that wall."

Colleen scoffed. "And you do?"

"Yes," Theo retorted. "I do. I was up on the graffiti wall the entire time they were back there, and I saw everything."

"Theo." Marna's voice was quiet, but loaded with judgment.

"Bro." Alejandro leaned past Marna to look at him. "You watched them? Yikes."

"It was an accident." Theo felt himself getting hot. "I was just trying to be alone, and then they started hooking up, and I got trapped."

"What did you see?" Colleen demanded. "What did they do?"

"Basically nothing." Theo let out a hard breath. "All they did was kiss."

"So AJ lied." Tuyet hadn't moved her eyes from Theo. "Shock."

"Well, just because Rook didn't sleep with him doesn't mean she didn't hit him," said Colleen, tossing back her red hair. "She's really strong. She could easily have hit him hard enough."

"Alejandro's really strong," said Theo, gesturing to Marna's massive boyfriend, his debate logic kicking in. "Maybe it was him."

"How am I in this?" Alejandro asked, bewildered.

"Then what about the texts?" said Colleen, leaning forward. "Those definitely came from her."

"Did they? *Definitely*? Anyone can text and say they're someone else," said Theo, and he leaned in too, meeting her energy. "Someone could have used a burner."

"Why are you defending her?" Colleen demanded. "What's going on? I thought you were with Ana, from Highland."

"What?" Theo asked, startled. "I am."

His stomach flipped. Where had that even come from?

"It's just you're awfully worried about Rook," said Colleen, seeming to realize she'd struck a nerve. She smiled at him. "So *that's* interesting. Maybe there's more going on with the two of you."

"No, there isn't. So don't make that one of your posts," Theo snarled. He looked at Tuyet. "And just because I don't want to talk about him doesn't mean I think I'm special. So you don't need to come at me like you're the only one with a right to grieve either."

He regretted saying it when Tuyet froze. Tears jumped into her eyes.

Colleen put a protective arm around her.

"Get out," she said to Theo. "Go somewhere else. You can't sit here."

Theo got up and left.

He was halfway across the cafeteria when he had to stop short to avoid a collision.

Rook was suddenly in his path. She didn't look empty like earlier—her eyes had energy in them. Guarded, but alive. She pushed a sticky note into his hand, and Theo looked down at it in confusion—it was covered in bullet points and phrases—nothing that immediately made sense. His brain was all over the place, jumping from anger to anguish to self-blame.

Tuyet was in pain, just like him—he was horrible. He glanced back and saw her sitting motionless, Colleen's hand on her shoulder. Marna met his eyes, and hers were righteously angry. He didn't think he had ever seen her so angry.

"There," Rook said, "we're even for the food. Bye."

Theo tried to refocus on her, but he was spiraling. "Wait—I don't understand."

She let out an irritated breath. "It's some stuff I found out."

"What *stuff*?" he demanded. "Just tell me what this is."

Rook's face closed off. The line of her mouth hardened. Was she mad at him too?

Theo gave up.

He sat on the nearest available cafeteria bench and put his head down on the table. He had told on Rook to the cops. He had yelled at random girls in the hall about her. He had stood up to his friends for her. Now he didn't have friends, and here *she* was—with a weird sticky note—and Colleen was going to post something underhanded. And Mateo was dead. And he had made Tuyet cry. Everything was wrecked, and it was his fault. All of it.

"No," he muttered. "*Damn* it."

"Jesus," said Rook, "what did I do?"

"It's not you," he said, his voice muffled against the table. "It's everything." He took a couple of deep breaths but didn't bother to sit up. He didn't have it in him yet. "Just talk to me. I don't have any Brussels sprouts, but maybe this once you could do it pro bono, because I'm having a pretty bad day."

Rook stood there, one fist clenched on her backpack strap, the other on the handles of her gym bag, looking down at Theo slumped on the table, and struggling to understand herself.

She had spent all of third period ignoring geometry and writing down everything she could think of that might matter. Everything she'd learned from staking out Mr. Magnusson's room. Everyone she suspected, and all her reasons. She had made that stupid sticky note, and she had come here to find Theo, and now she felt like an idiot.

She had thought he'd be glad to talk to her about it again. She didn't know why the hell she'd thought that—he had confused her with the chicken, he had acted like talking to her mattered to him, but now he was in some kind of mood, and he clearly didn't want her there. So.

"Never mind," she said. "See you."

"Sit *down*," Theo mumbled, before waving the sticky note at her. "Just sit down for two minutes and tell me what this thing is supposed to mean. I want to know, okay? I do." He sighed and sat up, looking at the note in his hand. "Ring and chain," he read aloud. "Care to explain?"

Rook gave him a wary look, barely resisting the urge to walk away. The way he was acting—she didn't know how to respond. What was wrong with him? Did he need help, or something? Was she supposed to ask if he was okay? They weren't friends. Was she still supposed to ask? Was that the normal thing to do?

Oh man, this should be good. You, attempting normal.

"Should I guess?" Theo asked, when Rook stood silent. "Ring and chain—I don't know. Sounds like a pub in a fantasy game. Is it a pub in a fantasy game?"

Rook snorted.

Even when he was being weird, he was still pretty funny.

"No, okay, serious guesses....obviously it's jewelry," Theo went on, frowning down at the sticky note. "A fancy clasp on a necklace or—"

He sucked in a breath. Looked up at her.

"AJ's baseball ring," he said. "On the chain. I saw it when you two—" He stopped. "I saw it. Why does it matter?"

Rook couldn't help it now. He had hit the nail on the head, and she wanted to tell him, she needed to hash it out.

She perched on the bench beside him. "The evidence in Sareth's locker," she said. "It was—"

She got no further.

Ice water crashed down over her head, soaking her hair. Her shirt. She jolted back on the bench.

River water. Cold. Black. Seatbelt.

Ice cubes lay scattered all over the table in front of her. They pooled in her lap. Wet her jeans.

Move. Get up.

She managed to stand, but her legs felt weak. She turned.

"Rookie!" Chad Perkins shouted, holding up an empty Big Gulp cup. He dropped it to the floor, where it clattered onto its side and rolled in a circle. "Payback, baby."

His friends laughed. The cafeteria hushed.

Theo felt them all zoom in, watching the scene, waiting for Rook's reaction, but he could see it in her face. She had switched off. Gone.

He, on the other hand, had had enough. This whole day had been enough. Fury and guilt and grief boiled over and crashed right out of his mouth.

"Is it Be An Asshole day?" he yelled, not caring, all of a sudden, that Chad was bigger than him, that all Chad's friends were bigger too, and that the entire cafeteria was looking at him like he was a complete loser.

He got up anyway—breathing hard, hot all over, ready to punch something.

"Relax," said Chad, putting a hand through his hair. "It's a joke, it's just water."

"What's *wrong* with you?" Theo kept shouting, too far gone to pull back. "Grow the hell up, you moron. Leave her alone."

Somebody tittered.

"Leave her alone," one of Chad's friends mimicked in a high voice.

"Simp," another one laughed. "Look how red he is."

Theo flushed hotter. Chad snickered.

"Hey," yelled a teacher. "Perkins, clean that up and get over here."

Chad puckered his lips at Theo a couple times like he was blowing kisses. "Later, sidekick," he said. Still laughing, he walked away with his crew.

Theo grabbed Rook's gym bag and backpack and shoved them into her arms. She hugged them to herself. He grabbed his own stuff and put a guiding hand on Rook's back. She stiffened, but allowed it, and he steered her past Chad, out of the cafeteria, and into the hall, where he realized what he had just done.

He had shouted down Chad Perkins in front of half the school. Like Mateo would have.

So that was what it felt like.

"I'm fine," said Rook. "I can change, I have gym clothes."

"I'll walk you."

Rook stepped back, out of Theo's reach. His hand dropped to his side.

"I don't need protection."

"I might, though," he said, only half joking. "Chad's trolls will come for me now. You'll bodyguard me, right?"

She gave no flicker of a smile.

Theo sobered. "He's always been like that. Ever since T-Ball. I'm sure it kills him that you're stronger than he is. I bet it eats all those guys alive."

"How do you know I'm stronger than them?"

"Well, look at you."

Rook seemed to like this answer. Her eyes grew friendlier.

Theo's pulse was still quick. He had never done anything like that before.

They'd get him back now. Chad and his crew would never let this go. He didn't know what it would look like, but he was sure it wouldn't be fun.

The bell rang, harsh and loud.

End of lunch. End of whatever *that* just was.

"Meet me after school by the baseball field?" Theo held up what remained of Rook's sticky note, which was too wet to read. "I still want to know what this says."

"Okay."

"Cool." He stuck it in his pocket and turned to go to class.

"Hey. Theo?"

He checked back over his shoulder. Rook hugged her bags to her chest, still soaked like she'd come in from a downpour.

"Thank you."

His insides grew warm. He saluted her, pivoted, and made his way to class.

NINETEEN

After school, they walked across the baseball field. Rook cast a moody look at the graffiti wall as they passed it, wishing she had never let AJ Ellsworth anywhere near her.

Theo's mind was also occupied. Mateo was the last person who had walked him home from school. It had been months since he had taken this shortcut with another human being and invited them to jump the fence into his backyard. Funny that it was Rook.

He jogged to the fence, hoisted himself over—and was halfway to the back door before he realized Rook hadn't followed. She stayed back from the fence like it would shock her on contact.

"What is this?" she asked.

"My house."

"Why are we going to your house?"

"So I can drug you and harvest your organs." He paused. "Kidding. Come on, Rook. Nothing will bite you in here, except my sister, but she doesn't usually do that anymore."

Rook didn't move. His house was his space, and the last time she'd been in Theo's backyard, she'd had handcuffs on.

"I thought we were just hanging out," she said. "We can do that outside."

"If we go inside, we can talk without being overheard. Also, there's food."

That was true.

Stop being a freak. It doesn't mean anything, it's just a house.

Rook threw her backpack over the fence, placed one hand on top of it, and vaulted it with ease. She landed softly in the tall grass.

"Badass move," said Theo. "Watch your step." He navigated the treacherous obstacle course created by Savannah's abandoned yard toys, and he opened the sliding glass door that led into his home.

Theo's house had some charm, Rook thought. Two stories, light blue, spacious yard. But the yard was overgrown, the paint chipped, the gutters green with moss—nobody seemed to care much about upkeep.

Inside, the situation was no better. They wove their way through piles of clothes in the untidy laundry room into an even more untidy kitchen. Rook glanced from the pots and pans, stacked high in the sink, to the cluttered kitchen counters. Not a single inch of surface was clear. Homework, tools, books, medications, a hairbrush—everything was everywhere. A soccer cleat lay abandoned on top of a pizza box. What the hell was this place?

Theo pulled a Hot Pocket out of the freezer and stuck it in the microwave, then rummaged in the refrigerator. He came up with a bag of baby carrots, a couple of celery stalks, Greek yogurt, and an orange. "You want peanut butter?"

"What kind?"

He opened the pantry door. "My mom eats the natural stuff, if you want." He tried to hand the glass jar to Rook, who balked.

"I can't eat your mom's food."

Theo laughed. "Please. If she thinks I ate something healthy, she'll throw a parade."

"Are you sure she'd be okay with me being here? Doesn't she think I'm a felon?"

Theo hadn't considered that. "She won't be home from work for a while," he said.

Snacks in hand, they made their way to his bedroom, where Rook realized that the mess in the kitchen had only been a warm-up for the real disaster. Theo kicked open his door, which wouldn't open completely, and Rook stepped in.

His room was so gross, she almost walked right back out.

Mountains of clothing, books, and assorted discarded items swamped the floor. Unwashed cups, plates, and used utensils lay scattered across his desk. His bedsheets looked like they hadn't been changed since before he'd entered puberty, and the reclining chair that pointed at his television set and video gaming consoles had a permanent human-shaped depression in its duct-taped, food-stained, crumb-covered surface.

"Christ," said Rook, disgusted. "Really?"

"Make yourself comfortable."

She took him at his word and started picking up junk food wrappers, counting as she went.

"What are you doing?"

"Making myself comfortable. Jesus, I've picked up fifteen of these things and I haven't even started. You're going to die of a heart attack before you turn thirty. Where's the trash can?"

He pointed to it. "You don't have to do that."

"I need space to work."

"School project?"

"I'm working out."

"What, here?" said Theo, bemused. "How? I don't have any weights."

Rook crushed a few dozen wrappers into the tiny trash can and started kicking laundry into the corners. "I knew I shouldn't come over," she grumbled, as a pair of Theo's boxers flew off the toe of her shoe. "Why would you let me witness this?"

Theo took the crumpled sticky note out of his pocket and held it up. "So," he said, "what do you know?" He pulled out his notebook and took notes as she spoke.

"One." Rook shoved a pile of video game magazines under his bed with the side of her foot. "The evidence in Sareth's locker was AJ's gold chain, with his baseball ring on it. Two, Chad Perkins got Sareth's locker searched. He sent an email to the principal, and that's why there was a lockdown."

Theo listened, sickened, as the crime played out in his head—an object thudding against AJ's skull, his body crumpling, a hand reaching out to yank the necklace off him.

Rook checked his expression. "What's the matter?"

"They ripped his chain off," said Theo, not sure why that was the part that bothered him so much. "And then they just left him there, bleeding, likely to die."

"Looks that way."

"It's so callous." Theo stared down at his notebook. "Who could do that?"

Rook shrugged, unbothered. "Plenty of people," she said. "Violent crimes happen all the time."

Theo shook his head. "Yeah," he said. "I guess so."

"The question is," said Rook, "how would that person get the chain into Sareth's locker? Wouldn't they need the combination?"

"Maybe not, if the ring would fit through the slats from outside."

"That's a big ring, though. Why would a guy like Sareth take weight training anyway?" Rook wondered aloud. "He doesn't seem to like it much."

"Because it wipes out a P.E. credit without taking up a valuable class period during the regular school day," said Theo. "It's exactly what I'd do, if I had to take P.E."

"Why don't you have to take P.E.?"

"I just don't," said Theo, who didn't feel like discussing his epilepsy at the moment.

Rook gave him a curious look that Theo didn't meet.

"How'd you find out about the evidence and the email?" he asked.

"I spied on a meeting between Mr. Magnusson and Principal Kim."

Theo looked up at her, stunned. "You *what*?"

Rook explained what she had done.

"Damn," said Theo in awe, when she was finished. "You are au*da*cious."

Rook tossed her ponytail. She liked how he was looking at her.

"Could you set a two-minute timer?" she asked.

Theo did, and Rook started squatting and jumping up.

"So if Perkins sent that email," she managed, as she worked, "then he knew the evidence was there. Which means either he planted it, or he saw who did."

Theo nodded, writing fast. "And since Sareth got him suspended from the weight room, Chad might have a grudge and want to frame him."

"True," said Rook, panting. "But also? Maybe no one's getting framed."

Theo raised his eyebrows.

"Sareth got arrested," said Rook, "and Sareth had the evidence." She was finding it harder to talk and breathe now. "So maybe the answer is obvious."

"You're suggesting Sareth did it." Theo shook his head. "He didn't."

Rook stopped talking and went full out with her jump squats, and when the timer beeped, she stopped and shook out her legs, sucking for air. Sweating now, she peeled off her sweatshirt and tossed it onto her bag.

Theo looked away, then his eyes moved back to her. Rook pretended she didn't see him taking her in. She let him gaze, enjoying his interest. She had always liked making boys look, when she felt like it.

Dumbass, she thought. *Don't go there.*

She glanced around his room. Now that she was over the shock of walking into it for the first time, she was able to see past the mess. She couldn't remember being in a place that felt so *lived* in. Books of all kinds science, poetry, world history—filled the shelves that lined his walls. They weren't just for show, either; they were battered and dog-eared, and he had clearly read them all. Trophies and medals stood among the books, along with certificates and plaques, celebrating his intellectual abilities. Winner of the Lincoln-Douglas Debate, Theodore Locke. Mental math finalist, Theodore Locke. Junior mock trial, Future Cities challenges... This guy was all kinds of smart.

On his desk stood a framed picture of him with another boy. They beamed at the camera, arms slung around each other's shoulders. Rook studied it more closely. Theo was younger in the picture, with a mouth full of braces, and the boy beside him was someone Rook had never seen before. If she had, she would have remembered. Even though he was young, he was already beautiful—brown and broad and vivid, square-jawed and dark-eyed, his smile infectious and inviting.

"Who's *that*?" she asked, pointing.

"That," said Theo quietly, "is Mateo."

The best friend. Rook was sorry that she would never meet him. He looked like he was really something.

"Do you like competing?" she asked, changing the subject.

It was the right question. Theo's face lit up.

"I love it. I get so wound up, sometimes I puke beforehand."

"Me too," said Rook, before she'd thought about it.

"So you compete in weightlifting? You must, right?"

Rook shrugged, sorry she'd said anything. She pointed to his carpet. "What's that orange stuff?"

"That was probably once a nacho cheese chip of some kind."

"Do you have a towel? Like a clean one?"

Theo got one for her, and Rook laid it out. She got down on the floor.

"Would you run a stopwatch this time?"

Theo brought up an app, and Rook lay on her back on the towel.

"Tell me when to go."

"Go."

She did sit-ups as fast as she could.

"You said something about Keanu," said Theo. "I guess it could make sense, if he really wanted QB."

"Yep," said Rook, reaching for her toes again. "Perkins was talking at The Lighthouse. There might be a college scout at the Homecoming game. Maybe Keanu wants the attention."

"It's just so hard to imagine," said Theo. "Keanu, AJ, and Chad have been friends since kindergarten. They're all Varsity Baseball too, and I don't know if you've picked up on this since coming to Lakeview, but our baseball team?"

"State champs," Rook panted. "I'm aware."

"Would a lifelong friend really do that?"

"Hundred percent," said Rook, breathing hard but unhesitating. "Anyone—can hurt anyone. Nobody knows—anybody. Keanu—could've done it. Sareth could've done it —I could've done it—you could've done it."

She was so resolute that Theo looked askance at her.

She sat up for the hundredth time and grabbed her knees.

"Time," she gasped.

"A minute and fifty seconds."

She was getting slower. Eating poorly, sleeping poorly, training on her own—it didn't matter anymore, but she still hated the idea of being average. She dipped a carrot in the peanut butter and chomped it, annoyed.

Theo watched her, dwelling on what she had just said. He disagreed. Deeply. But she clearly believed it to her core.

"That isn't true," he said. "Some people wouldn't hurt each other. Some people really know each other."

She gave him a look like he'd just said gravity didn't exist.

"No," she said. "You think you know people, but you never do. Ever."

"You really believe that?"

"I *know* that."

Theo shook his head. "Someone must've really hurt you."

Rook said nothing. Her instinct not to come here had been right. She had already said too much, and Theo was too smart. She had to leave.

He saw it in her face before she moved. Her eyes changed—she was shutting down, switching off.

She got up and picked up her bags.

"Don't go," he said quietly. "I need to tell you something."

He didn't want to. But if she thought nobody was trustworthy, then he had to be different.

He took a deep breath and said the truth.

"I told the cops you lied."

TWENTY

Rook's hands tightened on the straps of her bags. Her internal walls began to close. If she had heard him right, if she had done this to herself again—

"You did what?" she asked. Her voice came out higher and softer, like a kid.

Lock it down. Right now.

"You said you warm up on the field. That you have a routine." Theo met her eyes. "You lied. You're never out there in the morning—I would have seen you."

Rook flushed. "You told the cops that?"

"It was the truth."

"I'm going to get *arrested*," she said angrily. "How about that for truth?"

"You didn't do it," said Theo, "and I told them that, too."

"Awesome," said Rook sarcastically, "you saved the day." She let out a miserable laugh. "At least you did it fast, right? Two seconds in, and boom, you're a liar."

"When did I lie?" Theo demanded, standing up. "I could have lied, I could have said nothing, but I'm literally telling you the whole truth. I went to my friends today, and

I told them you didn't sleep with AJ. I told Colleen to stop spreading it around."

"Did I ask you to do that?" Rook shot back. "No, I told you it wouldn't make a difference—"

"It does make a difference," said Theo. "People have you wrong, and I don't like it."

Rook lifted her chin and looked away.

He didn't know her. Nobody did. For all he knew, his friends had her right on the money.

"I had to talk to the police," he said. "Sareth is my friend, and I owe him doing everything I can to get him out of custody. If we work together, I think we have a chance at it. Don't you?"

"Together?" Rook replied, cutting him with her eyes again. "You'll probably tell the principal I spied on her—Jesus Christ. I'm going to get expelled. I'm out of here."

"Don't go," he said again.

"Give me one reason," she said, "and make it fucking good."

Theo drew breath.

Truth, brother. Stick with it.

"I don't know what I'm doing," he said. "I have no idea how to do this."

"Do *what*?"

"Deal with this stuff. AJ, the police, my friends, Chad—you—I'm in over my head, and I keep screwing up, but—" He cut himself off. "This is what I've got. I'm trying."

"Trying?"

"To do the right thing."

She literally rolled her eyes at him. "The right thing," she mocked, like he was the most naive person she'd ever met. "And that is?"

"How am I supposed to know? If I knew, I'd do it."

She narrowed her eyes and studied him like she was trying to decide if he was for real.

"Why don't you think I did it?" she demanded.

"I just don't. You're not lying about that, I can tell."

"No you can't," said Rook. "I was on the scene. I could have sent AJ the texts. I'm strong enough to hurt him. And I did hook up with him—so maybe I was jealous."

"Now you sound like everyone else at school."

"Tell me where I'm wrong."

Theo considered carefully. Somehow, this was a test.

"You lied about why you were there," he said. "But you weren't there for AJ."

Her face colored instantly.

"You were doing something else," said Theo, leaning in. "What was it?"

"I was taking a walk," said Rook firmly. She wasn't going to tell him anything about the stuff behind the wall. That was for damn sure.

Theo let it go. Based on her posture and the look on her face, he knew that if he pressed the issue, she'd walk out the door.

"Fine," he said, "but you didn't send those texts. You wouldn't have asked AJ to meet you at the wall again, because you don't actually like him. At all."

"Then why did I hook up with him?"

"Great question, why did you?" Theo answered, swift. "He's an asshole, and you knew it the whole time."

Rook broke eye contact. He had been able to tell that?

"And yes, you're strong enough to hurt him, but if you were the kind of person who does that, you'd have put *me* in a coma by now."

She snorted softly. "I still could."

"As for the jealousy thing," said Theo, "I think we should talk about it."

"You just said I don't like AJ. Now you think I'm jealous?"

"No, but what if someone else is? Think about it. Somebody else is jealous that you were with AJ, and that somebody baited AJ to the wall and then turned on him. That would give them motive to hurt AJ *and* frame you."

Again, Rook's gut told her he was onto something.

"Chad Perkins sent the email to the principal," she said. "That part doesn't track. Why would he—"

"Because he has a problem with you," said Theo.

"But he didn't before," said Rook. "He never bothered with me until I told him off at The Lighthouse."

"He flicked ice at your stomach, I heard."

"So?"

"So that's probably his idiot, fourth-grade way of saying he's into you," said Theo. "He's probably liked you since you got here. Maybe he's frustrated."

"You're saying maybe he's mad AJ got a turn, and not him."

Theo winced. "I wouldn't say it like that," he said. "But basically, yes."

"And Destiny's acting like I'm a homewrecker," said Rook. "When I passed her and Nolan the other day, they were standing really close. He looked at me, and she turned his face away. With her hand."

"Maybe she's scared of losing him," said Theo. "She already lost AJ, at least from her perspective."

"So now she thinks I'm stealing Nolan next," said Rook. "And Sareth? What about him? Where was he that night?"

"Sareth didn't do it."

"Proof?"

"None, but I know I'm right." Theo studied her eyes. "So. What now?"

We keep talking, Rook thought instantly. *We figure this out.*

It was a terrible answer. She couldn't do that. Why was she even still in his bedroom? He had messed up. Bad.

But he hadn't hid it. He hadn't waited six months to let it blow up on her. He hadn't waited until she was raw, then plunged her into the acid.

No blindsides. That was the rule. If he could stick to it, then maybe...

Maybe what? You'll be pals? You're the sucker of the goddamn century.

"*If* I stay," she said, "are you going to keep talking about me to people?"

"If you stay," said Theo, "and I think something needs to be said, I'll talk to you first next time."

It wasn't the answer she wanted.

It wasn't a lie either.

Rook dropped her bags. Then she ripped open the carton of yogurt, ate it in two bites, tossed the empty carton into Theo's overflowing trash can, and got down on his floor again, this time onto her hands, because if she didn't do something physical, right now, she was going to come out of her skin.

"Time me again," she said. "Stopwatch. Say when."

"When."

She did push-ups, launching herself up off the floor in between each one to clap her hands. Without her sweatshirt on, wearing the tight tank top she'd changed into thanks to Chad's Big Gulp full of ice water, her arms and shoulders and part of her back were exposed. Her muscles rippled beneath her skin, and Theo let himself gaze, awed. He was fairly certain that if he tried to do even one clapping push-up, he would die, and she just kept knocking them out.

Her power was mesmerizing. He forgot he was staring. He only remembered when his door banged open, and his sister marched in wearing a bicycle helmet over her strawberry-blonde braids.

"Knock," said Theo, blushing in spite of the fact that he was sure Savannah wouldn't notice anything.

Savannah gawped down at Rook, who continued to work. Sixteen, Theo counted. Seventeen. Eighteen. She hadn't slowed at all. She was a machine.

"You're the girl," Savannah said, "the one from when the police came."

"Time," said Rook.

"Thirty-six seconds."

Acceptable. Rook rubbed her triceps and looked up at Theo's little sister.

"Savannah, right?"

Savannah nodded, looking both scared and important. "How come you're not in jail?"

"Because I didn't do it."

"Oh." Savannah played with one of her braids. "Who did, then?"

"I don't know yet." Rook searched her young, freckled face. "I'm sorry you saw that stuff the other day."

"I didn't really see anything."

"Did the cops scare you?"

"No, he was nice. He said I was brave. I liked those push-ups you were doing."

"Yeah? You like push-ups?"

"I do push-ups in P.E. I can do ten in a row."

"Good job," said Rook. "Do eleven."

"Why? How many can you do?"

"Doesn't matter how many I can do." She met Savannah's intense expression with her own. "All that matters is, if you can do ten, you push for eleven."

"It burns after ten."

"That's your muscles getting stronger. That feeling is important; it's how you know you're growing. Keep training."

Savannah looked impressed. "Okay. I'll go do eleven right now." She left the room and slammed the door shut.

"You'll be her favorite person now," said Theo, who would not have pegged Rook as someone who was good with fourth graders. "She loves it when the big kids take her seriously."

"How old is she?"

"Nine."

"You should take her seriously." Rook got up and shook out her arms. "Maybe I can find out more if I ask around. I'm a journalist for the *Seventh-Inning Stretch*, so I can use that."

"The what?"

"The school news show."

"We have one of those?"

"It's a new elective."

"Well, that's handy. You can interview Keanu about the Homecoming game and sneak some extra questions in, try and catch him off guard—speaking of which, what about Homecoming?"

Rook raised her eyebrows. "What about it?"

"It might be a good time to talk to people."

Rook bent down for her water and sneaked a look at Theo to find his eyes on her, checking her out again. She stood up, keeping her back to him for a minute to let him enjoy the view. Then she turned halfway toward him and watched peripherally as she tipped back her water bottle and drank. His gaze moved from her chest to her midriff, where her shirt rode up.

Rook capped the bottle and turned toward him again. The second she did, he shifted his eyes to the notebook in his hands, as if he hadn't been full-on ogling her.

He had a perfect mouth, she thought, studying it. Beautiful eyes. And kind of a young face. She wondered if he was a virgin.

Stop it. Leave it alone.

Theo got up. He dug his phone out of his pocket and started to text somebody.

"Homecoming, huh?" Rook asked. She pulled her hoodie over her head and smoothed down her ponytail. "You don't already have a date?"

Theo kept texting. "Wasn't planning to go."

She stepped closer to him. "But you're saying you *want* to go."

Theo glanced up from his phone. His breath caught. Rook was suddenly very close to him, sweating and radiant from exercise. The look in her eyes was thrilling. He remembered with absolute clarity how she had put AJ against the graffiti wall.

"Oh—no." He faltered. "I wasn't asking you to the dance."

"You want to, though, right?" she teased, and she leaned toward him, testing to see what he'd do.

Maybe it was a dumb game to play. But something in her wanted to see if he'd flinch.

His eyes widened. He scrambled backward, caught the heel of his foot on the desk chair, and flailed. He had to catch himself on his desk.

"Wait. I have a girlfriend."

Rook felt a flicker of disappointment but was also entertained. He looked terrified.

"Why aren't you taking the girlfriend to Homecoming?" she asked.

"We already went—at her school." The words spilled out of him fast. "She's at Highland. She was Homecoming Queen there."

"Wow. Royalty."

"Yeah," said Theo, still too discomfited to pick up on Rook's sarcasm. "She's the cheer captain. She's a senior."

Rook pressed her mouth shut on a smile.

"She better have straight As too."

"She does," said Theo earnestly.

Rook snickered and picked up her gym bag. "Cool," she said. "I'll go see what I can find out."

"By yourself?"

That was how she preferred it.

"Yep," she said, and she left his house behind.

TWENTY-ONE

The next day was Friday. The Homecoming game. Outside, a heavy gray mist hung over Lakeview. Inside, the school dripped with pink and black posters, window marker bubble letters, and spirit-day colors.

Rook waited for Keanu outside the locker rooms after zero period. He emerged in his football jersey, his backpack slung over one shoulder, his long, dark hair slicked into a topknot.

"Hey." Rook held up a notebook. "Could I get an interview?"

Keanu paused and ran his eyes over her. "An interview for what?"

"The *Seventh-Inning Stretch.*"

"What's that?"

"That's the show I mentioned," said Nolan, who had just emerged behind Keanu, football jersey on, buzz cut sharp, ready for game day—except that he looked exhausted.

Keanu peered at Rook. He seemed to be weighing

whether he wanted to engage. When he spoke, it was with suspicion. "Why interview me?"

Worried? Rook thought. *You should be. Laughing while your dumbass buddy threw water on me.*

"You're the quarterback," she said. "And it's Homecoming."

Keanu drew himself up a little taller. "What do you want to know?"

"I heard there might be a scout tonight. Ready to lead the team?"

"The team is missing important people," said Keanu, his deep voice grave. "I want to get a victory for AJ."

A shadow crossed Nolan's face. He nodded.

"You've been practicing QB for what, a week?" said Rook. "That's not long. Do you feel ready? You know the plays?"

"He knows them backwards and upside down," said Nolan.

Keanu shot him a grateful glance.

Rook raised an eyebrow. Keanu knew the plays that well? Maybe he hadn't just been ready—maybe he'd been waiting for this.

"Really?" She kept her tone nice and casual. "Did you study up in advance?"

"I pay attention," Keanu replied. "I'm a catcher on the baseball team too. I'm used to staying aware of a lot of scenarios."

"Smarter than some of your friends, huh?" Rook laughed. "Not naming names, but Chad comes to mind."

The flicker of a smirk crossed Keanu's face. Then it vanished. "Chad's a friend. I'm not talking about him with you."

"There's gonna be pressure tonight. How do you handle it?"

"I have people in my corner." Keanu glanced away. "Important people."

"Want to shout out anyone in particular?"

He shrugged.

"I heard you and AJ have been friends since kindergarten," said Rook. "It's got to be tough on you, having such a close buddy get hurt."

"Yeah." Keanu's face got sober again. He looked right at her. "Too bad someone smashed his skull in."

Rook said nothing in reply to this. She didn't want to drive him off. "Five-second favorites, you ready?"

"What's that?"

"Favorite class?"

"Weight training."

"Favorite song?"

"'Be Ready.'"

"Favorite play?"

"Full house."

"Favorite thing to eat at Shakemaster?"

He snorted. "I hate Shakemaster."

Rook leaned back and looked at him. "Really?" she said. "I heard you were there last Thursday night, after you left Tree's house."

Keanu's eyes flashed. "What?" His voice cracked slightly. "No—I mean—who told you that?"

That reaction. He was scared. He didn't want anyone knowing about Shakemaster—and now she knew it.

"Yeah," she said, "I heard you left the parking lot with someone. You got into their car."

"Who said that?"

Rook played dumb. "I don't remember. Why, what's wrong?"

Keanu narrowed his eyes at her. "You're walking around here like you didn't do anything to AJ. That's what's wrong."

He was going on the defensive, but that only meant she was close to something that mattered. Rook flipped her notebook shut and stuck her pencil behind her ear.

"I didn't hurt AJ," she said coolly, "which is why they didn't book me."

"Bullshit," said Keanu. "You were the one on the baseball field in the dark. You sent him those texts."

Nolan looked swiftly at her.

"And you threatened Chad in The Lighthouse," Keanu continued. "Telling him you'll break him? Who says stuff like that?"

"Who sits there and laughs while his friend throws ice at the waitress?" she retorted. "Check a mirror, get the answer."

Keanu stalked away.

Rook glanced at Nolan. "Do you think I did it?"

Nolan looked away. "No. I don't want to believe that."

"Do you actually know Keanu?"

"We're not close. It's all through sports. You know?"

Rook nodded. "Look, we both know it wasn't Sareth. It couldn't have been. But it also wasn't me, and... Keanu's kind of interesting. Could he have a problem with AJ? You've been around those guys in the locker room. What do you know?"

Nolan shrugged. "Lots of people don't like AJ."

"Why? Did he hook up with the wrong girl?"

"He's just... not a good guy. That's all." He looked at

her, and his ears reddened a touch. "But I guess you know that at this point. He bragged about you to all the guys. That's what he does."

"Yeah, I heard." She sighed. "Since we're being real here, can I ask you something?"

He shrugged.

"Destiny. You two are together now, right?"

Nolan's eyes softened. "Yeah."

"And you know her pretty well? You said in class that you're neighbors?"

"She's in the apartment by mine."

"Have you lived next door a long time?"

"A couple years. Her older sister took her in when we were in eighth grade."

"What about their parents?"

Nolan hesitated. "Faith's twenty-three," he said. "She's in college. She's doing her best. It's better like this."

Rook remembered Destiny stepping out of the Family Services office—she had mentioned Faith to that woman.

"Does she see a social worker at school sometimes?" she asked.

Nolan folded his arms like he wasn't answering that question. So the answer, Rook thought, was yes.

Destiny had been through some things. The glitter phone and the beach waves weren't the whole story. That stuff was her cover.

Rook felt a pang of uncomfortable empathy.

"She hates, me, right? For hooking up with AJ."

"Des doesn't hate anybody," said Nolan, "she's just trying to get through."

"Because I didn't know she was with AJ," said Rook. "I wasn't trying to start anything. You could tell her that. If you want."

Nolan uncrossed his arms. Gave Rook a brief, appreciative glance. "Okay."

"See you in Magnusson's class," said Rook, and she headed toward first period, wishing she had the same class as Theo so that she could run things by him.

Keanu was lying about Shakemaster. Chad had pointed the cops to Sareth. And Nolan... Nolan really didn't like AJ.

As for Destiny, Rook didn't know what to think. There was definitely more to that girl than she wanted to let on. And no matter what Nolan said, Rook was still sure that Destiny hated her guts.

BY FOURTH PERIOD, the whole school had traded rumors for glitter. Nothing existed anymore but the game.

Classes were shortened to make time for a pep rally. The gym thumped with noise and music as the Lakeview Salmon crowded onto the bleachers to hold up signs and pound their feet. Pom-poms shook, and metallic pink glared under the fluorescents. Football players roared, fists in the air.

On his way into the pep rally, Theo got elbowed once—then again, harder. He was sure it wasn't an accident. He looked over his shoulder to see who it was, but the sea of varsity jackets made it impossible.

He turned forward again and got shoved in the back. He stumbled, barely stayed on his feet, and heard laughter.

"Leave her alone!" someone squeaked.

He blushed, and gripped his backpack straps.

"Sidekick vibes," said someone else, followed by kissing sounds.

Assholes.

He didn't remember Mateo ever dealing with this. But

maybe he had—and just hadn't said anything. Mateo wouldn't have cared. He would've laughed. Shrugged it off.

Mateo had been on varsity, though. He had played football with them, and baseball too, just as skilled and talented as the rest of them. He'd been able to walk on both sides of that line.

Sidekick vibes.

It was true that Theo had never stepped up, until yesterday. He had let Mateo take point, and Mateo had never seemed to mind. He'd never pushed Theo to say more, or do more. He had simply been who he was.

They both had.

He searched for Rook in the fray. He found Colleen sitting with Marna and Tuyet, and he didn't like the look on her face as she pointed a stare at him and smiled. That was not a good smile.

He finally found Rook sitting at the farthest end of the bleachers, in the uppermost corner, her expression flat and detached.

When she saw him, she switched on. Sat up taller. Jerked her head slightly—a gesture that meant *sit here.*

He climbed to the top of the bleachers. "Isn't this great?" he said lightly as he smushed in beside her, trying not to think about Chad, or Colleen, or the rest of them. It was kind of hard, when he saw Colleen turn and snap a picture of the two of them, smirking as she did so.

"Uh-huh," said Rook, who didn't appear to see the photo happen.

"How overjoyed are you to be part of this wholesome tradition?" Theo went on. "You know what, don't answer, you don't have to. School spirit is just coming right off you in waves."

She didn't quite smile—but it was close. Encouraged, he pressed on.

"You want me to teach you our fight song?" he asked. "'Fight, fight, fight for Lakeview High! Pink and black and proud!' Tell me when you're ready for the second line, it's pure poetry. It involves Salmon getting loud, which, if you know anything about salmon, makes total sense. Also, there are hand gestures." He made his hands swim like fish, then shook his fists in the air in imaginary victory. Rook had to look away so she wouldn't laugh.

"Let's sneak out," she said. "Jesus."

"I'm not much of a sneaker-outer. I'm more your classic teacher's pet—hey, is that Destiny?"

Down behind the bleachers, Destiny Bray sidled along the wall toward the back door, her phone in her hand. She checked both ways when she reached the door, then slipped out of the gym.

Rook flooded with energy. If she followed Destiny right now, she'd find out what she was up to—but it was going to be tough to do it without drawing attention. The pep rally had started. If she got up and made her way down the entire set of bleachers and tried to walk out, teachers would notice.

If she slid between the bars next to her at the end of the row, though...

She wiggled them. The uppermost section of bars was meant to keep students from falling, but it was in no way up to code. It was old, and it had plenty of give.

"Watch my bags."

"What? Why?"

She didn't answer, but wriggled through the safety bars, gripped them tightly, then dropped out of sight.

It happened so fast, Theo wasn't even sure he'd seen it right. He gaped over the side of the bleachers as Rook dropped several feet to the waxed gym floor, landed in a crouch, and bolted out of the gym after Destiny, leaving her bags behind.

"Holy crap," he said to himself, "who *does* that?"

Video game avatars did, he thought. Action heroes did. And so did the girl who went by Rook Radcliffe.

TWENTY-TWO

Destiny's blonde waves had nearly vanished around the far corner of the outdoor hallway by the time Rook made it out of the gym. Rook trailed her all the way to the north parking lot. She crouched behind the nearest vehicle and peered through the windows of the car that gave her cover, watching Destiny climb into the passenger seat of an old green Jeep. It idled near the exit of the lot, bass thudding heavily enough to be felt ten cars away. A man with long, dark blond hair sat at the wheel smoking a cigarette. The sticker on the back window read *CPCC—Your Future, Your Choice.*

The man handed something to Destiny. She hesitated—then took it with both hands, looking down at it.

He leaned in close and put a hand on her shoulder, and Destiny went still. Rook froze with her. He looked too old. For several heartbeats, she could not move.

Do something. Anything.

She stood up and let herself be seen.

The guy in the Jeep turned and spotted her. Destiny did too. She scrambled out of the Jeep and slammed the door, and the driver peeled out of the parking lot so hard that Rook smelled rubber.

Destiny stood several parking spots away, staring at Rook, clutching something black and rectangular in her hand. She stuffed it deep in her coat pocket.

"Don't," she said.

Rook opened her mouth.

"*Don't,*" Destiny repeated. She strode toward the stairs that led back down to campus.

Rook followed. "I thought you were with Nolan," she said. "Who was that?"

"I *am* with Nolan," said Destiny. "You stay away from him."

"You don't want me to tell him what I just saw?"

"Nolan is my best friend," said Destiny. "There's nothing you can tell him about me that he doesn't already know. I want you to stay away from him because you're just going to do what you did with AJ—"

"I didn't do *anything* with AJ," said Rook, and she got in front of Destiny. "You think I took him? You think I want Nolan?"

"You're working on getting Chad from Jill, too," said Destiny. "I see how you operate."

Rook laughed, furious. "How the fuck do I operate?"

"You should know, pick-me girl," said Destiny maliciously. "You think guys think it's cool that you can lift all that weight? You think they all love how tough you act, like you're one of them? You think they're all talking about you, saying, 'Oh *wow*, she's so *different* from the other girls, she's so *strong*.' You're such a joke."

Rook stood rigid with fury. She had heard it all before, every word, but it always burned her right down to the core, because the insult was so deep, and the people who leveled it at her didn't even understand it.

They thought she went to the gym to impress guys. That she lifted weights for *boys*. That she did the things she did so that men would like her, so that she would fit in with them. They couldn't see and did not believe that she did it for herself.

It made her want to break shit.

Rook took a step toward Destiny, who stepped back at once. Fear lit her eyes.

"Don't hurt me," she said. "Don't hit me."

The fear in Destiny's voice was real. And totally out of proportion. Rook hadn't even lifted her hands, but she stepped back.

"I'm not going to hit you," she said. "I didn't hit anybody."

"Liar," Destiny whispered. "I know you sent AJ those texts and told him to come to the wall. Everybody does."

A school security officer came toward them. "Get back to the gym, girls," she called out. "Let's go."

Destiny ran.

When Rook caught up with Theo leaving the pep rally, he handed over her bags.

"Your super-spy escape from the gym was impressive, but I am chilled to my core by the condition of our bleachers. I will never sit in the top rows again..." He trailed off at the look of anger on her face. "Whoa," he said, "are you okay? What happened with Destiny?"

Rook caught him up. Partly. He didn't need to know Destiny's exact words, or how much they had bothered her.

Theo listened with evident concern.

"How much older was the guy in the Jeep?"

"I don't know."

He jotted something in his notebook.

"So we don't know where Keanu went after Shakemaster, or who he was with," he said. "He could have been on the baseball field."

"Yep."

"And Nolan? Do we know where he was?"

"No idea," said Rook. "Maybe I can find out at the dance tomorrow."

The bell rang. School was out. Students surged for the doors, shrieking, blasting music, ready to shake the stadium with their go-team energy.

Rook hesitated before heading to her car. She half hoped he would invite her over. It was dumb, and it didn't matter if he did, but if he did, then she might go.

"Heading home?" she ventured.

"Math club," said Theo. "Want to hang out after? Meet me at my house—or pick me up, we could grab food. You have a car, right? I have a bunch of homework, but I should be free by around six—oh no, actually, Ana's cheering a game tonight, I'm going to Highland. Call me, though. Wait, do I have your number?"

"Never mind." Rook headed toward the north parking lot, feeling—to her great irritation—embarrassed. She had forgotten he had a whole life. Clubs. Girlfriend. She should never have said anything. "I have work anyway. See you next week."

"Wait, wait." Theo walked faster to keep up with her. He tried to balance his books and take out his phone, which was tougher to do while practically jogging—she moved fast. "Phone number, I'll text you."

"I don't have one."

Theo did not seem to process this. "You don't have..."

"A phone."

"Oh. I guess it's not that big of—so how do I get a hold of you later? Discord?"

"No internet."

"Your grandfather has no *internet*? You're *joking*."

"Nope."

"Good lord. What do you *do* at night?"

"Sleep."

"But does your grandfather have a landline, or..."

Rook didn't answer this. She did not want people calling Oscar's apartment; her grandfather used her real name.

"Oh wow."

The softness in his voice made her pause. She looked over to find him gazing at her like he was seeing something new. His expression made her hold her gym bag a little tighter, to anchor herself. Why was he looking at her like that?

"What?" she demanded.

"You actually couldn't have texted AJ," he said slowly. "You don't have a phone. It's impossible that it was you."

"Right."

"But... you never said that. To me, or anyone. You didn't even try."

Rook shrugged a shoulder. "People are going to think what they want."

"Why wouldn't you defend yourself?"

"Why should I explain myself?"

Theo gave his head a slight shake. "To make your life a little easier?"

She laughed, soft and humorless. "See you next week," she said, and when she headed to her car, Theo didn't follow. He stood and watched her leave, trying to make sense of her—and failing completely.

TWENTY-THREE

That night, after her Friday shift at The Lighthouse, Rook sat in the tiny kitchen of Oscar's apartment, only half-concentrating on her geometry homework. Her eyes kept drifting to the olive-green phone on the wall—Oscar's only link to the outside world.

Part of her wished she had given Theo the landline number. She wanted to talk to him. She didn't *want* to want that. Why was she being weak?

Anyway, he was busy. The girlfriend was cheering a game. It was already eleven, though—did he have an early curfew? He seemed like he would have an early curfew.

She tried to stop watching the phone. It wasn't like he was going to call.

He was bright, though, Theo. She had mentioned Oscar's name to him, and he would definitely remember. If he looked up Oscar Radcliffe, it couldn't take him long to track down the number.

Theo could probably track down a lot of things, if he wanted to. The idea nauseated Rook. If he decided to find out who she was, she was sure he could do it. And then he'd ask questions. He'd want details. He'd see her differently, he'd act all weird, and she wouldn't be able to hang around him anymore, because it would suck too much.

Not that she wanted to hang around him.

She went to her room. It was good he had the girlfriend, she thought, as she took out her ponytail and pulled off her bra. Theo being off-limits in that way was better. It kept things simple. They were acquaintances with a shared goal, and that was it. She put on pajamas and got into bed.

When the phone did ring, she jumped so bad she almost left her body. Oscar's recliner creaked, and then the second ring stopped halfway through.

"Hello?" Oscar said gruffly. "Who?" A silence followed this. "Brooke?"

Rook leaped out of bed, flung open her door, and catapulted herself into the kitchen.

"I don't know," Oscar was saying. "Do you—"

Rook snatched the receiver out of his hand and hung up the phone.

"Easy, kid," Oscar protested. "Why?"

"Sorry." Rook felt foolish, even though it wasn't. "At school, the kids don't know who I am. I use a different name." She heard herself say it and winced. Not many people knew that. Now Oscar did too.

Oscar frowned. Just for a second, Rook saw her father in his expression. That deep frown was the same look Brian Radcliffe's face had settled into during long hours at the wheel of the truck.

Then it shifted, and her father was gone.

"I get that," he said. "I guess."

Rook glanced at the receiver. "Who was on the phone?"

"He didn't say."

He. Had it been Theo? Who else could it have been?

The phone rang again. Rook grabbed for it, fumbled it, and dropped it. The receiver hit the linoleum, and the plastic cover of the speaker popped off and rolled across the floor.

Oscar gave an irritated sigh and walked out of the kitchen. His recliner creaked, and the volume on his racing channel went up. Rook picked up the speaker cover and snapped it back into place, then put the phone to her ear.

"Hello?"

"Rook?"

Theo. He had found Oscar's number. What else had he found? What else did he know?

She tried to say something, but it stuck in her throat. She picked up a bottle opener that Oscar had left on the counter, *PETTY 43* printed down the handle. She flipped it in her hand, trying to keep her mind focused on stuff that was real. That was a thing one of the therapists had taught her. Name things in the room. Ground yourself.

Bottle opener. Window. Fridge. Phone.

"Did we get disconnected?" Theo asked.

"How did you get this number?"

"I looked up Oscar Radcliffe, and his number was on a list of local car-show volunteers. I just got back from the game, I figured if you were still up, we could talk—was that your grandfather? Is it too late to call? Sorry if I woke him."

His voice was too close.

Right in her head.

The last time she'd talked to a guy on the phone, it had been Gabe, and now his voice came in. It still lived under her skin. Warm. Deep. Real.

Brooklyn, I know it's late there. But I'm here.

She shut her eyes to stop the feelings. She felt dizzy. Sick.

"Hello?" said Theo, when she didn't answer. "Are you there?"

"Yeah." Her voice pitched up, breathy and unsteady. "What did you—" She couldn't remember what he had just told her. Nothing rational would come. "Hi, I'm not... I don't remember. It's late there."

"What do you mean?" His voice was instantly alert. "Rook? What's wrong?"

Her heartbeat roared in her ears. He should have waited—he shouldn't have called. She hadn't given him the number. She didn't want him to have access to her like this. She didn't want anyone to have access to her.

She couldn't let him hear her slip.

"You said—what?" she managed. "You were—where?"

"I said I just got home," he said. "Rook, do you need help? Tell me. Where are you?"

His voice was warm. Worried. Kind.

Hang up. Hang up.

She was cold. Her mind was scrambled. She had been doing so well, she had been able to keep the pain in a box, but now Theo's voice was in her ear, too intimate, too familiar; he had pushed himself too close, and she couldn't pretend, and he couldn't know.

She hung up. She took the phone off the hook and left it on the counter so it couldn't ring again, and she sat there, alone, silent, fighting to breathe. She gripped the edge of the kitchen counter, barely conscious of the din of sports talk from Oscar's TV, trying to talk herself down as her heart sprinted, relentless.

You're safe. You're alone. He doesn't know.

She breathed. Shuddered. Gripped harder.

Nothing bad. Just a phone call. You're okay.

Breathe.

She obeyed, shakily. Inhaled with intention.

When she knew she could do it without falling, she let go of the kitchen counter and uncurled her fingers. Focused on each muscle, relaxing each part of her body, until the panic attack finally passed.

Once she had herself under control, she went into the living room.

"Oscar, listen," she said. "If anybody calls here—they shouldn't, but if they do—you have to call me Rook. I know you're already doing a lot for me, but will you do that? Please?"

Oscar's eyes flicked to her. Blue, like her dad's. "Sure," he said. "You look like you could use some sleep, huh?"

Rook nodded and shut herself up in her bedroom, but sleep did not come easy.

TWENTY-FOUR

The phone went dead.

"Hello?" Theo insisted. "Rook?"

No answer. Silence. Something was definitely wrong—she sounded like she'd seen a monster. He redialed Oscar's number and got a busy signal.

He didn't like it. If he had known where she lived, he would have asked his dad to drive him there so he could check on her.

His phone buzzed. He almost dropped it in his hurry to check it.

The text was from Ana. Not Rook. Of course not Rook. Theo gazed at the phone for half a minute in disequilibrium. Ana had sent him a photo of a purple gown, laid out on her bed. What was this supposed to mean?

Theo texted back.

[THEO] That looks like Akari's casino dress from episode 44.

[ANA] Why do you think I bought it?

He grinned, thumbs already moving on his keyboard. She was the best.

[THEO] Where are you wearing it?

[ANA] Homecoming.

Theo looked at this text in confusion. Homecoming?

He called her.

"I didn't think you wanted to go to Homecoming at Lakeview," he said when she picked up. "I didn't get tickets because I thought we were doing a *DK* marathon. We could probably still get them at the door—"

"No," Ana said, "I still want you to come to my house. I just thought... we could dress up. If you want."

"You want to wear that dress and watch anime with me?"

"And maybe also *not* watch anime," Ana replied, her voice soft.

"Oh," he said, flustered. "Well then. I'll see if my suit is um, clean." He glanced at the heap it made on the floor by his closet, where he had discarded it after Ana's Homecoming dance.

He stuck the suit on a hanger, hoping that it would somehow de-crumple overnight, and he got into bed with his phone still in his hand. It was almost midnight when he decided to dial Oscar Radcliffe's number one more time.

Busy signal again—Rook didn't want to talk to him.

Or she couldn't.

Was she in trouble? Was she safe?

He rolled over and shut his eyes, and he tried to make himself sleep, because there was nothing else he could do.

The next day, he tried again. This time, it rang. Oscar picked up, voice gruff.

"Hello?"

"Hi, this is Theo Locke. Is Rook—"

"Working," said Oscar. "Gimme your number, I'll tell her you called."

Working. So she was at The Lighthouse. If he could get a ride, he could go.

You really think she wants you to do that?

Theo didn't know. He thought of the way Rook had stepped out of reach, after Chad had dumped the water on her at school. She had flat-out said that she didn't want protection.

Maybe she needed it, though.

Was that his decision to make?

His mom knocked on his door but didn't open it. "We just got back, honey. I can take you over to Ana's. Ready to go?"

Theo threw on the suit and opened his door. His mother looked him over in silence. She pressed her mouth shut.

"What?" said Theo, defensive.

"Nothing," she replied, "your choice."

She dropped him off at Ana's enormous house in Highland Hills. Ana met him at the door, her dark curls piled up on her head, her gown clinging to her.

"Wow," he said, now very much wishing his suit weren't wrinkled. "Eres hermosa."

Ana pulled him into the house and led him to the entertainment room, which was dark except for the episode of *Death Kingdom* playing on the big screen on the wall.

She had also lit one candle.

"It's our six-month anniversary," she said, as they sat together on the couch.

"That's *next* weekend."

"I know, but we're doing it tonight. I mean, celebrating our anniversary." Ana's eyes widened. "I didn't mean—although later—" She stopped, sounding strangled. "Maldita sea. I had it perfect in my head."

"It's perfect," said Theo, whose full attention was now focused on the words *although later*. What did she mean? What did she want to do later? "I like the candle," he said, trying to sound normal.

"At first I was going to light a whole bunch of them, like in the movies. But to be honest, whenever they have those romance scenes with all the candles, I spend the entire time nervous somebody's going to catch fire."

Theo laughed. "Same. I hate that trope. First, where did they get the candles? Who has thousands of candles sitting around? And then it would take hours to set them up and light them, and then the fire alarm—"

"So for our anniversary," Ana said, "I decided I want to show you something."

"Episode 38?" Theo glanced up at the enormous TV on the wall. "Good choice. I love this episode. This is where everything shifts." He quoted along with the character onscreen. "Lies make beautiful men ugly."

"I know, but no." Ana muted the TV, then sprang to her feet. "Shoot, I need my phone, it's in the kitchen. Un minuto."

While she was out of the room, Theo reflexively checked his texts. Nothing from Rook. Because she had no phone. Why did he keep looking?

As he waited for Ana, he navigated to one of his social media profiles and flicked through his friends' recent posts. He stopped when he came to a photograph of Sareth. It had been taken last March, during a debate. Somebody had found and reposted it.

@lakeviewunfiltered this him?? the guy who smashed AJ
@bigchad69 IS IT EVEN ASAULT IF BRO CANT LIFT A GALLEN OF MILK
@salmonrun aj's glove weighs more than this dude

Theo's thumb hovered over the screen. He watched as the upvotes climbed and people responded like it was a joke. Like Sareth's suffering wasn't real.

He knew better than to reply. He was too angry to stop himself.

@lockeandload Sareth is innocent. Only an idiot would think anything else.

Saying it was pointless, but he hit *post* anyway. For a few seconds, nothing happened.

Then the flood came.

@quinnestofalltime sidekiiiiiick! coming in hot
@crusenberryblast como estas, softboy
@floreselmejor guys, grow up and leave him alone is it be an asshole day???
@bigchad69 LMFAOOOOOO
@colleenofcourse so cozy at the pep rally look how cute

Colleen attached a photo to her comment, and Theo cringed.

He had expected her to do it, but seeing it was horrible. Himself and Rook, sitting together at the pep rally, smashed close beside each other because the bleachers were overcrowded. To make it worse, he was leaning close to Rook so that she'd hear him over the crowd, and she looked halfway happy.

@bigchad69 ROOKIE LIKES TO PARTY HAVE FUN SIMP
@salmonrun her again? Why.

Ana returned with her phone.

Theo scrolled instantly up, past the photo Colleen had posted, until Sareth's photo was back on the screen.

Ana peered at it as she sat beside him.

"Oh!" she said. "That's Sareth."

Theo nodded, unable to look up at her, his heart thumping furiously. When he got to school on Monday, this was going to be the story. Everyone was going to think that he was with Rook.

The rumor would definitely make it to Highland. It would get back to Ana.

What was he supposed to do? Tell her? Show her the post, explain why Colleen had done it, and tell her that he'd been hanging out—kind of—with Rook?

No, he realized. He had no obligation to defend himself, because he hadn't done anything wrong. The rumor mill was churning, but he was innocent. He had sat next to Rook at a pep rally. That was all. Telling Ana would just make it worse.

Wouldn't it?

"I knew I'd seen him somewhere," Ana said. "I saw him last Thursday night right by the Lakeview sign, and his face was so familiar, but he had his hood up and I couldn't place him. I must have recognized him from your last round of debates."

Theo snapped out of it. AJ had been assaulted last Thursday night.

He looked at Ana.

"You saw Sareth near campus last Thursday?"

She nodded.

"What time?"

"It had to be close to midnight," said Ana. "At least eleven or so. I was at the hospital late, Ella sprained her knee at practice and I was sitting at the ER with her waiting for an X-ray."

That was interesting.

Theo filed the detail for later and turned off his phone. People could keep blowing up rumors about him—and he was sure they would. But he couldn't put out that fire. If he tried to defend himself, he'd only be dousing it with gas.

Which was exactly Rook's point, he realized. It was why she hadn't told anyone she didn't have a phone. She refused to add to the blaze.

Theo shoved her to the back of his thoughts, along with everybody else at Lakeview.

He was with Ana. She was right here, it was their anniversary, she was perfect, and he was not going to blow this, no matter what else was happening.

"Okay," he said, and he turned and gave her his full attention. "Sorry. I'm here. What did you want to show me?"

Ana took out her phone and looked shyly down at it. "The other day, I said I liked you for your face," she said. "I just want to make sure you know that's not all it is."

"I know," Theo protested. "I knew it was a joke."

"Just listen. Remember this?"

Theo leaned closer to see the photo on her phone. It was a picture of Ana, her cousin Juan, and Theo, taken at her quinceañera two years ago, the first time he had met her. He had been Juan's guest. Thirteen, even skinnier than he was now, and wearing braces—he looked goofy and young. It was Ana, fifteen and spectacularly pretty in her party gown, who had reached a milestone of young adulthood. Flanked by the two younger boys, she looked devastatingly mature.

Theo remembered. She had seemed an impossible ideal. "I had such a crush on you," he admitted.

"Do you remember the next time I saw you?"

"Evelin's wedding."

"Nope." Ana swiped through her photos, then held the phone to her chest. "I'm about to tell you something embarrassing and stalker-y, because I don't know how else to make it clear to you how much I like you."

Theo waited, curious.

"I was at the debate championships in March. I went to cheer for one of my friends at school, and I recognized you." Ana glanced shyly at him. "And I paid attention." She handed him her phone and pressed play.

In the video, Theo stood onstage in the middle of his debate about whether the United States should adopt English as its official language. Compared with the photograph from the quinceañera, he looked much older—the lack of braces helped, and so did the suit and tie. This was also after he had grown a couple inches and his voice had changed and deepened. And because he had practiced and researched and prepared, he sounded confident and passionate as he laid out his thinking.

"The question then becomes: what is reasonable? Is it

reasonable to insist 350 million people adopt and speak a single language in order to be secure?"

"How did you get this video?" he asked.

"I took it."

"But you didn't know me."

"I know. But when you started talking, I couldn't look away."

Theo in the video gripped the podium and spoke with the full force of his dramatic ability, which was not small.

"Those children will lose access to education. Safety. Choices. This law would officially, legally, stamp those children as second-class citizens—and that can never be called reasonable."

He sounded like he meant it. He looked like it too.

"You were brilliant," said Ana. "Your words—how does a ninth grader talk like that?"

"You liked it that much?" Theo asked, uncertain. He had won that debate, so he knew he had impressed the adjudicators, but he hadn't expected to touch anybody's actual heart. "I felt kind of weird arguing that resolution. I was glad I got neg, it's the side I believe, but—" He stopped. Gestured to himself. "What does someone like me really know about that?"

"I don't know, but I didn't care." Ana leaned against him. "I was a junior and you were two years younger, but I couldn't shake it. I never had a crush like that. Juan said you might come to Evelin's wedding, so I made sure I did too. And I'd already seen your social media, so I knew we both liked *Death Kingdom*, and the conversation we had on the golf course—lying there, talking about the show with you? It was amazing to me, because you never acted like I was weird or crazy for knowing every line and every episode. There's nobody else I can talk to like that. My friends don't understand, so I keep that part of myself quiet, but with you I'm like—" Ana gestured wordlessly at the air in front of her. "I'm free. I can say anything."

She took his hand.

"Me gustas tanto," she said softly. "Pienso en ti todo el tiempo."

He clutched her hand, feeling oddly insecure. He had known she liked him, but he hadn't known how much. He didn't believe he deserved it.

"No soy tan bueno," he said.

I'm not that good.

She gave him a laughing look. "Oh, come on," she said, "you don't have to fish for compliments—I'm giving you all of them."

"I'm serious."

His tone must have been convincing, because Ana looked at him with concern.

"Why would you say that?" she said.

"Because debate isn't real," said Theo. "It's an exercise. It isn't action. What's the point of arguing whether the US should develop more youth jails when Sareth is *in* a youth jail? What's the good in standing around talking about it? I want to *do* something."

Ana lifted his hand and kissed it.

"Lo sé," she said. "But some things... they just aren't easy. Some things are so messed up..." She gazed away at the screen, but she didn't seem to be seeing the episode. "It just feels like they're beyond you. Like you could try as hard as you can, and it wouldn't change anything. ¿No cierto?"

Theo nodded. That was right.

Maybe she would understand, if he told her what he was up to. Talking to the police. Trying to find the truth with Rook. Even though Ana had told him to be careful, she cared about justice. She might understand.

What had Sareth been up to on campus last Thursday night? What could have had him there so late?

He would have to tell Rook about that. He didn't want to, because she would think it meant something, even though it didn't.

"The fact that you even think like this?" said Ana. "That you want to be better? It sets you apart." She reached up and played with his hair. "Although I really don't see how you could be better," she said. "Eres perfecto."

He knew he wasn't that.

"You could do way better than me," he said, with a self-deprecating laugh. "You never act like it, but it's true. You could have anyone you want. You know that, right?"

Ana put her lips to his ear. "Tengo a quien quiero," she whispered.

Theo kissed her—first softly and then with passion—and Ana lay back on the couch and pulled him with her. When Theo settled on top of her, she looked up into his face, her expression serious—and nervous. Her breath came faster.

"Theo—tonight—"

She stopped. It felt like an age before she started again.

"I still don't want to have sex," she said, "but..."

There was a long, tense silence while Theo waited to find out what the *but* might be.

"My parents are out of the country. And my brother is spending the night at his friend's. So I can—we can—"

Another agonizing wait. Theo gently kissed her, hoping to ease her into whatever it was she wanted to say. Because whatever it was, he was sure it was going to change his life.

"I want to just—go farther than we have," she whispered. "I don't know how far, I just want to see how I feel. ¿Está bien?"

He nodded, electrified. It was more than okay. It was *glorious*.

He hoped he didn't screw it up.

They got to their feet. Walked to the stairs. They were halfway up when Ana paused on the steps and cast another nervous look up at him. Theo reached for her hand.

"It's okay," he said quietly. "Let's stay downstairs and watch *DK*. I'm happy just being with you."

"You don't want to—?"

"No, I do." He had never been so hot in the face. "But there's no pressure."

"I know." Ana tugged his hand and kept walking up the steps. "You either, okay? No pressure."

The pressure inside him was like nothing he had ever experienced. The closest he had come to this mixture of terror and exhilaration was on a debate stage. This was worse. But also much, much better. The world and its complications were suddenly far away. Everyone at Lakeview—even Mateo—felt distant. For once, the noise in his head was muffled. There was only Ana.

TWENTY-FIVE

Rook's shift at The Lighthouse dragged. Everyone was off getting ready for the Homecoming dance, so there weren't many tips, but that was okay. She'd get her first actual paycheck soon, and she'd be able to join a cheap gym, avoid the douche patrol at school, and lift as much weight as she damn well pleased.

She'd have her own groceries too. She wouldn't need Oscar's—or Theo's.

A few groups of Lakeview kids showed up in their Homecoming formals, but they didn't eat much. Nobody wanted to get sloppy before it was time for pictures. They mostly ordered sodas and shakes.

One of them held up a phone and took a picture.

Rook frowned over at the guy whose phone was up. Quinn—one of Chad's friends. It looked like he was snapping a picture of *her*.

She waited until his date went to the bathroom, then walked over and stopped behind his chair. His long waves fell forward as he typed on his phone—he didn't see her, but she could see his screen.

It was some kind of thread. She saw a picture of herself and Theo at the pep rally, followed by comments she couldn't read because Quinn scrolled past them too fast. He posted the photo of her he'd just taken and started typing something on his phone.

> **@quinnestofalltime** rook's at the lighthouse, no locke here
> **@crusenberryblast** he's prob with the highland hottie. that girl is a 10, he's dumb if he's w rook
> **@colleenofcourse** right? I hope no one tells his gf...
> **@bigchad69** ID HIT THAT
> **@floreselmejor** which one rook or the 10
> **@bigchad69** YES

Rook's fingers tightened on her tablet as she watched the comments roll in.

So the new rumor was her and Theo?

She had gone to his house exactly once. Sat by him in the gym once. But of course that was all it took, because everybody sucked.

Quinn looked up and saw her. Tried to hide his screen.

"Too late," said Rook. "Fun chat?"

"It's nothing," he said, looking nervously at her as his date returned to the table. "People are just talking."

Rook slapped the bill down on the table. "Maybe one day they'll be talking about you," she said, and she gave him a cool once-over. "Probably not, though, let's be honest."

He turned red. She walked away to clean milkshake rings off empty tables with angry swipes of her rag.

At the end of her shift, she hung up her apron, and her boss handed her a new work shirt. It was huge—she'd swim in this thing.

"Hey, thanks."

"Sure." Barney took off his ship captain's hat and scratched his head. "The other night? The kids who were harassing you?" He paused. "If it happens again, you tell me."

Rook nodded. "Okay."

She put on the giant t-shirt over the tight one and headed to Homecoming in her work clothes.

The spirit committee had decked out Lakeview's roundabout in white Christmas lights and giant pink mylar dolphins—probably the closest thing anyone could find to salmon. Rook headed to the entrance of the gym, where a couple of cheerleaders decked out in short, shiny gowns sat at a ticket table.

"Um, okay," said the smaller of the two, glancing over Rook's t-shirt and jeans.

"I'll take your ticket," said the other.

"I don't need a ticket. I'm just gonna run in and talk to someone real quick."

The small girl tapped the sign by her cash box. "It's twenty-five dollars at the door."

It was the last place she wanted to spend her money, but Rook dug out her tips from the slow evening at The Lighthouse and dropped them ungraciously on the table.

"Twenty-three. Best I can do."

"Then you can't go in."

"Sure I can."

Rook walked into the gymnasium and stood inside the double doors for a minute, needing time to adjust to the bad decor. Hot-pink crepe paper drowned the room under the light of a rented disco ball. Body spray stung her nostrils.

The worst part was the huge picture of AJ displayed on an easel near the stage, surrounded by fake flowers, like he was dead and this was his tasteless memorial. *GET WELL SOON!* sparkled in silver letters under his face.

"Rookie!" Douchebag Perkins sidled up to her, smelling like he'd mistaken a bottle of Jack Daniels for cologne. His suit looked soggy, like he'd taken a shower while wearing his clothes, and he surveyed Rook's giant Lighthouse t-shirt in obvious distaste. "Best dressed," he slurred. "*Clear* winner."

"Touch me and die," she replied, scanning the room.

He laughed and reached a hand out like he was going to tickle her.

Rook caught him by the wrist and closed her grip with all her strength, like he was a 400-pound barbell she was about to pull off the floor. The douche tried to wrench his hand away, and when he realized he couldn't, he made a short, whining noise.

"Ow, I pitch right-handed—"

"Apologize."

"I'm sorry!"

He wasn't, but Rook was satisfied. The fear in his face was real. She let go of his wrist, and he clutched it to his chest and rubbed it, sulking.

"You're so mean," he complained.

Beyond Chad, leaning against the bleachers, Rook saw Destiny watching her, a black phone in her hands, its glow illuminating her face.

Their eyes met. Destiny tried to hold Rook's stare, but couldn't do it for long before she lowered her gaze. She turned off her screen and pocketed her phone, then hugged herself.

The instant her posture changed, Nolan leaned close. He touched her arm. Destiny jerked back. He withdrew, looking hurt, and she reached for him—she spoke, and Rook thought she could read her lips.

I'm sorry.

Nolan didn't lean in again right away. Not until Destiny put a hand on his cheek and stroked it with her thumb. He looked at her with such tenderness that Rook felt a pang in spite of herself.

He thought he was really in love.

Flecks of mirrored disco-ball light passed over them, and music thumped hard enough to make the bleachers vibrate, but in spite of Homecoming all around them, Nolan kissed Destiny like they were alone in the world.

"Hey," said a chaperone loudly, "break it up, kids."

Nolan put a hand on Destiny's waist and steered her out of the dance, into the parking lot.

Rook's eyes traveled the dance floor. She found Marna Hauterman laughing, surrounded by a group of friends, including Colleen O'Hare, who raised her phone and appeared to be filming Rook and Chad.

Marna spotted Rook, saw what Colleen was doing, and put a hand over her camera. She smiled and waved to Rook. Beckoned to her to join them.

"Ugh," said Chad. "She's so happy all the time. Who's that happy? It's fake."

Rook glanced at him. "Why is your suit wet?" she asked.

"Because Hauterman's boyfriend has zero chill," he said. "He threw me in the fountain because I'm *rude*." He put it in air quotes. "I'm like, relax, it wasn't a fat joke, and even if it was, Marna's not that fat. Colleen's the fat one."

He really did suck. But he was a chatty drunk, and he

clearly didn't have his guard up. She decided to be blunt with him.

"You know what I don't get?" she asked.

"Me, if you keep dressing like that."

"Why mess with Sareth, then turn around and tell on him?"

Chad looked blankly at her. "Huh?"

"First you tried to crush him, and then you sent the email about the evidence."

"Are you still talking to me?"

"Sareth," said Rook. "From zero period. You pinned him on the bench, remember? He got you thrown out of the weight room."

"The Indian kid? I was messing with him."

"By trying to crush his windpipe?"

"I didn't know he was *that* weak. I only took it up to one-ten. Who can't bench one-ten?"

"And the email?"

"What email?"

"You sent the principal an email. You told her Sareth had the evidence in his locker."

Chad looked genuinely thrown. "You're high."

"You're saying you didn't email the principal?"

"Do you want a drink?" He lowered his voice. "There's a flask in my pants."

"Admit it, douche. You framed Sareth because he got you in trouble."

"How am I in trouble?"

"You're suspended from the weight room."

"Do I care? I can skip zero period for two weeks. Now, if it were baseball season and I got benched for a game, *then* I'd get mad."

"The night AJ got hurt," said Rook, "did you know he was coming to school to meet me?"

"Yeah, we knew."

"Who's *we*?"

"Keanu and me and Tree. We were over at Tree's. I was watching the end of an old ALCS game. The pitcher throws this crazy fucking slider, catches the guy looking—"

"Focus up, douche. AJ got some texts, right?"

"Yeah, from you."

"You said he showed them to you—why? Why were you two even hanging out? Weren't you mad at him for telling you to apologize to Sareth?"

"What?" Chad looked briefly stumped—then laughed. "Oh *that*. No, afterward I was like, you suck, bro, all that shit about how I should apologize? And he was all, bro, calm down, I was just trying to get some." He snickered. "He meant with you. He acted like a simp, and you fell for it."

Rook gritted her teeth. If AJ ever woke up from the coma, she was going to put him right back in it.

"So yeah, I'm cool with Ellsworth," said Chad. "But not Nolan, fuck that dude, pushing me into the wall?" He gave his right shoulder a couple of shrugs. "He carries in bio though, he's my lab partner. I don't do jack shit in that class; he turns in everything for me." Chad cackled. "Loser."

"So AJ left, right?" Rook pressed. "And Keanu did too?"

"And then me and Tree went to Shakemaster."

"Wait, you did? Did you see Keanu there?"

"No, are you listening? He went home. I saw Jill's car there, texted her to hang, but she was with her friends like fucking usual. I'm about done with her." He gave Rook a cocky look. "You're on deck."

Rook didn't bother to reply, because that was the

dumbest thing he'd said so far. She looked around the dance for Chad's girlfriend, who was nowhere in sight.

"Why are you and Jill even together?" she asked, remembering the look Jill had shot him in the cafeteria the other day. "You don't like each other."

"Whatever," said Chad. "Jill's chill. Plus, she can drive —and she's Homecoming princess for our class." Chad looked smug. "People think she's hot."

Rook thought of Theo describing his own girlfriend. Homecoming Queen, cheer captain. Somehow, though, he hadn't sounded like an ass.

"You know what *I* don't get?" Chad asked suddenly. "How come you're not in jail? Everybody knows you went crazy jealous girlfriend on AJ."

"You sure *you* didn't attack him?"

"Me?" Chad looked affronted. "He's a great shortstop. I need that arm."

"What about Keanu?"

"Why would he mess with AJ?"

"Maybe he likes being the winning quarterback."

At that moment, Keanu walked into the gym with his tie loosened and the top buttons of his suit shirt undone, chest out and head high, like he was the king of Lakeview. Students on the dance floor converged on him, getting close, high-fiving, hugging, punching his arm. He laughed and let it happen.

He's at the mountaintop, Rook thought. *Long way down...*

"There was a scout at the game," Chad said, watching him. "A coach talked to him, I think. But I don't..." He gave a low hum. "*Damn,* Pham."

Rook followed Chad's gaze, which had shifted to Tuyet

Pham. She stood across the gym beside Colleen, staring at AJ's oversized photo. Her haunted expression only amplified her exquisite prettiness.

"Look at her," said Chad. "*That's* the real ten."

Jill chose this moment to walk up to them.

"Uh, *what*?" she said, putting her hands on her hips. She checked Tuyet briefly, then Rook, then returned her attention to Chad.

"What happened to your corsage?" said Chad, annoyed. "That thing was expensive."

Jill glanced at the crushed corsage on her wrist. It looked like it had been mauled. "Whoops," she said, but she didn't sound sorry at all. Just smug. A few strands of black hair had come loose from her updo, and she tucked them back into place and dabbed at the corner of her mouth. Popped her lip gloss open and reapplied it.

She smelled, Rook thought, like something organic. Familiar. She could almost place it... Why did it remind her of the weight room?

Was that *coconut* oil?

The details started to click. Jill's car at Shakemaster. Keanu getting into a car. Both of them walking into the gym at the same time. Rook looked from Jill to Keanu, pretty sure that she was right.

Oh damn. Drama.

"Let's get the picture and leave," said Jill. "Come on."

Chad groaned. "Fine." He put his arm around her.

Jill shrugged it off. "Gross, don't, you're still all wet," she said, and they headed off to the photo line.

Uh-oh, Douche, Rook thought, *too dumb to know what's up, huh?*

Was he that dumb, though, or was he just playing? How

much had he lied, just now? Had he really not sent that email? He had seemed believably confused...

Which made no sense. If the principal thought it had come from him, then it must have come from him.

She needed a minute of quiet. Somewhere she could think.

She also needed the bathroom.

Rook headed there, her next move unclear. What did she need to know—and who could tell her? She still didn't know where Nolan had been on the night of the assault. She didn't know where Destiny had been either. Neither of them was going to snitch on the other, so she'd have to ask somebody else. Who knew them—or knew enough about them to know who their friends were?

Rook locked the bathroom stall, used it, and was about to emerge when she heard footsteps approach the restroom.

"Tu," she heard someone say. "Wait." It sounded like Colleen.

Silently, Rook pressed closer to the stall door. She could see pretty well through the crack.

Tuyet walked up to one of the sinks and pressed the heels of her hands to her eyes. Colleen stood beside her, and for once, her phone wasn't in her hands. Her eyes were on Tuyet.

"How could they put AJ's picture on that board?" Tuyet asked angrily. "That is the exact same poster board—did they just *rip* Mateo's picture off there, and rearrange the letters, and—"

"It's awful," Colleen's voice was quiet. "Why did you even come?"

Tuyet uncovered her eyes. The darkness in them was disturbing. "Because I'm supposed to move on," she said.

"Says who?"

"The grief counselor. He also tells me death is natural. But it isn't natural. Mateo should be alive."

"It's only been two months," said Colleen. "You don't have to do stuff like this yet, everybody understands—"

"*Nobody,*" said Tuyet, her voice like gravel, "understands." She lifted up the skirt of her gown, revealing bike shorts with a small plastic bottle of vodka tucked into the waist. This she yanked from its place, opened, and tilted into her mouth.

"Love," said Colleen, with a laugh. "Share."

The two girls passed the bottle back and forth until someone else entered. Colleen sputtered and shoved the vodka at Tuyet in panic, but the person wasn't a chaperone. It was the dark-haired girl in the wheelchair who had stood up for Rook at The Lighthouse.

"Delilah," said Colleen, wiping her mouth. "Um, hi. We were just..."

"Having a special secret party in the bathroom," Delilah replied, rolling up to the only sink that had a mirror low enough for her to see into. "So fun. So sanitary."

"Come on," said Colleen. "Let's just go home."

She and Tuyet left.

In the quiet, Delilah took out a tube of lipstick, looked into the mirror, and carefully repainted her mouth dark red. She capped the tube, smacked her lips—and went still.

"Who is that?" she demanded, looking into the mirror at the reflected bathroom stalls, her eyes focused right at the spot where Rook was standing. "Stop watching me and come out."

Caught.

Rook stayed still. She didn't have to show herself.

Delilah wheeled around and rolled to the stall door. She looked up through the crack, saw Rook—and froze again, this time in recognition.

"Oh wow," she said. It was hard to tell if she sounded impressed—or afraid. "If it isn't the headbasher."

TWENTY-SIX

Delilah rolled back out of the way as Rook emerged.

"Spying on me?" she demanded. "Am I next in line for a coma?"

"Just using the bathroom."

"You were standing there, looking through the door crack," said Delilah. She flashed a sharp smile. "Oh *wait*—were you spying on Colleen?" she asked. "Hear anything good?"

Rook shook her head. What she had overheard hadn't constituted gossip. It had been rough. Private. She wished she hadn't eavesdropped on it.

"I figured," said Delilah, tucking her lipstick back into her bag. "Colleen thinks she knows everything, but she missed the best part. The parking lot."

"What's happening in the parking lot?" Rook asked, unable to resist.

"Well, there was your typical drama. People fighting, people crying. Nolan and Destiny doing a little of both." She changed the inflection of her voice, put a hand to her heart, and gave a low, melodramatic reenactment. "'I can't do this anymore.'" She raised her voice and made it breathy. "'You have to, there's no going back!'" She snickered. "She was pushing him away, pulling him closer, poor guy looked like he was on a bungee cord. Those two are their own little soap opera."

"No going back to what?" Rook demanded.

"Who knows? By the way, did you see my review?"

Rook had no idea what she meant. "What?"

"I posted a review of The Lighthouse a couple days ago. Gave it five stars. Mostly because the waitress is entertaining."

"Hey, I should be giving *you* five stars," said Rook. "I never got to say thanks for what you did—you were out of there pretty fast."

"No need to thank me," Delilah replied. "I'd help anyone who wants to break Chad Perkins."

Rook gave her half a smile. "Not a fan?"

"Of the reigning king of the tools?" Delilah snorted. "We're *very* close. Sometimes he even calls me Wheels, or that chick in the wheelchair. Once he referred to me as the hottie with a half-body—and honestly? I didn't hate that as much."

"Jesus."

"Yes, he's missing the part of his brain that has a filter," said Delilah, her expression now mirthful. "He has the emotional awareness of a lawnmower. He doesn't even know his girlfriend's at Homecoming with somebody else. Jill's backseat is going to need a detail."

"You saw her?" said Rook. "With Keanu, right?"

"You already knew?" Delilah laughed. "Well, at least some of us know where to pay attention."

She wheeled out of the restroom.

Rook stared into the mirror, not seeing herself. Just

thinking. She had been right. Even in the weight room last week, Keanu had been the one telling Chad to get Jill a corsage, and saying that her team had made it to regionals. And Chad had said that Jill was always busy with "her friends"—so this wasn't just something that had started in the parking lot tonight. Keanu and Jill had been going behind his back for a while.

It didn't help her understand what had happened to AJ. Still, she had to tell Theo. He would think it was hilarious. Or maybe he'd think it was kind of sad—he was probably too sweet to laugh at someone else's problems, even Chad's. She had to tell him either way, though. Because if Keanu had been with Jill the night that AJ was attacked, then he hadn't been attacking AJ.

These thoughts came in so naturally that at first she didn't realize what was happening. When it registered, she looked into her own eyes in the mirror, stricken.

What was she thinking?

She wasn't telling Theo anything. He had called Oscar's, he had almost learned her real name—no. He was too smart, too attentive. He had known right away, on the phone, that she was struggling. That focus was dangerous. She had to cut him off.

Why did that feel like a loss?

Give Brooklyn a little attention, and she'll give you anything you want.

God, what was wrong with her? What would have to happen to her before she would finally stop trying? Hadn't she been burned bad enough? Theo acted innocent, and he had the face, and it was a good performance, but she had seen it before.

Not this time.

She could do this alone. She *would* do it alone. What

did she still need to know? Nolan and Destiny. Who could tell her more about them? Not Colleen—not tonight, anyway. Colleen and Tuyet had been about to leave the dance; they'd be gone by now.

Marna, though. She had friends, she knew people.

Rook walked out of the restroom and back to the dance. She cut across the floor toward Marna, who waved to her from the snack table the instant she saw her.

"Where's her dress?" somebody said. "What's with that shirt?"

"Who cares?" someone else replied. "Psycho head-basher. I can't believe they even let her in here."

Rook stopped walking and turned to see the speaker.

Keanu. Standing in a pack of his teammates. Looking like he owned the night.

"What?" he demanded, stepping forward like he wanted a fight. His eyes gleamed. High on adrenaline, and victory, and the satisfaction of being with his best friend's girl. "You think you can take me like you took AJ? Try it. Right here, right now."

Rook gritted her teeth.

"No?" Keanu taunted. "Not so tough in public, huh? Need to text someone and catch them alone?"

"You'd know," Rook retorted. "Isn't that how you got Jill?"

Keanu's face sagged. The victory light went out of him. His teammates turned and stared at him.

"Whoa," said one of them. "She serious?"

"You want to tell Chad, right here, right now?" Rook pressed, too furious to stop. She was done with all these Lakeview assholes and their accusations. "No? Not so tough anymore? Didn't fucking think so."

She gave Keanu no chance to reply or retaliate, but turned and walked out of the dance.

Outside, the gloom had turned to darkness; the mist to rain. Rook put her head down and made a straight line to her car.

"Wait—wait, oh, my hair, oh, *eff*—"

Rook looked back to see that Marna had followed and was holding her hands over her abundance of glossy brown curls, trying to shield them from destruction.

"You're so *fast*," Marna gasped. "Are you okay?"

Rook took out her keys.

"No, wait—oh, forget it, my hair is ruined anyway." Marna tugged up her strapless yellow gown. "That was so mean, what Keanu said to you—everyone's being so *mean* to you."

"It's fine."

"It's horrible! And I know you didn't do anything wrong, because Theo is a good person—even if he's being insensitive—and *he* likes you so much that I know *you* have to be a good person, and I'm just so sorry, and I want to help. How can I help? And if you wouldn't mind, can we just step right over by the theater so that I don't get completely soaked, because I borrowed these shoes from my brother's girlfriend—thank you, I really appreciate it."

She ushered Rook into the shadowy overhang outside the theater building.

"I was hoping you'd be here tonight." Marna briefly touched Rook's arm. "You're the best—what you did at The Lighthouse? Amazing. We *have* to be friends. I think all of us have wanted to do that to Chad at some point, because he is *such* a dee-bag, but nobody ever does."

Rook folded her arms. "Didn't your boyfriend just throw him in a fountain?"

"Well, okay, but he's a boy. It's different when a girl does it. Also, Colleen sent me a video of it happening—do you want to see?"

Rook couldn't bring herself to say no.

Marna took out her phone, and they watched together as gigantic Alejandro Rosa lifted Chad like a struggling toddler and dropped him in the water. Chad splashed down with a terrified yelp, and Rook couldn't help snickering. For the first time all night, she felt like she was getting her twenty-three bucks' worth.

"I shouldn't laugh," said Marna anxiously. "Alejandro really could've hurt him." She put her phone away. "Is Theo all right?" she asked quietly. "Is he sleeping? I'm worried that he's still blaming himself, and I want to be there for him, but he won't let me."

Rook had no idea what Theo would be blaming himself for. She shook her head.

"I've known him since we were little," said Marna. "And he's so smart, you know? He gets so far into his head, which is fine sometimes, but right now..." She trailed off. "You never met Mateo, did you?"

Rook shook her head.

"He wasn't the kind of person you can get over." Marna's eyes sparkled with tears. "None of us ever will. There's no way to tell someone who never knew him what he was. He was just different. He had this unshakable..." She stopped again and looked up at Rook. "He would have done the same thing you did in The Lighthouse," she said. "It makes sense that Theo likes you."

"Uh, no," said Rook, before she could stop herself. "We're not—"

"Oh, no, I know. Theo's with Ana Castillo—she's great, have you met her? But he's ridiculously adorable, isn't he?"

Rook wasn't about to answer that. "How well do you know Nolan Becker?" she said instead.

"Oh, I've known him forever. We're not *close* close, but he comes to my house sometimes for parties. Why?"

"Who are his real friends?"

"He mostly hangs out with the football guys, but his closest friend is Destiny. They've been tight for years," said Marna. "I think he's liked her for a really long time, but he didn't think she'd ever like him back. It's so sweet that it worked out." She paused. "Although it's funny."

"What is?"

"Well," Marna said slowly, "ever since they got together, it doesn't seem like they're that happy. I thought they would have been happy."

"When did they get together? Wasn't Destiny with AJ right before I hooked up with him?"

"Well, that's what Colleen says." Marna wrinkled her nose. "But she said that about you, too."

That was the truth. Rook nodded, absorbing. "So Destiny might *not* have been with AJ?"

Marna looked hesitant. She toyed with the little silver cross on her necklace like she was trying to decide whether to say more.

"A lot of people want to be with AJ," she finally said. "He's good-looking, and he's great at sports, and everybody knows him. I think some girls—they think being with him makes them special. But with AJ, no one's special. Everyone's just..."

"Getting used?"

Marna made a soft sound of sorrow. "Did he hurt your feelings?"

Rook looked away. "Who would know whether Destiny and AJ were really together or not?"

"Maybe Adel or Fernando," said Marna. "They live in the same apartment complex as Nolan and Destiny." She gave Rook a curious look. "Why do you ask?"

Rook shrugged.

Marna's phone buzzed. She checked it. "Um, Alejandro thinks I died or something. I need to go back in," she said. "But we're friends now. No take-backs. I'll throw another party soon, and you're coming—and please, since you're the one he'll talk to, take care of Theo."

Marna hurried back to the dance, hands over her hair.

Rook went to the Civic. She sat for a while without starting the car, both hands on the wheel, thinking.

She had to call Theo.

She couldn't call Theo. And she definitely wasn't taking care of him.

She drove back to Oscar's but barely remembered getting there; she was too busy berating herself for being a stupid baby. She could talk to Adel and Fernando by herself. She could handle the rest of this thing on her own. That had been true for a long time, and it wasn't about to change now.

Even if she hated it.

TWENTY-SEVEN

Monday at Lakeview was easy—or at least, avoiding Theo was. Rook hid in her car to eat lunch, and as far as she could tell, Theo didn't try to find her.

The rest of the school, however, had eyes on her as usual—only now, the center of gossip had shifted from AJ to Chad. Keanu was absent from school. Football players gave Rook sidelong glances. She passed Jill in the hall at one point, surrounded by a knot of softball girls.

"Coldest breakup I've ever seen," one of them said.

"I can't believe Chad dumped you at Homecoming," said another. "How are you even here today?"

Jill just laughed. She looked totally unbothered. When she caught sight of Rook, however, her expression darkened. She played with one of the softball patches on her letterman's jacket, cutting Rook with a stare.

"Watch out for that one," she said.

Her teammates all turned in Rook's direction.

Rook booked it to class.

On Tuesday, after zero period, Rook waited for Destiny to leave the locker room so that she could talk to Adel alone.

Destiny, however, moved slowly. She held her makeup bag like it was heavy. When she tried to draw on her eyeliner, her hand shook. And when her phone buzzed, she jerked like it frightened her. She pulled the phone out of her bag and checked it. It wasn't just black anymore—there was one sticker on it now. One big, pink, sparkly heart, slapped right onto the middle of the case like it was trying to make up for the darkness.

She left the locker room without a word.

Rook approached Adel. "Do you know Destiny outside of class?" she asked.

Adel pushed back the long side of her short dark hair and fixed it in place with her aviators. "She's in the apartment right over mine. Why?"

"The night before I found AJ, did you see her anywhere?"

"Yeah, when I came home from Imani's," said Adel, taking her letterman's jacket from her locker. "She was on the steps outside with Nolan, crying and showing him her plastic princess phone."

"Her..."

"That's just what I call it, because you've seen it. With all the glitter and the stickers."

Rook had seen it, but not for awhile. Since Homecoming, Destiny had carried the black phone.

The guy in the Jeep had given her something black and rectangular.

Rook's internal machinery spun up. Destiny had gotten a new phone from that guy—and then shoved it in her pocket so Rook wouldn't see.

"What was she showing Nolan?" she asked.

Adel pulled on her varsity jacket and fixed the collar.

"She said something like, I knew it, I'm so tired of it, I'm not letting it go this time."

"And Nolan?"

"He told her she shouldn't go."

"Go where?"

"How would I know?"

"People say Destiny was with AJ," said Rook. "Could that be a rumor?"

"Nope. I saw him come over to her place late a couple times. They had a thing."

"Last time you saw them together?"

Adel grabbed her softball duffel and banged her locker shut. "The night before you went out to the graffiti wall with him," she said, as she headed for the door. "After that, she switched to Nolan."

SINCE SATURDAY, Theo had barely touched the internet. Sunday disappeared in a kind of weightless fog, soft and beautiful and strange. He and Ana called and texted throughout the day, staying connected after a night of being closer than they'd ever been. Theo still couldn't quite believe it had happened.

When he finally checked his phone, he did it through his fingers, like he was watching a horror movie. But no one was talking about him anymore—or Sareth, or even Rook.

The story had moved on. Jill. Keanu. Chad. He skimmed through posts until he understood the social bomb that had exploded at Homecoming—and knew that Rook had dropped it.

What else had happened? Did she know anything new? Was she okay?

He still couldn't shake the way she had sounded over the phone.

On Monday, he couldn't find Rook at lunch, and he didn't see her in the halls.

On Tuesday, he tried waiting outside her second period class—he knew she was part of the *Seventh-Inning Stretch* and that she'd have to show up there eventually. But either she was late, or she was absent, because he didn't see her anywhere. He gave up right before the bell and ran to precalculus.

On Wednesday, Theo got to campus early enough to wait at the bottom of the weight-room steps before zero period. If Rook was at school, he would find her here.

She came through the gym doors. Saw him.

Pretended not to.

"Hey," he said. "How was Homecoming?"

She also pretended not to hear him, and neatly avoided contact by walking into the girls' locker room. He waited almost the entire period, but she didn't come out.

Angry, Theo left the gym and strode to the front office.

"Theo Locke." The office manager peered over her glasses. "Winning any debate medals for Lakeview today?"

"Hi, Mrs. Dixon," said Theo. "Nope, trying something new. A news program. Mr. Magnusson's running it."

"Oh!" Mrs. Dixon sat back, looking pleased. "He's resurrecting *The Wolf Howls*? Ah, the Wolves. We had more dignity back then."

"I need to find one of his students—Rook Radcliffe. We're doing a story on the justice system. Can you tell me where to find her?"

"We could certainly use more kids like you." Mrs. Dixon turned her attention to the computer as she typed. "Radcliffe, Rook. The names some parents give."

Mrs. Dixon listed out Rook's classes and the rooms they were in, and Theo jotted down the information.

Third period Geometry. He'd try to catch her there.

After precalculus, he waited at the door of Rook's classroom until he saw her. The moment she realized he was there, she turned on her heel and bolted.

He followed fast.

Dimly, he knew his frustration wasn't entirely justified, and what it really signaled was fear. He didn't want her to shut him out, but he didn't know how to stop her.

She made for the doors at the end of the hall and pushed her way through. He walked outside right after her. The moment they were out of the school building, he spoke.

"Why are you pretending you're not home?" he said, trying not to sound as upset as he felt. "Why are you avoiding me? Have I done something wrong here?"

Rook stopped walking, bags on her shoulders. She kept her back to him.

"Just go away."

"*Why?*"

She didn't move. Didn't answer.

He walked around her and stood in front of her.

"Tell me what I did. Is it because I talked to the police? Or my friends? Because I thought—"

"No."

"Then what?"

Rook fixed her eyes on one of the poles that held up the roof of the covered walkway.

You called me, she wanted to say, but it sounded stupid. He would never understand. People called each other, it was normal. She knew she was weird for getting so upset about it.

"Is this because I called you?" he asked, like he could read her mind. "It is, isn't it? Why was that bad?"

This was the problem with him. He could read her. He could tell things. And she didn't want anyone to be able to tell anything. But how was she supposed to say that?

"I didn't give you the number," she replied slowly, "because I didn't want you to have it."

"Fine, I'm sorry."

But he didn't sound like he thought it was fine. Or like he was sorry.

"You think I have to answer you," she said. "I don't."

"No, I thought we were helping each other. I thought we had a goal. I still want to figure things out, don't you?"

She gave a disdainful shrug.

"Yes you do." Theo pointed a finger. "You *know* you do, you even staked out a classroom!"

"*Shhh*! Jesus!"

"Did your grandfather say you can't talk to me? Is it against his rules, or something?"

"What? No."

"Then I don't understand," he said. "I'll go away if that's really what you want—but this is weird, Rook. You're acting like I hurt you, and I don't get it."

The bell rang for first period. Rook shifted her weight.

"I need to go to class."

"You think I don't?"

"So go."

"No. This is important."

Rook shook her head. "We barely know each other."

"I know, but—"

Theo wasn't sure how to finish that sentence, he only knew that he was right. Whatever this was, it mattered. Too much for her to sever it because he had made a misjudgment.

He took out his phone.

"Deleting Oscar's number. There, it's gone. Are we good?"

She looked away and crossed her arms.

"How was I supposed to know how much that would bother you?" he asked. "Most people text each other all the time."

"I'm not most people."

That was for sure. Theo studied her. Her brown hair was down from its ponytail for once, softening the super-defined lines of her face and jaw. Her eyes, unwilling to meet his, belonged to a predator with a thorn in its paw. Injured but still dangerous.

He wished he could ask her why. What had happened to make her so aloof? So determined to wall herself off? But her flat expression and her closed-off body language told him to keep his questions to himself.

Maybe she had been abused.

"I'm sorry," he said, and this time the apology was real. "I didn't mean to invade your space. I won't call again, I promise. We can hang out at school, or at my place, if that's what you're comfortable with."

Rook wanted to accept. She pressed her mouth shut.

"Just one thing, though." Theo paused. "I know you won't like me asking this, but I have to."

She flinched and tried to brace herself for impact.

"Are you safe, at home?" he asked.

Now she looked at him, and the vulnerability in her eyes took him by complete surprise. She looked the way she had sounded on the phone the other night. Young and small. He had the urge to reach out for her.

He quashed it. She would only tear his arms off. Emotionally speaking.

"I'm fine," she said.

The words were automatic, like he'd pulled a string, and Theo knew they were a lie. He wished he could press, but it wouldn't work. Her boundaries were real, and he couldn't force his way through.

"Okay," he said. "I'll drop it. But if you ever want to talk, I'll listen."

Her stomach ached. Gabe had known how to say the right thing too.

She told herself to scorch the earth. To tell him to fuck off for good.

A teacher walked past them. "Third period started five minutes ago. Go."

Rook headed back into the school. Theo walked beside her.

"Lunch?" he asked.

No. Don't do it.

"Lunch," she said. "But not the cafeteria."

"Okay, where?"

She glanced at him. "Meet me at my car. Gray Honda Civic. Corner of the north parking lot. Baseball field side."

The invitation surprised him. It felt like progress.

"Sounds great," he said. "See you there."

TWENTY-EIGHT

Rook sat in the driver's seat of the Civic, chewing her chicken breast and waiting for Theo. She saw his blond hair first, shining optimistically under the gray and rainy sky. He waved, jogged toward the car with his backpack and stack of books, and let himself in on the passenger side.

As soon as he shut the door, Rook felt the stifling intimacy of the situation. The rain intensified, pattering on the windows, shutting out the world. Everything inside the car felt closer now. His breathing, his slight sniffle as he wiped rain from his face, the sound of his backpack zipper as he opened it to get out his lunch. His friendly, easy "Hi." All of it was right inside her head.

She had admitted him to the only truly private retreat she had. She hoped he wouldn't make her regret it.

But he seemed to understand about calling Oscar's. Or at least he understood that her privacy mattered to her, even if it didn't make sense to him.

"Okay," he said. "Homecoming. I know about Keanu and Jill—are people exaggerating? Did you really get onstage and announce it to Chad in front of the whole dance?"

"Not quite." Rook explained what she had figured out and Delilah had confirmed, and how Keanu had picked a fight he couldn't win. Theo worked his way through half a sleeve of Oreos as he listened.

"The idea of Delilah turning her powers to gossip is absolutely frightening," he said. "She's so smart it even scares *me,* but she usually sticks to world domination via robotics." He glanced at Rook. "You okay?" he asked.

"I'm fine."

Theo popped a whole Oreo into his mouth and offered the sleeve to her.

"Gross."

He shrugged, downed a paper box of milk, and opened another one. "What else happened?"

"Well, I had to threaten the douche again."

"Who?"

"Perkins," she said, and she told him about their conversation.

"That sounds like an unholy length of time to spend with Chad," said Theo, when she was finished. "Will you ever recover?"

"Unlikely."

He laughed and gave her a warm look that made her want to squirm.

"He really didn't sound like he knew about the email," she said quickly, looking away from him. Her breath fogged the passenger side window, and she dragged her thumb through it just to have something to do.

"He was drunk, though," said Theo. "Everything he said is probably compromised." He hesitated. "I found something out too. From Ana."

Rook drew another line in the window fog. "Oh yeah?"

"She saw Sareth the night of the attack, somewhere between eleven and midnight. He was by the Lakeview sign. But he didn't do it," he added quickly, when Rook looked at him.

"Then what was he doing here?"

"I'll ask him when we get him out," said Theo. "He's my friend, Rook. It wasn't him."

Rook wanted to tell him he was a sucker for thinking that friendship meant anything, but she couldn't quite get herself to do it.

Nearly midnight by the Lakeview sign was pretty damn close to the scene of the crime. Maybe the police had gotten the right guy after all.

"I also talked to Marna," Rook said. "She says Nolan's been into Destiny for a long time, but they've been best friends, so he didn't think Destiny would ever like him that way. Maybe that's why he always looks like he's letting her do what she wants. He's afraid."

"Of what?"

Rook chose her words carefully. "Of having it go away," she said. "If he didn't think she wanted him, and now she suddenly does, he might feel like he has to go along with her or lose her. The way he looked at her—I think he really feels it."

Theo shook Oreo crumbs into his mouth. "So they were at Homecoming?"

"Yeah, and Delilah said she heard them in the parking lot. He said he needed to do something, and Destiny told him there was no going back."

"No going back to *what*?"

"I don't know, but I heard the night AJ was attacked, Destiny was crying to Nolan about how she was tired of something and she wanted to go do something about it, and he was telling her not to."

Theo stuffed the empty Oreo wrapper into his lunch bag and pulled out his notebook and pen so that he could jot this down.

"And there's something else weird," said Rook. "Destiny used to have this princess phone. Really sparkly and obvious. Now she has a black one. And when I saw her with the guy in the Jeep, he gave her something black that could've been a phone–she shoved it in her pocket when I saw it. Like she wanted to hide it."

Theo finished writing and reviewed his notes, chewing on the pen cap.

Rook adjusted her seat to lean back a little. She gazed out through the windshield at the rain.

For a minute or two, they were quiet together.

"So... up to that night," Theo said slowly. "Based on what we know, Destiny was with AJ."

"The last time they were seen getting together was the night before he met me at the graffiti wall."

"Then that was a fresh cut, for her," said Theo. "She felt betrayed."

And like she deserved it for being stupid, Rook thought.

"Yep," she said.

Theo jotted something. "And you think Nolan's in love with her?"

Rook dug some sliced apples and almond butter out of her bag. "Sure," she said. "It's the real thing."

"Couldn't it be?"

"In high school?"

"Yes." Theo's color heightened. "Some people fall in love early, and it sticks. A percentage of people marry their high school sweethearts."

"What percent? Two?"

"Well, yes. But—"

"How do you even know that?"

"Debate. And don't change the subject. Even a small percentage means it's possible, doesn't it?"

Rook didn't see the point of arguing with Theo, although it was fun to see him all heated up and indignant. She stuck an apple slice into the almond butter and chomped it. "You know Marna Hauterman thinks you're adorable," she said eventually, watching his cheeks grow pinker like she'd turned up a dial. He was so white he couldn't hide a blush for anything.

"Did she say that? That's so funny."

"Why?"

"Oh, I had a huge crush on Marna, back in the day." He ducked his chin and put his fingers through the thick, light hair that waved over his forehead. "She was the first girl I ever kissed—just a game at a party. Beginning of eighth grade. Mateo was there. He kissed a girl for the first time too—Tuyet."

"Spin the bottle?" Rook hesitated. "Sixth grade," she admitted. "Same."

"Your first kiss was a party game?"

"If you could even call it a kiss."

"That bad?"

"That *wet*. I had to wipe my face on my shirt."

Theo made a noise of disgust and laughed at almost the same moment.

"Almost makes AJ look adequate," he said, and then he winced. "Sorry if I shouldn't—"

"No, you're fine. It's true. He sucked." She raised an eyebrow at him. "What about Marna? On a scale of sloppy to life-changing."

He looked flustered. "Oh. Marna—she's always—really warm." He cringed. "I mean her personality," he rushed to say. "Not her, uh. Although—never mind."

Rook laughed. "Wow. Memorable, huh?"

"But it wasn't really *real*," he said, strangled. "It's just... you know. Firsts are firsts." Theo looked down at his hands, unable to continue speaking for a few moments. When he did, his voice was softer. "Actually, that's not true. It was real for Mateo and Tuyet. They were together after that kiss. Until he died."

"It seemed like she was struggling with him being gone," said Rook.

Theo glanced at her. "Tuyet went to Homecoming? With who?"

"Nobody, I think. She didn't want to be there, she just thought she had to be. She talked about the grief counselor telling her to move on."

Theo's face tightened. "Move on," he muttered. "If they knew him, they'd never say it."

Rook fully understood.

"Hey, uh." She cleared her throat. "Marna asked me if you're sleeping. If you're okay."

"I'm sleeping," said Theo vaguely, his eyes focused on something Rook couldn't see. "I'm not okay."

Rook offered him an apple slice and her almond butter.

He glanced at it.

"Gross."

Rook half-smiled and finished her lunch. "You spent Homecoming with her royal highness, right?"

"Who?"

"Your cheer captain." Rook cast a sly look at him. "The senior."

"Yeah." Light shone in his green-yellow eyes. "I did."

"Fun weekend?"

He didn't answer. He would have told Mateo every detail of the most incredible night of his life, but that was different. Mateo had been a safe person for those secrets—Theo wasn't sure if Rook was. Plus, he didn't think he could talk about these particular details without melting. He hadn't even been able to form a complete sentence about Marna, and that had been one kiss. His evening with Ana, on a scale of sloppy to life-changing, had been epic. Off the charts.

"That's good," Rook said.

"What is?"

"That you won't brag about it."

When the bell rang to start fourth period, neither of them moved to leave the Civic.

"I've never been late to so many classes in my life," Theo said, as he paged slowly through his notebook. "Chad and Destiny." He gnawed on his pencil. "If it wasn't Keanu, then maybe it was one of them. Chad would have motive to frame Sareth, and possibly to hurt AJ. Destiny would have motive to retaliate against AJ, and to frame you."

"If it was Chad," said Rook, "why would he send the email?"

"He says he didn't. Just like *you* say you didn't send a text to AJ."

"I couldn't have."

"Exactly. What if somebody else sent both of those messages?" He tapped Destiny's name with his pencil. "Her phone," he said. "She had one, and then it vanished, and she got someone to give her a new one. Right?"

"Right..."

"Okay." Theo looked suddenly animated. "Let's pretend she did it. If we accept the premise that she texted

AJ and lured him to the wall, and then she hit him over the head—what would she do next?"

"Uh... get rid of the weapon?"

"And also?"

Rook's mouth opened. "The phone," she breathed. "She might get rid of the phone."

"Yes. If she panicked, she might think, better ditch the evidence. I don't think it would matter, because the police could still seize phone records... I don't really know how that works, but if she wasn't thinking straight—"

"You're a fucking genius," said Rook. "Utter. Fucking. Genius."

Theo looked like he wanted to be modest but couldn't quite pull it off. "Thanks."

Rook had a sudden instinct. She needed another genius. One whose wheelhouse included robots. Computers.

Emails, maybe.

She opened the car door. "Come on. I have an idea."

"What?"

"It's kind of a long shot," she said. "I'll tell you if it works."

TWENTY-NINE

Rook returned to class with no intention of staying there. Ten minutes in, she excused herself, claiming nausea, and headed to the office to see the nurse. Instead, she went to the attendance desk and dropped a note in the TA basket.

She went to the bottom of the weight room steps, sat down, and waited.

Near the end of the period, Delilah rolled through the gym doors, holding the note Rook had sent to her.

Hey Gossip Girl—

Thanks for the 5-star review.

Meet me ASAP in the gym.

—The Headbasher

"Yes?" Delilah said, coming to a stop at the bottom of the steps, where Rook sat, leaning back, elbows propped on the step behind her.

"You're into robots, right?" she asked. "Seems like you're good with computers."

"Depends what you mean."

"Can you get me into Chad's email? His sent mail, specifically."

"His *sent* mail?" said Delilah. "You're assuming it exists. I struggle to imagine him stringing written sentences together."

"So can you do it?"

"Why? What do you want with his email?"

Rook lowered her voice. "Whoever reported the evidence in Sareth's locker? They sent the email from Chad's account, but he says it wasn't him. I want to see if he's lying."

"Chad's the reason Sareth's in juvie?" Delilah demanded, incensed. "Why the hell would he do that?"

"Sareth got him suspended from the weight room."

Delilah made a noise of rage. "That *prick*," she ranted. "That self-absorbed waste of human life. Sareth is one of the few people around here who doesn't deserve any trouble—how dare he?"

"Right, so can you hack in, or whatever?"

"I build and code robots, you meathead," Delilah snapped. "Hacking is a different skill set."

"Meathead?"

"Aren't you? Don't you spend your free time moving heavy objects to make your muscles grow?"

"Don't knock it till you try it."

"As if I can try it."

"Okay, hold on," said Rook, annoyed. "You could try it. What's stopping you?"

"I'll give you one guess."

Rook looked over her shoulder and up the stairs.

There was no ramp here. No elevator either. She hadn't thought about it.

"Wait," said Rook, getting uncomfortably warm. How had she missed that? "But that's not legal, right? They have to give you access, don't they?"

Delilah sighed. “Forget it,” she said. “Let’s do this. I’ll get you into Chad’s email.”

“I thought you weren’t a hacker.”

“I never said that, I said they were different skill sets. And I’m not doing it on the school computers, or on my own laptop. Meet me at the public library after school tomorrow, and we’ll see if Chad has ever sent an email in his life.”

THIRTY

It was almost one o'clock in the morning when Theo's phone buzzed, nudging him out of light slumber. He rolled over, rubbed his eyes until he could read Colleen's text, and sat straight up in bed.

[COLLEEN] aj is awake!

Theo texted her back at once.

[THEO] Is he talking?

His phone rang.

"He's okay," said Colleen. "Grant says he's acting like himself, he's able to talk and move like normal—he's got a headache, that's all."

"Does he know who hurt him?"

"He doesn't remember that part, *but* he remembers that the last person he talked to, the person he met at the wall, was *Destiny*." She paused. "I almost didn't even call you, because you're being such a jerk right now. But this is too important."

Theo wasn't fully awake, but he couldn't let that pass. "I told you to shut up because you were spreading rumors about Rook," he said. "And then you started spreading rumors about *me* and Rook—"

"You think that's why I'm mad?" said Colleen. "Say whatever you want to me, I don't care, but you better make it up to Tuyet, because she is *breaking*. She can't handle this. And before you start in on how Mateo was your best friend and you can't handle it either—yes you can. You'll be okay—it'll be horrible, but you'll come out on the other side, because you're you. Tuyet is—I don't even know what she is. She's losing it. So fucking be nice to her, because you have no idea what I can do if I really decide to go after you."

Colleen hung up.

Theo stared at the phone. He couldn't go back to sleep. He knew he should be focused on what he had just learned—Destiny had been there, he'd been right.

Instead, his brain latched like a tick onto the illogical thought that perhaps Mateo should be in a coma instead of dead, so that he, too, might wake up and have a second chance.

If he had started walking sooner, maybe a coma. Maybe not dead.

If he had put down the controller just a few minutes sooner. Hadn't made assumptions.

Hadn't left him alone to die.

Theo curled up in bed and pressed his hands over his face, digging his fingertips into his forehead, painful.

It had been several days since his brain had done this to him. Now the monster returned in a twisted form, offering him a nonsensical solution. A bargain. A coma. If he could go back and get it right, Mateo could be in a coma.

Grief is a shapeshifter, the counselor had said. *It'll change on you, and sometimes, logic will fail. If it gets worse, if it becomes overwhelming, the best thing you can do is tell someone else. Don't stay in it alone.*

Still in the fetal position, he texted Tuyet.

[THEO] You heard?

[TUYET] I heard.

He called her. Tuyet answered, sounding distant.

"So *he* lives."

Theo knew exactly what she meant.

"I can't think," he said, and he realized that his teeth were chattering. "My brain makes no sense."

Tuyet made a low, wordless sound that helped him more than anything else could. A sound that could have come from the chasm in his heart. At least she knew what they had lost.

"I can't do it without him," he whispered.

"No," said Tuyet.

They were silent. Just breathing.

"I'm sorry," Theo said quietly. "I'm so sorry."

For being unfair, he thought. *For not being there for you. I don't know how to help you, I can't even help myself.*

"I just wish we could somehow trade," she said eventually. "I'd trade anyone."

Theo was sure she meant him included.

THIRTY-ONE

The news of AJ's return to consciousness spread so fast that by the time zero period started, everybody already knew. Adel pulled Rook aside in the weight room.

"The cops came to our complex at three this morning," she whispered. "They took Destiny. I guess they found her prints on a baseball bat in the school dumpster." She shook her head. "Her poor sister was crying so hard."

Nolan shuffled into the weight room alone, gray faced and sweating. He sat against the wall, eyes shut, breathing unevenly, rocking like he could not remain still.

"Gotta be rough," said Adel quietly. "You think he just found out this morning that his girl's a psycho?"

It was a good question, and Rook's instinct was that Nolan had known everything.

"Hell yes," crowed the douche, on his way into the weight room. "My shortstop lives."

Keanu Faletogo slunk into the room a few minutes later.

The second Chad saw Keanu, he turned his back. Most of the other guys in the weight room took his lead and did the same. They clustered together, talking in low voices.

Iced out, Rook thought, watching as the dynamic shifted in real time, leaving Keanu completely in the cold.

Keanu's eyes found Rook. He stalked toward her, hands in fists by his sides, balled so tightly that his arms shook.

Rook stood and squared up, ready.

"I don't care if they arrested Destiny," Keanu said angrily. "She didn't do anything to AJ, and we all know it. It was *you*. You're the one who framed Sareth, his locker is *right* next to yours."

Nolan opened his eyes. Pinned them on Rook.

Keanu got right in her face. Rook didn't move an inch.

"You lied about her," he said. "You lied about me—"

"Hey!" Coach Gonzalez was out of his office. "Both of you, step back."

Rook and Keanu did as told, never taking their eyes off each other.

"Radcliffe, sit down," said Gonzalez. "Perkins, what are you doing here? You're banned until next week, get out. Faletogo, my office. Now."

"I didn't even—"

"Now."

Keanu shot Rook a look of pure loathing, but obeyed the teacher.

"Dang," said Adel. "Kinda wanted to see that happen." She strolled off to the dumbbells.

THIRTY-TWO

"I was dead set on retiring," Mr. Magnusson told the *Seventh-Inning Stretch* group during second period. "But working with you kids is changing my mind. It's been a long time since I've woken up excited to come to work every day."

"Plus, you get more retirement money if you stay longer, right, Mr. M.?" Elijah called from the back of the room.

Rook went into the newsroom, where Fernando sat at the end of the desk. He leaned back in the swivel chair, and tipped his baseball cap up to fix his eyes on her.

"Oh listen, I had an idea for a sports segment. You versus Perkins, weight room throwdown. Everyone knows you two have a rivalry going—people would love it."

Rook didn't answer, but the expression on her face was apparently enough.

"If Rooks could kill..." said Fernando. "Damn, okay, never mind."

"Do me a favor, though," said Rook. "Let me borrow your baseball ring. Just five minutes—I need to check something."

Fernando rubbed it protectively. "Check *what*?"

"It's for the *Stretch*."

"Okay." Fernando tugged the ring from his finger. "For the *Seventh-Inning Stretch*. Five minutes," he warned.

Rook took the bathroom pass, hurried to her locker, and tried to fit Fernando's ring through the slats.

It went through. So that was that. If Destiny had wanted to frame her, she easily could have made a mistake and stuck the evidence in Sareth's locker. No combination required.

Everything lined up. Except Perkins's email.

She headed back to class.

"Rook who's back," said Fernando, and he stuck out his finger. "Ring me."

Rook pushed the baseball ring back on. "You live near Nolan and Destiny, right?"

"Same complex," said Fernando. "Why?"

"The night AJ was attacked, did you see either of them?"

"I saw Nolan," said Fernando. "Probably around eleven-thirty."

"Doing what?"

"Getting in his mom's car."

"Alone?"

"I think so."

"Where was Destiny?"

Fernando shrugged. "She shares a car with her sister, but I don't think it was there."

"Why would you notice that?"

"Their parking spot faces ours." Fernando gave her a keen look. "What are you up to?" he asked.

"Investigative journalism," Rook replied, and she went back to her computer station, her brain whirring.

THIRTY-THREE

That afternoon, at the public library, Rook sat beside Delilah at one of the computer tables.

"Before we start," said Delilah, rapping her fingernails on the table. "I've been thinking. If Chad says he didn't send an email, then how do you know the principal got an email from Chad's account?"

"Who cares?"

"I do. Because you could only have that information if you did something underhanded to get it," said Delilah. "Which means I might actually like you." She turned back to the computer screen. "Here we go. Chad Perkins's sent mail, where logic and reason go to die. Any idea what his password is?"

"I thought you could hack it."

Delilah snorted. Her fingers moved over the keyboard. "Let's try 'boobs' with zeros instead of Os."

Entry denied. Delilah minimized the screen with alert swiftness when a librarian walked behind them.

"Okay," she whispered. "We'll go through a teacher account, I have a password. We'll take a look at Chad's login info, and his failing grades, and given how much this district fawns over sportsball, probably all his pitching highlights—*oh*," she said, and muffled a laugh behind her hand. "Got it."

She typed in PERKINS#1 and clicked with a flourish.

They were in.

"Nice," said Rook. "He wrote that at the diner. You saw it from where you were sitting?"

"I didn't have to," said Delilah. "He tattoos it everywhere. So of course he uses it as his password, because he is an exception to the rules of natural selection." Delilah clicked his sent mail. "Nope, nothing. A wasteland, as predicted."

"Check his deleted files."

"Oh, is that what I should do? Please, share more tips." Delilah navigated to the trash.

"Empty," said Rook. "Fuck." She jumped a little when a library cart squeaked. She glanced over her shoulder, but nobody was looking at them.

Delilah navigated to a subfolder.

"School servers hoard everything," she said. "You think you're safe, but nope. Your deleted mails go into a recoverable items folder right here."

A window popped up when Delilah tried to access it, demanding authorized user credentials.

"Denied," she said. "*Unless...*"

She typed in a username that wasn't Chad's or her own.

"I told you I have access to a teacher account," she said, when Rook gave her a questioning look. "Mr. Booker's password is taped under his keyboard."

"How'd you find it?"

"I offered to clean up his desk for him when I was done with an assignment, and he thought it was altruism. And here we are."

Chad's recoverable items folder opened. There was only one item inside it.

"Subject header: check locker 702," Delilah read quietly, checking to make sure no one was near enough to listen. "Sent by Chad Perkins to Principal Regina Kim. My my, what an upstanding young man. It's boys like him who make me feel safe alone at night."

She hit print. Rook snatched the email from the printer.

Subject: CHECK LOCKER 702
From: Chad Perkins
To: Principal Regina Kim

DEAR MRS PRINCIPLE ITS
ABOUT AJ. THERES STUFF IN
LOCKER 702 THE COPS
SHOULD SEE BUT DONT
TALK TO ME ABOUT THIS I
CANT BE A SNICH
-CHAD

He had seemed so confused at Homecoming. It could have been a lie, of course—anyone could lie, Rook knew that—but Chad didn't seem bright enough to lie so believably.

"Rook." Delilah's voice had changed. Sharpened. "Look at this."

Rook returned to find that a second email had appeared in the recoverable items folder.

"It just showed up," said Delilah. "It must've been queued, and it just synced." She glanced up at Rook. "And it's not great for you."

Rook bent down to read over her shoulder.

Subject: IT WASNT HIM
From: Chad Perkins
To: Principal Regina Kim

MRS PRINCIPLE
THE CAMBUDIAN KID DIDNT
HIDE THAT EVIDINCE IT WAS
THE GIRL WITH THE LOCKER
NEXT TO HIM ROOK
-CHAD

Rook stared, her heart chugging.

Chad had pointed the finger directly this time. There was no more wondering who he'd been trying to frame. It had never been Sareth. He had messed up the locker number—because he was Chad.

Why would he send this now, eight days after the first one? Why not immediately correct the mistake, and tell them that she was the one to look at? Had he been afraid of her? Afraid of someone else? Was somebody making him do this?

"It was sent sixty seconds ago," said Delilah grimly. "Perkins is at a keyboard right now. I'm out."

She hit print, cleared cookies, logged out, and headed for the library door. She paused just for a moment, to look over her shoulder.

"Good luck," she said, and she was gone.

Rook went to the printer and snatched up the second email, and she looked from one printout to the other, feeling like she'd just shot caffeine straight into her veins.

Now the cops had another reason to come for her—first the texts, now this—and Theo had told them she never warmed up on that field. Definitely enough evidence for them to make a move.

How long did she have before the principal saw this and forwarded it? How long before the cops saw it? How long before they arrested her, and actually booked her this time?

They'd fingerprint her. Take her picture. Put her in a jumpsuit.

Just like her mother.

If she'd had a phone, she would have texted Greta. She would have called Theo. She had no idea what to do next.

But somehow, she had to get her shit together and serve burgers. Her shift started in ten minutes.

Clutching Chad's emails, Rook walked down the block to The Lighthouse.

THIRTY-FOUR

Theo stepped out of grief counseling and into Ana's Audi, shivering.

Ana turned up the heat. "How was it?"

"Fine," said Theo, because for once, he'd gotten through a counseling session without crying his eyes out and blaming himself for Mateo's death. He'd spent the whole session talking about Rook and AJ instead—an easy way to detach from the ugly grief that had clawed back since Colleen's text.

The doctor had suggested that Theo might be fixating on the crime because of his guilt issues with Mateo. He couldn't go back and change what had happened to his friend, so his mind had wrapped around a problem it had a chance at solving. And though the doctor had a point, Theo didn't care. Since August, grief had trapped him in his head, obsessing over what-ifs, but these past two weeks, he'd felt alive again.

He wanted to stay that way. Needed to.

He took out his notebook and dragged the tip of his pen over the short lists of key information he'd synthesized on his own last night, unable to call Rook and talk to her about it. He hadn't seen her today at school, either. She'd said she had an idea, and then she had never come back to find him.

He texted Tuyet.

[THEO] Rook said you saw Keanu at Shakemaster last Thursday.

[TUYET] Yes.

[THEO] Did you see Chad there?

[TUYET] Yes...

[THEO] What time?

[TUYET] Around 11.

[THEO] When did he leave?

[TUYET] 11:30.

[THEO] Alone?

[TUYET] Yes.

[THEO] Did you see where he went?

[TUYET] No.

There was a pause, and then:

[TUYET] Theo, what are you doing?

Theo jotted these items in his notebook under Chad's name, then flipped the page back to Keanu.

"What's that?" Ana asked, when she reached a red light. She leaned closer to read the list he was looking at. "Keanu—greed, ambition, attention. Is this Lit homework?"

Theo considered saying yes. Instead, he ventured, "What reasons could a person have to hit another person?"

Ana sat back, looking interested. "Is this for debate? Okay—self-defense. That's one. Protecting someone else, a loved one. That's two. Or maybe you're stopping someone from hurting themselves."

"You're a good person," said Theo, "so your answers are good-person answers. What if you were a terrible person?"

"Then greed," said Ana. "Revenge. Jealousy. Anger. Or if you're really a sicko, maybe you just torture other people for fun." She shuddered. "And there are really people like that," she said, almost to herself. "Just walking around."

"Now what if you're a normal person?" said Theo. "A little good, a little bad. Just an average human being. What could possibly motivate you to club somebody over the head?"

"Theo, is this about AJ?"

"Yes."

"Those lists in your notebook are about AJ?" Ana sounded worried. "I thought you were staying away from that."

Theo shifted in his seat. "Remember how I told you about Rook?"

"The girl you were *also* going to stay away from because she might have committed assault?"

"We've been hanging out."

Ana looked at him.

"She didn't assault anyone. I'm sure."

Ana changed lanes without responding.

"Are you upset?"

She stopped at a red light. "I guess I should admit something," she said. "I saw a picture of you with her. Somebody forwarded it to me and said there was a rumor at Lakeview about the two of you."

Theo groaned. "There was," he said.

"I figured if it was anything, you'd tell me."

"There's nothing to tell," he said. "Colleen posted that picture because she was mad at me, and that's how she always retaliates. Rook is—I don't know if I can even say she's a friend. We've hung out a few times."

"You're not afraid she's dangerous?"

Ana's voice was quiet. Careful. Like she was asking more than just that question.

Theo hesitated. Rook had an edge. But not the kind Ana was thinking.

"She didn't hit AJ," he said, "but she should've. He told people she slept with him. She didn't."

"I hate guys like that," Ana muttered. "So... I shouldn't worry?"

"About what?" Theo looked down at his notebook again. He wished he could call Rook.

And then he remembered. She was at work—and if they went right now, he might still catch her.

"You hungry?" he said. "Want to grab something to eat?"

"At Shakemaster?"

"No, The Lighthouse. I'll introduce you to Rook."

THIRTY-FIVE

Rook bussed soda glasses from table eight, eyeing the little bell that hung over the diner door. All night, every time that bell had rung, she had expected the cops to walk in and march her out, and now her nerves were frayed.

She was on her way to the pass with the empty glasses when the bell jingled again, shrill in the near-empty diner. Rook jumped so hard she nearly dropped the tray, and looked over her shoulder to see who was there.

Theo. Her spirits lifted. She could show him the emails.

He waved, and Rook headed over, checking out the girl who stood close beside him, looking around at The Lighthouse like she wasn't sure why she had come. She had to be the Homecoming queen, still in her cheer skirt, CAPTAIN emblazoned down one arm of her hoodie. She was short, fit, and pretty. She and Theo were the picture of the perfect high-school couple.

"Ana, this is Rook. Rook, this is my girlfriend, Ana."

Ana looked up at her with dark eyes that were not entirely charitable.

"Hi," they both said at the same time.

"Have a seat." Rook handed them menus. "Not that booth—somebody puked there. What can I get you?"

"Shakes." Theo slid into a booth and pointed to himself and Ana. "Chocolate, strawberry."

Ana sat across from him. Her dark eyes flicked over Rook—quick, assessing.

Theo missed it. Rook didn't.

"Got it. Hey—can I show you something after I'm done? If you can wait," Rook added, when Ana's expression tensed.

"We can wait," said Theo, oblivious.

Rook put in the order and waited by the pass for the shakes.

"Are those friends of yours?" Barney asked her, pointing to Theo and Ana. "Go ahead, join 'em. Your shift is up in five anyway."

Rook delivered the milkshakes—and hesitated. It seemed weird to sit next to Theo with Ana there, but the idea of sitting next to Ana was somehow worse. She dragged over a chair and plunked down at the end of the booth.

There. Not awkward.

But the silence that followed was. Ana played with her straw as Theo sucked down his milkshake, not sure why he felt nervous.

"Chad was definitely at Shakemaster like he said," he told Rook. "He left at eleven-thirty, alone."

"That fits." Rook pulled the emails out of her pocket. "Here's what I found."

Theo unfolded them and read them. His eyes widened. "How did you *get* these?"

Rook didn't want to get Delilah involved if she didn't have to.

"From a recoverable items folder," she said. "They were deleted from his sent mail, and then from his trash."

"Like he wanted to cover his tracks."

"Yep. One of them is from eight days ago, right before the lockdown—"

"The other is from today," said Theo, frowning. "Why would he send it now?"

"That's what I don't get."

"But this isn't good, Rook," Theo said, as the full weight of the second email struck him. "This makes it look like you actually..." His eyes met hers. "They'll arrest you. They'll use what I said."

"It's okay."

"Wait, wait." Ana put up her hands. "Stop." She looked at Rook. "Why do you have emails from somebody's deleted folders?" she demanded, and she turned her eyes on Theo. "What do you mean, she's getting arrested because of something you said? What *is* all this?"

Theo looked apprehensively at his girlfriend. "We've been—sort of—asking around at school and trading theories, trying to figure out what happened to AJ."

Ana blinked. "Trying to figure it out," she repeated. "What, like Nancy *Drew*? Are you for real right now? You're talking about someone who put a guy in a *coma*—there's a police investigation!"

Theo didn't know where to look.

Ana turned on Rook, her eyes hostile. "You've got him convinced that you didn't attack anybody—and maybe you didn't. But whatever this is?" She pointed to the printed emails. "It's *not* okay. Theo's a good person. He's smart, and he's been through enough. Don't drag him into something that could hurt him."

"Ana—"

"What? Look at you. You're going to end up in trouble—you're going to get hurt." Ana stood up. "I'm going to the car. If you two know anything about what happened to AJ, then you need to tell the police."

"He did," said Rook. "He called them and told them what he knew. Don't be mad at him. He did the right thing."

Ana turned to Theo. "What did you tell the police?"

"It's not important," he said, but he hated saying it. It wasn't true. He just couldn't explain it to Ana, because that secret belonged to Rook.

"It's not *important*." Ana stared at him. "But they could arrest her for it?"

"Theo caught me in a lie," said Rook quietly. "Not about AJ, but he didn't want to risk it, so he reported it." She glanced at Theo. "He was honest with them. And with me. And it's really okay," she said, at the guilty look on his face. "Hey. I mean it."

"Theo, come on," Ana said. "We need to leave."

When Theo didn't move right away, Ana spoke again, this time in a way that Rook couldn't follow.

"Esto no es como tú. Estoy preocupada." She gestured for him to follow her. "¿Vienes conmigo?"

"Ya voy," Theo replied. "Primero tengo que pagar, ¿está bien?"

Ana gave Rook a look and walked out.

"I'm so sorry," Theo began, once she was gone. "I should've told her more before we came. I have to go, but we're close now, I know it. We're almost there—and if the cops bring you in, I promise, I'll find the answer. I won't let it drop."

Rook watched Ana's straw sink down into her untouched shake.

"Rook?" Theo said. "Did you hear what I just said?"

"She's right," Rook replied.

"Really? You think we should go to the police now?"

Rook shook her head. "I think you should go back to doing your own thing."

"What thing?"

"I'm not someone you should hang around with."

"Why not?"

But Rook couldn't answer that. "You're a nice guy," she said. "And the cheerleader's waiting. You better go, or she'll think... whatever, I'll see you around, okay?"

Theo put his money on the table and looked at Rook, his eyes intense.

"AJ was assaulted. Sareth's locked up. You're implicated. I'm not quitting. Are you?"

"No."

"Then I'll see you tomorrow." He got up. "Lunch? Your car?"

Rook pushed her chair back over to the table where it belonged. It would be better—for him—if she ended this. Anything else was selfish.

"You speak Spanish?" she said. "I'm surprised."

"¿Porque parezco un güero básico?" Theo grinned.

"No clue what you just said."

"Because I look like a basic white boy?"

"Yeah, pretty much." Rook laughed—and then she froze. Shocked into stillness by an idea. *The* idea. Around her, the diner blurred out. She heard no sound except her own heart.

Did she have it?

Was she right?

"I basically lived half my life at Mateo's house, so I learned a lot through immersion," Theo said. "And then I joined the dual-language program in elementary so I could get better and practice at school, so that helped too. ASL was my first language, actually—my older brother is Deaf, so when I was born..." He kept on talking, unaware that Rook had checked out and could no longer hear him.

She pulled out Chad's emails and reread them. She focused on the second one.

MRS PRINCIPLE
THE CAMBUDIAN KID DIDNT
HIDE THAT EVIDINCE IT WAS
THE GIRL WITH THE LOCKER
NEXT TO HIM ROOK
-CHAD

Certainty bloomed in her chest. Warm. Satisfying. It spread through her, buzzing, until she was lightheaded with it.

She had it.

She was *right*.

Everything fit. Destiny's phone. The baseball bat with her prints on it. The timing of the second email. All of it.

"Meet me at my car tomorrow morning," said Rook, interrupting Theo in the middle of a sentence. "Parking lot. Six a.m. We need to plan."

"Plan?" His eyes gleamed. "Why?"

Rook held up the email, triumphant.

"Because I know who did it."

THIRTY-SIX

The next morning, Theo showed up at her car right on time. He made an amusing picture so early in the morning: flushed and agitated, his blond hair sticking up on one half of his head.

"*Who*?" he demanded, before his door was even shut.

Rook explained, step by step, how she had come to understand it. The more she talked, the surer she was of her answer, but she liked that Theo was a critical listener. He asked smart questions and tried to dismantle her theory until finally he ran out of ideas and concluded he agreed.

"Mr. Magnusson has first lunch," Rook said. "His room will be empty. All you have to do is get one of those passes from the attendance office and deliver it when lunch starts."

"You'll only have about twenty minutes," said Theo. "Cutting it close."

"Plenty of time for a confession. It's perfect."

"Remember, two-party consent. If you don't tell him you're recording, it's useless in court, and he has to knowingly agree—"

"Got it, counsel."

"Which means he might not say anything," said Theo anxiously.

"He will."

"And afterward, we *have* to call the police," Theo went on. "Or I am going to be down one girlfriend. Ana's freaking out. She thinks the attacker is going to target me next, and I'm going to end up clubbed to death in the cafeteria."

Rook checked the clock. "Time for school," she said, pulling her keys out of the ignition.

"Are you *sure* this is the right move?"

"I'm not waiting until they drag me in and interrogate me," said Rook. "When I go back in there, I'm going with the details."

Theo nodded. "Okay," he said. "I know my job. Front office. Note."

"Yep. I'll be in the tech room at lunch, you deliver the note, and then wait right outside while I do the interview."

"You shouldn't be alone in there."

"I'll be fine. Let's go."

During second period, she checked in with Mr. Magnusson. "Can I work in here today while you're at lunch?"

He looked shrewdly at her. "I suppose," he said. "Just respect the equipment."

At the lunch bell, Mr. Magnusson let her in before leaving for the staff room. Alone, Rook set up the cameras, and waited.

When the door opened several minutes later, a wave of terror hit, just like it did before every lifting meet—but she locked it down.

Focus. No fear. Do what you came here to do.

"Hi, Nolan," she said as he walked in.

Nolan held up the pass Theo had delivered.

"What's this about?" he asked, glancing around. His tall frame was hunched, his face tense.

"You almost got me arrested," Rook replied.

Nolan froze.

"I think it's time you told the truth."

Only his eyes moved. He met her gaze.

"You want to sit down?" Rook asked. "Talk about what really happened to AJ? Because I think you probably do. I get the feeling you've been wanting to tell the truth ever since this went down, but Destiny told you not to. She told you to shut up and let her take the fall, didn't she? Because she figured she'd get sympathy, or maybe she just thought she could handle it better than you could. But you don't want to do that. Because you love her."

Nolan remained locked, unmoving, like she had cast a spell.

"This is on record," said Rook. "The red light there means the camera's recording us. We're going to talk this out, and when we're done, Destiny won't have to stay in jail. You can get her out of there."

He slumped. "Okay," he whispered. He put his face in his hands. "She didn't do anything wrong. She didn't hurt AJ."

"No," Rook said quietly, "you did."

He let out a soft cry. "It was an accident."

"Yeah, I think I know how it went." She gestured to one of the computer lab chairs. "Sit down."

Nolan thudded into a chair and slumped forward onto the table, face buried in his arms.

"The night before AJ got with me at the graffiti wall, he got with Destiny," said Rook. "And after I blew him off, my guess is he rebounded. Tried to get Destiny back. Told her he was sorry, gave her some garbage about how he really cared about her. Am I on the right track here?"

Nolan nodded once.

"But she had her pride, right? So she texted him like it was me," said Rook. "To catch him lying. And when he said he'd meet me, she knew she was getting played. She went to confront him—one of your neighbors heard you tell her not to go."

"I told her not to." Nolan's voice was muffled in his arms. "I told her of *course* he's cheating on you, of course he wants two girls at the same time, AJ's a *pig*, this is what he *does*—"

"So she went to tell him so," said Rook. "And a little later, you did too. You didn't like the idea of her alone with him. She took her sister's car, you took your mom's. You left around eleven-thirty. Destiny didn't know you were following her, did she?"

Nolan shook his head.

"She went to the graffiti wall. AJ showed up. When he saw it was her and not me, well... I don't know what was said. But based on what I know about AJ, it wasn't gentlemanly."

"He called her pathetic," said Nolan hollowly. "He said she's so thirsty she'll let him come over anytime he wants, it doesn't matter what he does."

Rook's stomach turned. "Well that's disgusting," she said. "And unfortunately, it tracks. And then he walked away. He must have—if he met her at the wall, he had to walk away, because he was out in the middle of the baseball field when I found him. So he left her there, walked off, and I don't know what happened. Maybe she followed him. Maybe he said something else nasty. Or maybe he was just walking across the field and you were waiting, and you had heard enough."

"He walked away," Nolan whispered. "She chased him. She put a hand on his arm, barely touched him, and he—he *pushed* her, he pushed her off so much harder than he had to—"

"Did she fall?"

"On the ground. She was crying. And he *laughed*."

"And you stepped out."

"I don't remember doing it." He lifted his face from his arms and looked at Rook, his eyes haunted. "I don't even remember picking up the bat. I think it was by the equipment shed, and I—I just remember she was crying, and then AJ was on the ground, and I looked at the bat and it—had blood on it."

"And Destiny's a survivor, I think," said Rook. "Scrappier than she looks. She saw you, and she understood the stakes, and she clicked into damage control. You probably stood there in shock, and she did everything."

Nolan nodded.

"She took the bat," said Rook. "Tried to clean it, chucked it in the dumpster. That's why the prints are hers."

"God," Nolan whispered.

"She took the ring and the chain," said Rook. "Snapped them right off his neck so she could blame me and have physical evidence to back it. Then she got you out of there. At some point, she threw her phone away because she was worried about those burner texts—maybe it's in the lake, maybe the woods."

"The lake," said Nolan softly.

"And she got a new phone from some guy in a Jeep who doesn't look like a great person to do business with."

"He's her sister's boyfriend," said Nolan. "He's a scumbag."

"But the one silver lining in all this," said Rook, "was that Destiny also found out that night that you love her. Capital L. And from everything I've seen, it looks like maybe the feeling is mutual. So the two of you came together in a way that you never thought you would, and you've been stuck like glue ever since. But this is what it cost you."

Nolan shut his eyes. "Yes."

"Last Monday, you tried to frame me. You were in charge of the evidence, because *you* are Perkins's lab partner, and you know his password. You planted AJ's necklace and sent the email to start the lockdown, and if you had gone with 703 instead of 702, we wouldn't be having this conversation, because I would be neck deep in juvie."

"I'm sorry," he whispered. "I didn't want to do that to you."

"What about Sareth?"

Nolan's eyes snapped open. "It wasn't on purpose!"

"I know. You stood up for him. You jumped on Chad in the weight room, after he hurt him. Just like you cracked AJ on the field, after he hurt Destiny."

"She's alone," he said. "You don't understand, she's been through so much, and now she's in trouble."

"So for the next week, you and Destiny stayed close," said Rook. "You tried to convince her to let you tell the truth. You didn't want Sareth to be hurt. You wanted to do something about it. But she said—and she was right—that there was no going back. But then she got arrested, and she couldn't stop you anymore—and you were so desperate to get her out of there that you made another mistake."

Rook took the second email out of her pocket and handed it to Nolan.

"You said the Cambodian kid," she said. "That's how I knew. Perkins always says the Indian kid, because he doesn't care about other people. The irony, right? If you'd been more of an ignorant dumbass, I might never have known you're a felon."

"You can't tell anyone." Nolan was shaking. His whole body trembling. His eyes were on her face, but he didn't seem to see her—they were empty. Terrified. "You can't tell *anyone.*"

"I told you I was recording," said Rook. "It's over, Nolan. Sareth's coming out. You're going in."

He stared at her, breathing hard. Then he was up, fast—too fast—the chair hit the ground behind him as he slammed both fists down on the table. He picked up the nearest tripod, ripped the camera off and flung it toward the wall, where it shattered. Shards skittered, but Rook didn't flinch; the camera on Magnusson's desk was still rolling.

"You can't take me from her, you can't put me where I can't help her—"

Rook backed toward the door, silent, trying not to draw his attention. She couldn't stay here. He wasn't rational now. He was the same guy who had picked up the bat and crushed AJ's skull.

Nolan turned and saw her leaving, and his face contorted.

He sprang.

Rook pivoted and sprinted for the door, but Nolan was taller and faster. He snatched her by the ponytail and flung her down. The floor slammed into her. She lay stunned, staring up at the ceiling, her breath gone.

Nolan picked up a chair and swung it up over his head.

Rook leaped to her feet and scrambled out of his orbit as he brought the chair down so hard that it smashed to pieces on the floor. Plastic and metal flew everywhere.

"Don't do this," she said hoarsely, moving behind a bank of computer tables so that something was in between them. "You don't want to go to real prison, and you don't know what you're up against right now—"

He popped one thumb knuckle. Then he took a large pair of scissors out of a supply bin near Mr. Magnusson's desk.

Jesus.

Rook felt her way around the tables, never taking her eyes off Nolan.

"Listen to me."

Nolan circled toward her, slow and deliberate, gripping the scissors in his hand.

"If you hurt me, you'll be *fucked*. You won't see Destiny again. If you love her, put the scissors down."

With agility frightening to behold in a person of his height and size, Nolan leaped onto the table, brandishing the scissors like a knife. In a moment, he would be on her.

Rook crouched, grabbed the table legs in her hands, and lifted with all the strength and force she possessed, flipping the heavy table away from her and onto its side.

Nolan shrieked. He fell. His legs flew up, and he landed with a crash among a pile of smashed computers. He lay there in the wreckage, unmoving. Rook shoved the table over the rest of the way and it landed, upside down, on top of him. She stepped onto it.

She had won.

And she had every single word on camera.

Rook looked around the tech room at the tripods she had set up. Nolan had shattered one of the cameras, and another had been broken in the table flip, but the one on Magnusson's desk was still standing. Still rolling.

They had him.

"Get off me!" Nolan shouted. He started to struggle, pushing at the table to free himself, and Rook leapt off it to avoid being tipped over. Then she locked herself inside the newsroom as Nolan stumbled to his feet.

He stared at her through the window, and the animal she had seen in him moments ago was gone. Now he was crying. Stricken.

"Tell Destiny I'm sorry," he choked, and he fled from the room.

Still high on adrenaline, Rook went to the camera on Mr. Magnusson's desk, and she stopped the recording and detached the camera from its tripod. She cradled it in her hands.

Proof.

For once, she had all the answers.

Theo ran into the classroom. "He ran for it," he said, and then stopped and stared around. The place was thoroughly trashed. "What happened in here? Are you okay?"

"Yeah. Got it all."

Rook's scalp ached, but she could barely even feel it. What she felt instead was a growing elation that threatened to lift her right up off the ground.

She had done it. They had done it.

She tossed her ponytail over her shoulder, picked up the classroom phone, and dialed zero. "Hi, Mrs. Dixon," she said. "It's Rook Radcliffe. Tell school security to head to the parking lot, and you're gonna want to call the cops. Nolan Becker's about to try to leave campus, and he's a wanted felon. Confessed."

She hung up.

THIRTY-SEVEN

"Ms. Chase."

"Officer Petros."

"It's Detective."

"Huh," said Rook. "Feels like maybe that should be *my* title."

Once again, she sat at the police station across from Nick Petros, and once again, he'd been having a sloppy day. Coffee ring on his file folder, grease stain on his collar.

"First real case, and I'm already living on vending-machine lunches," he muttered under his breath, flicking crumbs off his tie. He opened his file and looked up at her. "How well do you know Nolan Becker?"

"Not very."

"Is your relationship platonic?"

Rook guffawed. Even the warning look from Greta couldn't stop her. "Christ yes," she said, and she sat back, feeling good. She had figured it out. The cops hadn't been able to do it; they had gotten it wrong twice. But she and Theo had seen it through to the end.

It was good, knowing the answer. It was great being right. She didn't even care that she was stuck in another interrogation room—she felt like she was on a sunny beach somewhere, basking in her own rightness.

She was in the clear. So was Sareth. And Destiny too—partly. She was an accomplice, but not the one with the bat. Rook wondered how much trouble she would get in now. Juvie? Community service? What happened to a sixteen-year-old who obstructed justice?

"Enjoying yourself?" said Petros, annoyed.

"Feels pretty good," said Rook, with a grin she hoped would piss him off even more. "Haven't you ever caught a perp? Might want to try it."

Petros gave her a withering look that did nothing to dampen her attitude, and then he started to grill her. She answered his questions, giving only the necessary details. She never mentioned Theo. She didn't want him to have to go through this crap. He was a good guy, and he had already lost his best friend this year—and he didn't have a lawyer like Greta.

"How'd you know where Destiny Bray got that second phone?" Petros asked eventually.

"I followed her to the parking lot during a pep rally, and she got into a Jeep with a guy. It looked like he—"

"Brooklyn." Greta's voice was swift and firm. "Don't speculate."

Rook fell silent.

"How'd you know what the evidence was?" Petros asked.

Rook was not about to tell him about her tech room stakeout.

"Lucky guess," she said. "Remember last time I was here, I told you I thought I remembered something being taken from AJ, but I didn't want to say it, because I wasn't sure?"

Petros nodded.

"When I found him on the field, I thought I noticed his chain was gone. Turns out I was right."

"And the emails?"

"What emails?" she said flatly.

"The ones your principal received from Chad Perkins's account. How'd you know about those? Because I've spoken with Regina Kim, and she denies ever having spoken with any student about the matter."

Rook shrugged. She wasn't saying anything about Delilah, and she definitely wasn't admitting she'd broken into Chad's email. That was the kind of thing Petros could really nail her for.

"How did you have a physical copy of those emails?" Petros pressed.

"That's privileged, Detective," said Greta. "Unless you're charging her, we're finished."

"All right, all right," Petros grumbled. "Just a couple more questions."

"Wait." Rook put up her hand. "I need to say something first. Not about the emails," she said, when Greta gave her a razor-sharp look. "The guy in the Jeep with Destiny—he gave me a bad feeling. Nolan said he's her sister's boyfriend, and he just looked like he was getting too close to her. And like he's too old."

"Yeah, we've got our eye on him," said Petros. "Theo flagged it."

"Why are you questioning Theo?" Rook asked at once, frustrated. "He didn't do anything."

"I'm not questioning him," said Petros. "He called in the

license plate a week ago. Got in touch, told me there was something off about the guy."

"Oh. Okay. Good."

Rook sat back, warm through, glad to know that Theo wasn't getting dragged through all this. He could stay the way he was. Innocent. Somebody should be allowed to stay like that.

"Who's *Theo*?" Greta asked, checking Rook's face. "Something I should know?"

Rook wasn't listening. Theo had found the license plate on his own. Called the cops a week ago. Never said a word about it.

How had he even found it?

"He agreed to the recording on camera, so the DA's happy," Petros was saying. "Hello? Ms. Chase?" He knocked on the table.

"Sorry." Rook blinked. "What?"

"I said you did good with that recording," he said. "You got Becker's consent. We can use it. Makes things a whole lot faster for getting Sareth out."

That had been Theo's idea too.

Rook wondered where he was. Probably sitting in his room, in all his crumbs and plates and laundry, eating a Hot Pocket and drinking a Coke and doing some heavy precalculus in his unmade bed. She smirked to herself at the picture.

Or maybe he's with the cheerleader.

The picture in her mind changed.

Rook shut off her mind's eye with a snap, and tossed her ponytail. Yeah, he was probably busy. She'd see him at school on Monday.

"And you still got Becker to keep talking," said Petros, with grudging respect. "Not easy to do. Pretty good move, using his feelings against him, making him think it was all for his girlfriend—you have a knack."

"What?" said Rook again, only half listening.

"Don't play cop like that again, though," Petros warned. "That was dangerous. You're lucky you didn't get hurt."

Rook didn't think it was luck so much as strength and smarts, but she didn't bother saying so.

"What happens to Destiny?" she asked instead.

"Probably deferred disposition," said Petros, and at Rook's blank look, he added, "Six months community supervision if she keeps clean."

So Destiny would have to sit with it for a while. Think about what she let happen. And Nolan would have to sit in juvie, hoping Destiny didn't bail on him the first chance she got.

It was midnight by the time Rook got out of the interrogation room and stood outside the station with Greta, waiting to find out what legal hoops she'd need to jump through next.

Greta tapped a cigarette into her fingers. "You certainly enjoy drama."

"Where's my name change?"

"Soon. I'll send you the official papers when I have them, and you can have your driver's license reissued." She laughed through her nose. "*Rook*, though. Are you sure? What about Brooke? Isn't that a more appropriate girl's name?"

"Fuck being appropriate."

Greta looked oddly pleased with this reply. "So, are you ready to go back to Saint Catherine's? Or do you prefer the chaos and violence of the public education system?"

"You think Saint Catherine's was all fun and games?"

"I don't remember Caroline mentioning any assaults."

"Like Caroline cared what was happening to me."

Greta gave Rook a look both curious and cautious. "Why? What was happening?"

Rook had no desire to rehash it. "I'm staying here in Washington."

"Then what about Highland High? It's a much stronger school, and it's right nearby."

Rook thought of Theo, who was clearly getting a damn good education. He didn't need Highland High.

"Lakeview's good."

"Barely a step up from a GED," muttered Greta. "Are you still planning to go that route?"

Rook played with Oscar's car keys. "You think Caroline'll let me?"

"You could always ask."

But Rook found she didn't want to.

"Speaking of Caroline." Greta tucked her cigarette packet away and took out her lighter. "She's going to pay for all the property you destroyed during your little cage match. Nine grand in smashed cameras and computers."

"That was Nolan's fault," Rook began, but Greta held up her hand.

"You *flipped* him, and an enormous table of school equipment, completely upside down—I saw the video. The fact that he assaulted you notwithstanding, the damages are significant, and it's my job to make these problems go away."

Greta lit the cigarette and inhaled deeply.

"I admit it's impressive," she said, with a quick, interested look at Rook. "Only sixteen, and you've already solved a felony. Your mother always says you're smart."

"She wouldn't know what I am."

Greta exhaled smoke. "You're very similar, you know," she said, with a cutting smile.

Rook flinched like she'd been slapped.

"I'm sure it's a waste of breath to say this," said Greta, "but stay out of trouble."

She stalked across the parking lot to her town car, leaving Rook to wonder if Greta was being cruel, or if, in some small, horrible way, what she'd said was true.

THIRTY-EIGHT

It wasn't a crime scene anymore, and she was no longer a suspect. The security tape had been taken down. It was Saturday night, and campus was empty.

Rook still waited until dark to go back to the graffiti wall.

It had been fourteen days. Multiple rains. By now, it was possible that something was out in the open. She would reclaim it before it did damage.

She parked in the upper lot at Lakeview. Crossed the baseball field, Oscar's flashlight held high. Slipped behind the wall and knelt in the dirt and damp to excavate the evidence. Everything smelled green, cleansed, and earthen.

The letter came out whole. Folded, filthy, wet, but still intact.

The remaining, thumbnail-sized edge of her license, however, was gone. Rook dug, but couldn't find it anywhere. Washed away by the rain. Too small to make a difference anyway.

Brooklyn Chase was a ghost.

Rook drove to Smallmouth Beach. Walked across the

rocky shore and down the empty dock. She sat at the end, feet dangling, staring across at the glittering city, letting the cold late-October night sink through her hoodie and leggings and down into her bones.

The letter remained in her hands, cupped loosely. She wouldn't unfold it again. She knew it by heart.

I've never seen anything like you,
Brooklyn. Put that pain in the tank,
and you can fly.

She couldn't get rid of his voice. But she didn't have to carry it around.

She tore the letter into pieces and let the wind whip the shreds out over the lake. They fluttered and fell. Sank and were gone.

"You're dead," she said quietly. Not to herself, this time.

She lay on her stomach on the wooden planks and dipped her hands into the freezing lake to wash away the dirt. She listened to the water lap beneath her, feeling the empty darkness of the lake and sky.

When she got up and went home, she only felt tired. Not good. Not bad. But nothing inside her burned.

THIRTY-NINE

Theo saw the flashlight from his yard.

He had just gone outside to find his Converse—in an hour, he was going out for a Saturday night date with Ana, and he thought he had left his shoes by the sliding glass door. He found them, stuck his feet into them, looked up, and saw it.

A flashlight beam, jumping as it moved toward the wall.

Theo reached into the house and flicked off the mudroom light to make himself impossible to see. He went to his fence and jumped it. He didn't know who was out there, and he didn't want to be hurt, so he waited where he was for five minutes. Ten.

Twenty minutes later, the flashlight illuminated again. The light traveled back across the baseball field and up the steps to the north parking lot.

Against the parking lot lights, he saw a silhouette of someone with a ponytail. Then a car pulled away from Lakeview.

His feet moved without needing to be told.

Theo turned on his phone flashlight and walked out

behind the graffiti wall, heart thudding. Whatever she had wanted to hide, whatever her *real* reason had been for being on the baseball field that morning, it was here. Right back here.

He shone his phone's LED light around at the trees and the wall, then scanned it over the dirt. One area looked different. Raised and smooth, like someone had buried something.

He knelt and started digging in the dirt, but found nothing. He checked the time on his phone. Ana would be at his house soon—he had to go home and wash his hands and change his jeans or he'd look like a crazy person.

Later. He could come and give this his full attention later. Whatever she had done here, he would find it.

He got up, brushed the dirt off his jeans, and felt something hard and plastic fall from his knee. He shone his light on it.

Driver's license, he thought, and although it was only a very small piece of one, he was pretty sure that he was right. He picked it up out of the dirt and examined it carefully. It was the bottom left corner. No bigger than his thumbnail. The state of issue was unclear. A sliver of photo—nothing helpful. Just the beginning of a handwritten signature.

Broo.

That was it.

Whatever she was hiding, this was part of it.

He could find the rest. If he researched—if he used everything he knew? He could do it.

She wouldn't want him to do it.

She would stop talking to him if she found out that he had done it.

Theo went home. He stashed the tiny piece of license in his desk, changed his jeans, washed his hands, and was outside in front of his house by the time Ana picked him up. She drove them down to Smallmouth, and as they went down the hill that led to the beach, a familiar Civic drove past them in the other direction.

Rook. She didn't see them. Just drove on, unaware. Ana, too, was insensible of whom she had just passed.

Theo turned to watch Rook's car vanish up the hill.

He and Rook had done it. They had seen the thing through, and it was over.

But it didn't feel to him like it was over. It felt to him like something was just beginning. He couldn't shake the sense that, over the course of the past couple of weeks, he had exited one reality and entered another one; he was part of some new entanglement that had sent his life arcing in a direction he hadn't planned.

At the beach, he and Ana walked to the end of the dock. It was freezing, but he took off his hoodie and wrapped it around her shoulders, and she snuggled against him and kissed him, which made the cold more than worth it.

"We can go to a movie," she breathed, kissing him more deeply so that he was unable to reply right away. "Or Three Tree, if you want to do arcade stuff..."

Theo loved, as Ana put it, "arcade stuff", but there was no arcade game in the universe as good as what was happening right now. Ana lay down on the dock and hooked one leg around him.

He kissed her harder. It was perfect. She was perfect. Everything was good. Nolan Becker was under arrest, and Sareth would be released. Lakeview would go back to normal. Ana was beautiful. Smelled like flowers.

Rook was not who she said she was.

What was her name? Where was she from? What kind of person did the sorts of things she did? What sophomore girl waltzed into Lakeview, lifted hundreds of pounds, spied on teachers, faced down varsity royalty, got criminals to confess, trashed half the computers in the school in the process, and then tossed her hair like it was nothing? If superheroes had been real, then Theo would have assumed Rook was one. He wasn't entirely convinced she wasn't.

Ana made a soft, yearning noise.

He broke from the kiss.

"You okay?" Ana asked, sitting up. "You look sick."

"No, I'm... sorry." He shook his head. "I'm sorry, my head's all over the place. I'm still processing, I think."

"Of course you are. After everything you've been through—I'm selfish. I'm sorry. I'm here." She hugged him, and he leaned on her.

He needed his laptop. Now. He had to know.

"I know how I acted," said Ana, muffled against his neck. "When you told me what you were doing, trying to help Sareth, I know I was judgmental, and I shouldn't have been. You wanted to help someone, and you *did*. That's what people should do, and not enough people ever actually try." She hugged him tighter. "I was rude to your friend," she said. "I'm sorry I acted that way. I just didn't understand."

"I'm not upset."

"You're not?" Ana pulled back and looked up at him, distressed. "Because it feels like maybe you're mad at me."

"No. I promise." He kissed her gently. "I promise," he murmured.

"You'd tell me?"

"I'd tell you."

They kissed for a long time. No words. Arms around each other, growing colder all the time in spite of the heat they made. Theo finally shivered, and Ana rubbed her hands briskly up and down his arms.

"You need your hoodie back."

"No," he said. "You can keep it."

She snickered. "Look at you, all goosebumps and trying to be a hero." She looked lovingly up at him, and Theo didn't know what happened in his own expression, but Ana's faltered.

"You're really struggling, aren't you?" she said. "Do you need some time alone?"

He did.

He needed to figure out Rook, and that would take time. Alone.

"Or do you want to talk about it?" she asked. "We can go get some food and just keep it low pressure. Want to?"

Who *was* she?

How would she treat him, now that there was nothing left to solve? It was impossible to guess. It seemed to him, after what they'd done, that the two of them had established something like a friendship—but he knew Rook just well enough to know that nothing about her was certain. If he made one wrong move, she would have no qualms about switching him off like a light.

Ana prodded him. One gentle fingertip in his sternum.

"You're not home," she said. "You're in here." She lifted her fingertip and tapped his temple. "Come out, talk to me."

Theo focused on Ana's face. Her beautiful, kind, amazing face.

He was losing it.

"Food sounds good," he said, wrenching himself out of his unraveling thoughts. "Where should we go?"

They went to Three Tree, had fries and sodas, and played air hockey and mini golf—laughing at how bad they both were in the batting cages. They ran into friends from Lakeview and from Highland, and had so much fun that Theo was halfway able to push his relentless questions to the back of his mind.

Who is she?

What is she?

It was late by the time Ana took him home. She got out of the car so she could hug and kiss him properly before sending him to his door.

"Que sueñes conmigo," Ana said teasingly. *Dream of me.*

"Siempre," he replied. *Always.*

Hermano, said the voice in his mind. Quiet. Judging. *What are you doing?*

Shut up, Theo snapped back, *leave me alone.*

His mind went quiet.

Ana drove away.

Theo went to his room. Locked the door. Opened his laptop. It glowed in the darkness, half blinding him until his eyes adjusted. His chest went hot. A sick rush—fear and excitement. Whoever Rook was, he could find her. He pulled the shard of driver's license out of his desk and turned it over in his fingers. Maybe it was crazy, and it wasn't hers at all.

But it was.

He pulled up the search bar, not sure, at first, what to type.

Rook Radcliffe

This gave him nothing. Not a soul online went by that name.

Rook weightlifting

This brought up powerlifting gear, but no people.

Weightlifting categories

Now there were weight classes, age groups, federations—where did she fit? He didn't know. He tried an image search, but the volume of results overwhelmed him; weightlifting was a bigger sport than he had imagined. Most girls posted under usernames, or went by nicknames. The data was organized by meet, not by identity. And none of them were named Rook.

Could he find her, in all this?

He clicked through video after video, competition after competition. An hour passed. Two hours. His dad knocked on his door.

"You need sleep," he called. "It's late."

"I know," Theo called back. "Night."

Frustration mounted. Maybe he was way, way off here. Maybe Rook liked to lift, but she had never competed. But he had watched her lift—she moved just like these women. The way she snatched the barbell, the efficiency, the speed—she was championship level.

Theo put the cursor in the search bar and added one more word.

Champion

He hesitated, checked her license again, and added, *"Broo"*.

The search results returned.

He sat forward, staring at her picture.

There she was: in a deep squat, barbell locked out overhead, her face fierce and determined, her weight belt pulled tight around her firm middle, her smooth ponytail snaking over her shoulder, her body powerful and lithe.

Theo clicked the picture, his fingers jittering, and he enlarged the image to make sure that he was right—which he was. That was definitely Rook's face. He read the caption.

Brooklyn Chase, 15, beats her own record at the American Open Finals

Brooklyn Chase.

He gazed at her name—her real name.

She had lied to him.

Ever since Officer Petros had said that she went by her name, Theo had been sure there was something off. He didn't know why he felt so surprised.

Betrayed, even.

She didn't owe him her secrets. But she had turned blistering anger on him in the weight room when he'd told her what he'd seen on the graffiti wall. She had stood right here in his bedroom and threatened to walk out because he had gone to the police behind her back. Any flicker of a falsehood, any trace of untrustworthiness, and she went up in flames.

But she was allowed to hide *this*.

"Brooklyn Chase," he whispered, testing her real name aloud. It sounded wrong in his mouth. Phony.

"Rook Radcliffe," he said, and it felt real. Maybe because it was the first name he'd known her by—maybe because it fit her better. He couldn't imagine her as anything else.

But she *was* something else.

Theo clicked the search bar.

Weightlifting champion "Brooklyn Chase"

There were dozens of videos of her lifting in competition. He clicked through them, riveted, watching her step onto national and international platforms, belt pulled tight, eyes blazing. She washed her hands in chalk, brushed her hands methodically across the barbell in a ritualistic motion, and gripped it like a warrior. Shouted and clenched her fists each time she won.

She'd been at Nationals. At Worlds.

He found a video interview. Rook stood in front of the camera, so different that she was almost unrecognizable. It was dated over a year ago—her face looked younger—but that wasn't what made her look like another person.

It was her expression, he realized. He had never seen her openly happy.

"Team USA invited you to train with them," the interviewer said. "Everyone agrees that the Olympics are in your future. How do you feel?"

A wide, spontaneous smile lit Rook's face, and Theo's heart jammed. He paused the video and stared at her, knocked backward by the difference. He had never once seen her smile. Not like that.

She was beautiful.

He didn't mean to think it, but there it was, and it was true. She was beautiful, and her name was Brooklyn Chase, and not long ago she had been a bona fide champion on her way to the Olympic Games. Now she was here at Lakeview, she went by Rook Radcliffe, and she didn't smile like that anymore.

Why?

Theo heard her voice in his mind. Cool. Controlled.

I didn't give you the number because I didn't want you to have it.

This wasn't her real secret.

Being a world-class weightlifting champion on her way to the Olympics—that wasn't something to hide. She should have been showing this off everywhere. Everyone at Lakeview, everyone in Cedar Point, should have known that she was elite like this.

Instead, she had left it behind. She had turned her back on it. Changed her name.

Erased herself.

And anything that could make her do that had to be *bad* bad.

Theo's fingers hovered over the keyboard. He had enough information now to know everything.

Brooklyn Chase, he typed. *Trouble. Problem.*

He licked his lips and typed one more.

Crime.

He didn't press enter.

She doesn't want you to know.

Theo got up and walked away from his laptop. He made it to his bedroom door before he pivoted, came back, sat down, and almost pressed enter again.

She'll ghost you. She'll wreck you.

You do this, you lose her.

"Fuck," he said softly, and got up again. Paced back and forth, wringing his hands.

This was an invasion of privacy. Just because information existed on the internet didn't mean he should look for it. Just because he wanted to know more about her didn't mean it was his right.

But if there's public information, anyone could get it, he reasoned. *Why not me?*

Because you care about her.

He shut the laptop, staring into the dark.

He picked up the thumbnail scrap of her license, gripping it so tightly it hurt his palm.

Then he folded the scrap of plastic into an index-card sleeve, sealed it with tape, and slid it behind a row of old math trophies.

He walked out of his room and was surprised to find his mother still awake. She sat on the couch watching a movie. He sat close to her. Hugged her.

Franny hugged him back and kissed his temple. “What’s this for?”

“I don’t know.”

“Did something happen?”

“Not really.”

“Okay.” She kept an arm around him. “You’ll tell me if it does.”

He didn’t move again for a long time.

FORTY

Rook was in the Ford Ranger with her feet on the dash. She always had them on the dash. She was ten years old, and things were still okay. But not for long.

It was a dream. Sometimes, when she had this one, she knew.

Her dad hummed beside her. In her periphery, he picked up the styrofoam cup and slurped the remains of its contents.

"I could use another coffee." His voice was deep and warm. "You hungry, baby girl?"

She leaned against the window. "Kind of."

He changed lanes and yawned; she heard how tired he was. He should pull over. She should tell him to pull over.

"You go to sleep. I'll wake you up when we're at the drive-through."

"Okay."

But this time, she wasn't going to go to sleep. This time, she would stay awake and warn him. Make sure he stayed on the road.

"Dad?"

"Mmm."

"I love you."

His big hand ruffled her hair. "You're my softie. Love you too."

She wanted to turn and see him. She didn't know why she couldn't. She wanted to see his beardy face, and his crinkly blue eyes, and his smile.

"You did a good job, baby," he said. "A real good job."

Rook leaned against his hand, and she missed him so much, and the loss was so deep, that when she woke up, she didn't open her eyes right away. She curled up, aching, and tried to keep him there for just one more minute.

When she arrived at Lakeview that morning, she was reminded of what her life had been like ten months ago. Everyone asking questions, everyone wanting their minute with her. Several of the kids in zero period crowded around her, wanting details about Nolan and AJ.

"Damn, news reporter," said Adel Juárez. "You're *good.* How'd you figure it out?"

Rook had no intention of giving a press conference. She ignored people's questions and went toward the squat bar, where she loaded 180.

"You sure?" said Gonzalez. "Isn't that your max?"

"I'm fine."

"You need a spot."

"I'm *fine.*"

Gonzalez motioned to Chad and Keanu. They came to the squat rack and flanked her, glaring at each other. Rook glanced from one to the other of them. She didn't trust them for one second—not that it mattered, since she didn't need a spot.

"I thought you got kicked out of here," she said.

"I'm back, Rookie." Chad waggled his eyebrows at her. "And I'm here to supervise your snatch."

"I don't want your help," Rook warned.

"Fine with me," said Keanu.

Rook went back to her gym bag and rifled for her earbuds—because if the douche was going to stand right next to her, at least she didn't have to hear him talk. She turned her old music player up and walked back to the barbell. She gripped it, ducked under it, and pulled her traps tight against it. She unracked the weight and stepped back.

The barbell felt heavy. Really heavy.

Good heavy.

Rook braced and squatted, getting low, experiencing the beautiful sensation of being pressed down by real weight. Serious weight. The kind she had to fight back against with her whole body.

She pushed her feet against the ground and pressed her knees out; she squeezed her glutes, her legs, her core, and she exploded out of the hole, shoving herself upward until she was standing, breathing hard, her heart slamming with joy.

Had she accidentally loaded too much weight?

No. Of course she hadn't. Chad had tried to mess with her—he'd loaded extra plates on the bar, assuming she'd crumble. Instead, she had schooled him. Both of them. Chad stood there in open-mouthed shock, his eyes halfway out of his head. Keanu glared at her in disgust. Coach Gonzalez stood beyond him, staring at Rook from under the brim of his Seahawks hat like he wasn't sure if he was hallucinating.

She had no idea how much weight she was squatting, but whatever it was, it was a lot. So. Now they knew. No point in pretending. Rook dropped into another squat, fought to stand it up, and then did a third one, just to make it burn.

When she racked the bar, she took out her earbuds and stepped back. She checked the plates and did the math. They'd each added a 45 to her bar, bringing her up to 270.

Not bad. It had been a while since she'd hit 270 for reps. It was good to know she still could.

From across the gym, Adel whistled. "Damn!" she hollered. "Yes!"

Rook tried to smirk, but a grin broke through, irresistible.

"Your turn, douche," she said to Chad, and she gestured for him to step up to the bar. He just kept gaping like a dumbass fish. "No?" she said, turning to Keanu. "You want some?"

"Whatever," Keanu muttered. "Real girls don't do that shit."

Rook laughed. "Yeah we do."

He walked away.

"Hey Coach," said Rook, in a louder voice. "This class is great, I'm learning so much. I'm getting really strong this month, right?"

Gonzalez shook his head. But he had a gleam in his eye, and Rook knew he was impressed.

"So can I snatch now, or are you still worried about me?"

"Oh for the love of—fine." The coach threw up his hands. "Go ahead, Radcliffe, do your thing."

Rook had to force herself to walk to the other side of the gym. What she wanted to do was run. Skip. Twirl. She hadn't wanted to twirl so much since she was a kid, but winning had always been her favorite, and for the first time in a long time, she was stacking a lot of wins.

FORTY-ONE

Theo tried to find Rook at lunch. They hadn't spoken since she had left Lakeview on Friday, in police custody. Without an invitation to call her at Oscar's, he hadn't wanted to risk it, so he had spent the weekend stewing, knowing more about her than she wanted him to know, and needing to see her. Talk to her.

"Theo?"

Marna gestured to him from her table. Tuyet, too, looked at him like she hoped he'd come over and sit.

Theo took his tray and parked across from them, beside Colleen, who picked at her lunch, looking salty.

"Do it," said Tuyet.

Colleen let out a gusty sigh. "Oh *fine.*" She turned to Theo. "I apologize for being *wrong,*" she said. "And posting things that were *wrong.*" She looked at Marna and Tuyet in obvious irritation. "Good enough?"

"Theo?" said Marna. "Do you accept Colleen's apology?"

Theo snorted. "I feel like I'm in the kindergarten calming corner," he said. "But yes. I accept." He glanced at

Colleen. "Rook might need her own apology," he warned. "She's the one you really messed with."

"Ugh," said Colleen, "now you can apologize for what *you* did." She got up and swept away from the table, tossing her red hair behind her as she went.

Marna looked pointedly from Theo to Tuyet.

"I told you," said Tuyet, "he already apologized."

"But I'm still sorry." Theo met Marna's eyes. "I know I'm not being a good friend right now. I'm just..."

"Surviving," said Tuyet.

Marna sighed. "I know." She took Tuyet's hand and reached across the table for Theo's.

He gave it to her.

"Would you come over soon?" she asked. "We miss you."

Theo couldn't make himself say yes. He wasn't ready.

"You could bring Rook," Marna offered. "I'm inviting her too."

"Yes," said Tuyet, watching him. "Rook."

Defensiveness stirred in Theo's chest, the urge to throw up a wall. *Nothing's going on. Don't make it a thing.* But if he said it, it would only sound like there was something to defend.

Marna's phone buzzed, and she let go of their hands to check it. "Oh eff," she said. "I forgot, I told Alejandro I'd help him before his math test." She picked up her backpack. Touched Theo's shoulder as she passed him.

"Take your time," she said. "But not forever. Okay?"

He nodded. "Okay."

Marna hurried toward the library.

Tuyet stood and picked up her tray, but lingered for a moment. "Have you visited them since?" she asked. "Mateo's family? Have you been to his house?"

Theo shook his head.

He should have visited. Should have checked on them, after the funeral. But the idea of going to that house—of seeing Mateo's room—

No.

"Have you?" he asked.

"I tried." Tuyet's lovely face showed no emotion. She stared down at the cafeteria table. "But I didn't see them."

"They weren't home?"

"They were. I couldn't go to the door. Because I thought, what if he doesn't answer it? What if he's really not there anymore? And of course he's not, but if I accept that..." She met Theo's eyes. Hers were glassy. "I'm going crazy," she said, and she walked away, leaving him alone.

AFTER SCHOOL, the debate team came together in the AP History classroom for practice rounds. On the board behind Mr. Ramesh, in thick black letters, read *Resolved: The United States should promote the development of juvenile incarceration centers.*

Sareth limped into the room late, on a crutch, expressionless, his ankle in a cast that had been tagged with gang signs and other graffiti—obvious badges of his time in detention. The room fell silent as he took the chair beside Theo's.

Mr. Ramesh began speaking to the team, saying nothing of real importance, clearly trying to smother the silence for Sareth's sake. Students began to talk amongst themselves.

Sareth turned to Theo and fixed him with the most impossibly arrogant look he ever had. "Well?" he said. "Questions, Locke?"

"Actually," said Theo, lowering his voice so no one else

would hear. "Why were you on campus the night of the assault?"

Sareth gave him a look of real appreciation.

"Did my absence teach you the value of concrete facts?" he asked. "Well, I'm glad something could."

"That's no answer," Theo retorted. "Talk about abstract."

Sareth laughed. "I was with my brother," he said. "He's a QuickEats driver, I was riding along so I could pick up tacos." He gave Theo a curious look. "Did you actually think I attacked AJ?"

"Nope. Not for one second." He looked down at Sareth's cast. "What happened?"

"Irrelevant." Sareth glanced up at the resolution on the board. "Prepare, Locke. Your precious imperative is about to meet with hard data—and lose."

Theo grinned. He couldn't stop himself.

"Game on."

FORTY-TWO

"Goooooood morning, Lakeview, and welcome to the first episode of the *Seventh-Inning Stretch*! We're your hosts, Elijah Jones—"

"—and Blaine Bonderman—"

"—and it's almost third period on this gray and rainy Tuesday. Time for all you little Salmon to wake up and start swimming upstream so you can spawn all over the gravel bed."

"Let's keep this family-friendly, Elijah." Blaine smoothed his tie, straight-faced. Elijah flashed a smile at the camera. Every classroom screen at Lakeview was tuned to their channel; across the school, every student and staff member watched the two freshmen, engrossed.

"Here's a G-rated joke for you," said Elijah. "How long did the baseball player spend in the hospital?"

"I don't know, Elijah. How long *did* the baseball player spend in the hospital?"

"Not long. It was a short stop."

At his sound station, Liam Ballard played a rim shot.

Rook stood at the door of the tech room, listening to Lakeview's students erupt with distant laughter.

"Knock knock," said Elijah.

"Who's there?" Blaine replied.

"Coma."

"Coma who?"

"Coma on and put your hands together for AJ Ellsworth, who is back at Lakeview today, and we're glad to report that his coma is a thing of the past."

"Unless he's stuck in chem class," Blaine added. "Just kidding, Mr. Wilkerson, you know I love you. Please don't fail me."

"Hey, Blaine?"

"Yes, Elijah."

"I've got another special Salmon on my mind, and I'll bet you can guess who it is."

"Is she stronger than Chad Perkins?"

"Mmm-hm."

"More powerful than Nolan Becker?"

"That's what I heard."

"Able to lift big barbells in a single thrust?"

Elijah cleared his throat. "Family-friendly."

Blaine winked at the camera. "We must be talking about Rook Radcliffe, sophomore super-sleuth. Thanks to her, Sareth Sok is back at Lakeview where he belongs. Welcome home, buddy."

Rook stayed at the door, glad for the cold air on her cheeks, and gladder to hear the shouts of approval and thunderous applause that rocked the school in support of Sareth.

"Rook's an investigative journalist here at the *Seventh-Inning Stretch*," said Elijah. "So if you've got a lead on a story, or if you think your Homecoming date might be a felon, go ahead and send her an email."

"No case too big, no problem too small."

"Think she'll give us a live interview, Blaine?"

"I don't know, Elijah. Let's ask her."

"Rook?" they called out together. Then they waited, blinking at the camera, as Liam played the noise of singing crickets.

"Not very talkative, is she?"

"One might even call her inaccessible."

"Nice segue." Elijah leaned forward and quirked an eyebrow at the camera. "Why don't we play a fun game called *how many places at Lakeview are inaccessible to students with mobility issues?*"

The show cut to a pre-recorded segment, which showed two *Seventh-Inning Stretch* reporters standing on the stairs outside the weight room.

"I'm Ursula Choi."

"And I'm Tapeesa Bear."

"And we're here to talk about the fact that Lakeview High School's weight room is only accessible by stairs."

"This means that students in wheelchairs, or with any mobility limitation that makes stairs problematic, are excluded from weightlifting." Tapeesa put her hands on her thick waist. "Other areas of the school are technically accessible, but still hard to reach."

"We're calling on the Cedar Point School District and our own administration to address this problem immediately." The metallic pink ponytails of Ursula's cosplay wig sparkled. "Now it's back to you in the studio."

Elijah and Blaine reappeared on all the screens.

"Uh oh," said Elijah, "I think we're out of time. The bell's about to ring."

"It sure is. But we'll be back tomorrow—"

"And the next day—"

"Because remember, kids, if you're at Lakeview, and it's almost third period—"

They said the last line together.

"It's time for the *Seventh-Inning Strehhhtch*."

In the newsroom, the students running the equipment cut the feed. Elijah and Blaine fist bumped.

"Episode one is in the can," said Mr. Magnusson, beaming. "Well done, all of you."

Rook tried to move quietly from the door to her desk. To stay unnoticed in this room, as usual.

"Super *sleuth*," cried Elijah, clapping her on the shoulder. "Legend." He winked at Rook and kept walking toward Mr. Magnusson's desk.

Rook sat down, hot-faced. Colleen glanced up from the camera and gave her a clinical once-over.

"Not bad," she said. "I mean it's actually terrible that this was our first episode, because we'll never be able to top it, but... good segment."

It wasn't quite a compliment. It definitely wasn't an apology. But Rook got the feeling that it was supposed to be both.

"Gather up, team," said Mr. Magnusson. "Time to plan episode two. We are about to get busier than most of you have ever been."

FORTY-THREE

Ms. Winter called her to the counseling office for the last fifteen minutes of the school day, and Rook was in such a good mood that she didn't even mind. She didn't feel like talking, so she sank into the throw pillows and did her biology homework until school was out.

"It's been a big week for you," said Ms. Winter, right before the bell. "Need anything?"

"Nope," said Rook. "I'm good."

She went up to the weight room. Coach Gonzalez gave her an approving nod as she entered, and she felt the pleasure of being back in a space where her strength was known and respected. She warmed up. Loaded her barbell.

Eventually, the football team filed out for practice—all except AJ, who had been eyeing her, looking for his opening. Rook didn't give him one. If that guy thought he was ever going to touch her again, he was going to be disappointed. And possibly reinjured.

She braced for another heavy clean.

AJ stepped up and said something she couldn't hear. She stood up and took out an earbud.

"Yeah?"

"So that's the real you," AJ said, with a nod at her barbell. "You've been holding back."

Rook swigged water.

AJ ran his eyes over her, making his continuing interest obvious. "And you figured out who hit me. Guess I owe you one." He smiled, looking like he thought he was cute. "Let's hang out after practice."

Rook laughed at him. Turned her back on him. Put her earbud back in and kept lifting. She didn't know when he left.

THEO PASSED AJ on his way to the weight room. They brushed against each other at the bottom of the steps.

"Tease," AJ muttered, not quite under his breath.

Theo stopped. "Who are you talking about?"

AJ barely looked up. "Rook, obviously."

"Don't make the sidekick mad," said Chad, as he walked out of the locker room. "Locke thinks he's her bodyguard."

"That right?" AJ laughed. "Aww. Careful, you'll miss out—girl's got skills."

"Like you'd know," Theo shot back. "I saw you and Rook behind the graffiti wall, and you're all talk. Nothing happened. You asked her to Homecoming and she said no."

"She jumped me." AJ grinned. "Must've missed that part."

"She kissed you," said Theo, "and then she walked away."

"But she got naked, right?" Chad demanded.

"The only one with their shirt off," Theo held AJ's livid gaze, "was this guy."

Chad chortled. "Dude, is that true? Rookie shut you

down? No, you know what, that tracks. Bro got *blocked*." He walked away, still snickering.

AJ gave Theo a long, black look. He clapped his shoulder, harder than was friendly. "Oh, I get it," he said soft and vicious. "Mateo 2.0. Playing the hero. Have fun in the friend zone." He shoved open the locker room door and went in.

Theo continued up the steps, slow, needing time to get his heart rate back in check. Pressure coiled inside him. His shoulder stung from AJ's hand.

He would never be Mateo. But he hadn't hesitated.

Yes, brother. I see you.

When he entered the weight room, he found Rook already lifting, facing away from him. She didn't notice him take up a position against the far wall. They were the only students in the room, like the day he had tracked her down for answers two weeks ago.

It felt like so much longer.

She moved through a clean and jerk, calves tensing, hips snapping forward, explosive, relentless. All that power. All that discipline. All that training to earn her spot in a sport she couldn't even talk about anymore, for reasons Theo couldn't begin to guess.

He wished he could tell her that he understood her better now.

Rook jerked the bar overhead. She held it, shaking, for three full seconds, then dropped the barbell and released a guttural sound. She turned to grab her water, and she saw Theo. A flicker of surprise crossed her face—

And then she smiled.

It hit him like a sunbeam. He had no protection against it. Had anyone ever smiled at him like that?

Beautiful.

She pulled out her earbuds and jogged over to him, her expression relaxed. Younger. Like Brooklyn Chase in that interview.

"Hey, Theo."

"Hey, Rook."

Somewhere deep in his mind, not quite his subconscious but nowhere he was ready to look closely, he understood that he had brought that smile out of her, and that if he wasn't careful, it was going to upend him.

"How'd it go with the police?" he said. "Are you in trouble?"

"Not so far." She swigged her water. "You gave Petros the Jeep license plate, huh? How'd you find it?"

"My brother works at the community college," said Theo. "So I went with him one night and looked around."

"You didn't tell me you did that."

And you didn't tell me your name, Theo thought.

But that wasn't fair. He couldn't hold that against her—he only knew about it because he'd crossed the line.

"I know I said I'd tell you first if I talked to the police again," he said. "But this wasn't about you, it was about Destiny. It sounded like she wasn't safe, so I called it in. Sorry if—"

"No. Don't be sorry."

Rook was looking at him now like she was trying to see inside him. He glanced down, unsure of his next move. They had figured out the truth together—was that it for them, or were they friends? He didn't know how to ask.

Rook threw her water bottle into her gym bag. She would be done here in ten minutes, and if Theo was free, maybe he'd want to hang out.

Dumbass, she told herself. *Walk away*.

But she couldn't make herself.

Ask her over, he thought. *Worst case, she says no.*

He didn't want her to say no.

He met her eyes. She opened her mouth.

"So, after this, you and the cheerleader have plans, right?"

"Nope," said Theo. "I'm free."

Rook tried to block the relief that expanded in her ribs. "Should we hang out?"

"Yeah," said Theo, and tension came loose inside him. They could be friends. She wanted to. It wasn't over.

As long as he didn't tell her what he knew, it wasn't over.

"Come to my house," he said. "Savannah's been asking for you—she's dying to show you her push-ups."

"How many can she do now?"

"Fourteen."

"She's working hard—good for her. Okay, let me finish up."

When Rook was done, they walked toward the baseball field and crossed it in the falling twilight, making a straight line toward Theo's backyard. They reached the Lockes' fence, and Rook jumped it. When Theo didn't immediately follow, she checked back to find him looking at her in a way that made her stomach tighten and her muscles tense. He stood on the other side of the fence, his green-yellow eyes roaming her face like he was trying to bring himself to say something.

"What?" she said, fearful.

"Just glad you're here," he said.

Rook's neck got hot. She didn't know what to say.

"Oh," she managed, grinding the sole of her shoe into the dirt. "Um."

Theo relented and rescued her. "Wait till you see the

fridge," he said, as he climbed the fence. "I told my mom you're not an attacker and that, in fact, you *caught* the attacker, and then I told her how healthy you eat, and she went nuts at the store. There's two rotisserie chickens in there, and like twenty pounds of snap peas."

Rook grinned. "Kickass."

"She's hoping you'll influence me, but you won't. I will have popcorn and Coke like a decent American. Want to watch a movie, by the way?" he asked, as they picked their way through the yard.

"Depends which one," she said, nudging a plastic toy out of her way with her shoe.

"*Alien*? I've seen it a thousand times, but I love it."

She gave him a smile. Her dad had loved that movie too.

The hero's like you, baby, he used to say. *She's smart and she's tough. People who don't take her seriously get eaten.*

"Is that a yes?" asked Theo, as he opened the sliding door.

Rook tossed her ponytail. "Yeah, okay," she said. "Since there's chicken."

Together, they went inside.

ABOUT THE AUTHOR

E.J. Ridley writes emotionally grounded mysteries with barbells, damaged people, and long arcs of trust. She lives in the Pacific Northwest, where she drinks exactly the right amount of coffee, no further questions.

Out Cold is her first novel—and the first in an eight-book series.

For more about the series, visit ejridley.com.

ACKNOWLEDGMENTS

To my husband and best friend—you absolute legend of a partner. You read every single word, every single time. Your intelligence, integrity, and willingness to stand up for the story, even when you know I'll get defensive—epic. You're brave, sir. Your belief in this series, your patience, the way you haul the domestic load so I can write? You're a unicorn prince. No one would believe you're real.

To my wicked smart, golden-hearted, hilarious children—thank you for your eternal patience with your obsessed mom and for eating so many last-minute chicken nuggets.

To Maureen, Jamie, Ruth, and Lisa—over multiple decades and projects, your unflagging support and incisive feedback have made me a better writer and human. Thank you, my sisters, my friends, my secret keepers. For the last time: Read this one instead.

To Gerry, Mike, Joan, Jennie, Tara, Emily, Maria, Dom, David, Debbie, Cheryl, and DeeDee—you read this book and helped it grow. Your time and kindness live in the fabric of Cedar Point forever.

To my readers—thank you. If you're here, you're part of it.

To Rook and Theo. Thank you for choosing my head to walk into. Writing you is the greatest creative gift of my lifetime. The road will get rough, but don't worry. I got you.

—E.J.

www.ingramcontent.com/pod-product-compliance
Lightning Source LLC
La Vergne TN
LVHW091106080826
845145LV00008B/1825

* 9 7 8 1 9 6 9 8 6 3 0 1 1 *